The First Christmas After the War

a novel by

Alan Simon

the sequel to

The First Christmas of the War

&

Thanksgiving, 1942

Alan Simon

The First Christmas After the War

Copyright © 2015 Alan R. Simon. All Rights Reserved.

First Paperback Publication 2016
First Edition

ISBN: 978-0-9857547-9-2

PERMISSIONS

Cover photograph from author's family collection.

Epigraph quote from *"The Best Years of Our Lives"* furnished courtesy of The Samuel Goldwyn Jr. Family Trust.

By Alan Simon

An American Family's Wartime Saga (Series)
The First Christmas of the War (2010 – special Pearl Harbor 75th
    Anniversary Edition with new bonus content, 2016)
Thanksgiving, 1942 (2012)
The First Christmas After the War (2015)
The First Winter of the New War (coming soon)
Additional titles to follow

Unfinished Business (2010)

Gettysburg, 1913: The Complete Novel of the Great Reunion (2015 – USA Today Bestseller)

Visit Alan Simon's blog about the real-life Gettysburg, 1913 Great Reunion:
gettysburg1913.wordpress.com

Clemente: Memories of a Once-Young Fan – Four Birthdays, Three World Series, Two Holiday Steelers Games, and One Bar Mitzvah (2012 – Nonfiction Memoir)

Visit www.alansimonbooks.com for new releases and book extras

To be notified by email about future books: info@alansimonbooks.com

Author's Note about Newspaper Headlines and Stories

With one exception, the headlines and newspaper stories from *The Pittsburgh Press* used in the main body of **The First Christmas After the War** are genuine and were actually published as portrayed during December, 1945. The one exception, in the interest of our story's timeline: your author changed the date on which the "VETS TO GET ALL NEW '46 HOMES" headline appeared, and also moved that news story to appear in that morning's *Pittsburgh Post-Gazette* rather than the afternoon *Pittsburgh Press*.

The headline and the accompanying news story that appear in our tale's Epilogue are entirely fictitious.

A Note about the Period Usage of the Terms "Air Corps," "Army Air Forces," and "Air Force" in this Novel

The United States Army Air Corps became the United States Army Air Forces (USAAF) in 1941. However, the USAAF was frequently referred to by its predecessor's name of the Air Corps by many Americans – civilian and military alike – during the early 1940s, largely for reasons of familiarity because that change had happened a short time earlier.

Further, by the middle of the war and especially into the latter years of World War II, the term "Air Force" came into usage – still referring to the USAAF – even though the United States Air Force would not be formed as a separate service until 1947.

Thus throughout this novel – as was the case in *Thanksgiving, 1942* – your author frequently switches among the various terms and names in dialogue and in the thoughts of various characters, as those alive at the time would likely have done themselves.

Part I:
Am I Really Home?

"You know, I had a dream. I dreamt I was home. I've had that same dream hundreds of times before. This time, I wanted to find out if it's really true. Am I really home?"

"The Best Years of Our Lives," 1947 Academy Award® Winner, Best Picture.

Prologue – Sunday Morning, December 16, 1945

Charlene Coleman had barely opened her eyes. Though her vision was still fogged with sleep she could tell that the three G.I.'s sitting on the other side of the railroad car's aisle, two rows ahead of her but facing backwards towards Charlene, were staring at her. Even as she forced her vision into focus she willed a smile onto her face. After all, that was what was expected of her.

One of the soldiers, a corporal who looked to be about fifteen years old but was probably eighteen or nineteen, noticed that Charlene was now awake and smiling back at them. At least a little bit braver than his two comrades, the boy rose from his bench seat and walked back to Charlene's row, stopping in the aisle in front of her.

"Are you Carla Colburn?" he asked bashfully. Maybe he was a bit reticent because he was intruding on Charlene just as she woke up from her uneasy sleep on the train, but more likely his bashfulness was because of whom he had summoned his courage to address.

Charlene's smile broadened.

"Yes I am, Corporal," she replied.

The boy turned back to his friends and energetically nodded, his own face now bearing a huge grin. The soldiers must have had a discussion, maybe even a small bet, over whether or not this beautiful young woman on *their very train* was none other than one of the most popular new starlets in Hollywood!

The young corporal turned back to Charlene and suddenly seemed tongue-tied over what to say next; or if he should say anything at all to this starlet. Charlene sized him up. He was probably too young to have seen much action, but who knew for sure? After all, Audie Murphy looked like a high school kid on the cover of *Life* magazine back in July, even though he had actually turned twenty – barely. And look at all the combat he had seen and the heroics he had accomplished!

"Where are you headed, Corporal?"

The boy took a couple of seconds to reply.

"Back home to Cleveland, ma'am," he began nervously rambling. "We're – my buddies over there and me, that is…" – he quickly looked back at his comrades, and then turned his head back again to face Charlene – "…we're all from Cleveland, and we're coming back from San Francisco. We all got back from Hawaii, where we were training for the invasion, and then they sent us to the Presidio for a while, then down to L.A. to catch this train."

Charlene didn't need to ask what invasion the boy was referring to. She knew he meant the massive invasion of Japan that never had to happen now that the war was over.

Before she had a chance to ask him another question, the corporal continued.

"We were all over in the Philippines until April, but when things slowed down there they shipped a whole bunch of us to Honolulu to get ready for the invasion. We were over there until October, then we got shipped back to 'Frisco."

The boy sighed.

"And now they're sending us all home. Discharged, effective New Year's Day. We get furlough for Christmas and then we go to a processing center in downtown Cleveland, and then we're all done."

Before Charlene could even ask the question, the boy answered it.

"We all saw you in the U.S.O. show in Manila back in March, and you were great!" The corporal started blushing, as if he was reliving some intimate memory rather than a performance with dozens of Hollywood actors and actresses and something like 4,000 G.I.'s and sailors in the audience for just that show alone! But to this soldier and his friends, and probably to most of the others who had seen Charlene and the others perform, there no doubt was an element of intimacy given that the show provided a brief reprieve from the daily horrors they had faced during the Philippine campaign overall and the Battle of Manila in particular.

Charlene's memory settled on remembrances of the two-month U.S.O. Tour she had taken part in this past spring, and the Manila show in particular that had been held amidst the city's terrible devastation. Most of her numbers were as part of an ensemble chorus made of up of stars and starlets from MGM, Columbia, Paramount, and RKO. But she had also been given two solos in most of the performances, and ironically they were the very same numbers she had sung back in late '42 in the All-City High School War Bond Benefit show that had caught the eye of Pittsburgh's own Gene Kelly, the Broadway star of *Pal Joey*. Show after show, battle-hardened soldiers and sailors were mesmerized by the newly famous Carla Colburn softly singing a solo version of *I Could Write a Book* and then *Bewitched, Bothered, and Bewildered*. The songs weren't her own; she had still been in high school when

Pal Joey had been on Broadway, and so far no movie version had come out of Hollywood even though Columbia bought the screen rights way back in 1941. But to tens of thousands of G.I.'s that spring, her own identity as an up-and-coming starlet was immutably intertwined with those two numbers.

"Could I get your autograph?"

Charlene smiled again.

"Of course," she answered. "If your friends would also like an autograph they can come over as well and we can chat for a while."

The corporal wheeled in place, went back to the row and immediately fished in his duffel bag for a fountain pen and some paper. He quickly returned with his two friends in tow, each bearing their own artifacts for Charlene to scribble her name on.

She chatted with the soldiers for about ten minutes, and then they all reluctantly headed back to their seats on the train. Before doing so, though, one of the other boys received the privilege of lighting her Chesterfield for her; no doubt a tale he would tell one and all nonstop for days after arriving back in Cleveland, and probably every so often for months to come or even longer! Meanwhile, other G.I.'s and sailors and a few Marines on the train – now alerted to a real-life Hollywood actress being on board – wandered over to ask Charlene for her autograph. No doubt the ritual would be repeated many more times as military men boarded the train at various points across the country, most of them homeward bound just in time for Christmas. Right now, Charlene figured, the train was a little bit east of Phoenix; she had many more miles to go until she disembarked in Pittsburgh.

As she always did when she began signing autographs, she reminded herself to sign her name as "Carla Colburn" rather than "Charlene Coleman."

Even though more than two years had passed since she had signed on with MGM, Charlene still occasionally thought about the whole big to-do over what her screen name would be. The studio had come up with a surprisingly long list of possibilities, with many of the names bearing her genuine initials. The list was pared down, and then Charlene found herself sitting in a smoky room on the MGM back lot with Louis B. Mayer himself and a bunch of other studio big-wigs as they made their final decision on how their new starlet would be known.

The consensus was that both her first and last names should have two syllables each, just as many of the biggest starlets did: Betty Grable; Rita Hayworth; Lana Turner; Judy Garland; Ginger Rogers; and so many others including Carol Lombard, who had died in that terrible plane crash less than two years earlier. Even Dorothy Lamour's name was typically pronounced "Door-thee" rather than the three-syllable "Dor-o-thee," the way Auntie Em in the *Wizard of Oz* had referred to Judy Garland's character. Two syllables plus two more syllables it would be for this new girl, it was decided.

From the list, the selection turned out to be "Carla Colburn." Just the right amount of smoldering mystique combined with girl-next-door approachability, Louis B. Mayer had pronounced as he bestowed Charlene with her new name. While Charlene was thrilled to be considered important enough for these Hollywood men to grant her a screen name of her own, part of her was saddened that if she indeed became famous – as she had every intention of doing – it wouldn't be by the name her parents had given her and which she had carried all of her life.

Nonetheless, Carla Colburn she was to her fans; and no doubt the servicemen on board this long train journey from Hollywood back east were thrilled at the presence of one of their favorite new starlets, no matter what she called herself.

❄ ❄ ❄

On a different train, in a different part of the country, Joseph Coleman abruptly awoke drenched in sweat, his heart racing. In his dream – his nightmare – it was the end of April again. But in the dream it wasn't the American tanks and G.I.'s arriving to liberate the prisoner of war camp as had happened in reality, but rather Nazi Panzers and S.S. killers coming to eradicate each and every one of the more than 100,000 Allied prisoners crammed into Stalag VII-A.

So this was how Captain Joseph Coleman's wartime saga would tragically end, at least in his nightmare. It had begun with the forced fifty-mile march out of Stalag Luft III along with more than 11,000 other P.O.W.s, most of them British and American fliers, at the end of January through the snow and freezing temperatures with the Soviets and the dream of liberation less than 20 miles away. Next came the cramped train ride to another Stalag, where they remained until mid-April when the Germans abruptly evacuated the prisoners from that prison camp with the approaching Americans only miles away. Finally Joseph had endured that final march to Stalag VII-A, where more than 100,000 prisoners of war of all nationalities were crammed into a camp that had been meant to hold a fraction of that population.

But in this nightmare, as in so many others he had endured over the past seven months, the third time wasn't the charm when it came to liberation. Instead of Patton's tanks arriving on April 29th, it was the Nazis again and this time they had no intention of again moving their prisoners to another camp, one step ahead of the approaching Allied forces. Machine guns began blasting away; prisoners were cut down by the hundreds where they stood or as they futilely tried to escape; and Captain Joseph Coleman watched helplessly as he knew the bullet meant for him was only seconds away…

It's only a dream! Only a nightmare!

Joseph wasn't certain if he had uttered those mollifying words only in his thoughts or if perhaps he had spoken them out loud. He looked at the two G.I.'s sitting across from him on the Pennsylvania Railroad's *Iron City Express* about an hour outside of New York City, just beginning its westward journey that would terminate in Pittsburgh.

"You okay, Captain?" A weary-looking infantry staff sergeant asked Joseph when he saw the sweat-soaked Air Corps pilot's eyes pop open, the flyer's lips moving but offering only unintelligible murmurings.

After a few seconds, Joseph replied with a simple:

"Yeah…thanks, I'm okay."

The other G.I. – a technical sergeant who was also infantry from the patches on his uniform jacket, Joseph could tell – glanced at this pilot's drenched shirt, at least the part that could be seen underneath Joseph's "Ike jacket," as the waist-length officer's coat was called. The *Iron City Express* was freezing, and this captain's field jacket hardly provided much warmth against the outside December chill that refused to be supplanted from the train by the puny wartime heating system. Still, the two dogfaces couldn't help but notice that the flyer was sweating like it was the height of summer out on some Pacific island.

"Nightmare, huh?" the tech sergeant asked Joseph, knowing the answer.

"Uh...yeah," Joseph acknowledged.

"Well, don't worry, sir; you ain't the only one, ya know," the tech sergeant commiserated. "Even after V-E Day, I ain't slept a night without wakin' up dreamin' about some battle or another that ended up with me takin' a bullet right between the eyes or in the gut."

The tech sergeant rapidly shook his head, as if those images were making their way into his thoughts at this very moment and he was trying to keep them at bay.

"I'm hopin' that after I get home all those nightmares will stop." He looked over at the other G.I. then back at Captain Joseph Coleman. "I'm hopin' anyway..." his voice trailed off.

"Yeah, me too," the staff sergeant seconded.

"It wasn't a battle," Joseph suddenly blurted out. "In my dream, I mean. I was a P.O.W. after I was shot down back in late '43, and we were only a couple of hours away from the Russians liberating us in January when we got marched to another Stalag, and then another. I mean, that's what really happened; not just in the dream. Our tanks finally came through and liberated the camp a couple of days before V-E Day, but I dreamed that instead..."

Joseph paused, but the two G.I.'s knew exactly what he would have said; that for millions of American men and boys who had fought in this terrible war and survived to the end, the world of dreams would be haunted by horrible, painful death even when real life had actually spared them for – the Good Lord willing – a long time to come.

"So where ya headed, Captain?" the staff sergeant asked. Maybe getting this flyer to yack a little bit would get his mind off of his nightmare.

"Pittsburgh," Joseph replied. "Home in time for Christmas with my family."

"Yeah? That's great," the technical sergeant offered. "I'm headed to Harrisburg, and this guy" – he pointed a thumb at the other infantryman – "is gettin' off in D.C."

"Same for us," the staff sergeant added. "Home for the holidays."

Joseph looked at these two men sitting across from him. They were all coming home, but given what they had all gone through, what toll would be extracted from each one's future?

❄ ❄ ❄

Major Jonathan Coleman's train was only four hours behind the one his sister was aboard, though of course he didn't know that. His Southern Pacific train – the *Golden State* – was rolling into Phoenix, bringing a flood of memories to Jonathan. Back in '42 he had spent months at Thunderbird Field here, side by side with his brother Joseph as both went through their initial Army Air Forces flight training. They had traveled back home to Pittsburgh together for that first Thanksgiving of the war, and after a far-too-short furlough in which Jonathan had surprisingly become reunited with Francine Donner, the Coleman boys had boarded a train headed back to Phoenix to finish up their training.

So many memories of this place! Dawn was breaking over the desert, and from his window Jonathan could see the once-sleepy city that had grown to nearly 100,000 people begin to come to life. War had brought thousands – not just the flyers, but many civilians also – to the airfields in and around the city. Then, even as the war came to an end, many were staying to bask in the desert warmth and the excitement and energy radiated by the city's rapid growth.

Jonathan welcomed the flood of memories about Thunderbird Field, some 20 miles or so north of where he was now. He wished he could get off of the train and make a short side trip up to Thunderbird to make his recollections come even more alive. However, doing so would delay his arrival in Pittsburgh by at least a couple of days because he would have to wait for another train to come through. He knew his mother would be furious if that would happen, but even besides not wanting to enrage Irene Coleman, he desperately wanted to see Francine; to be with his fiancé for the first time in more than three years!

Less than two weeks from today, he and Francine would become man and wife...finally! Jonathan couldn't help but think how strange their relationship was, thanks to the war. Four years ago, only weeks after the attack on Pearl Harbor and on the first Christmas Eve of the war, he was just about to ask Francine to marry him when she confessed that she had drunkenly allowed Jonathan's best friend and her own former boyfriend, Donnie Yablonski, to have his way with her. And that was all for Jonathan and Francine, he had figured. But nearly a year after that, when he and Joseph had been home for Thanksgiving furlough, he and Francine had bumped into each other at a lunch counter. Before they knew it, they were not only back on good terms but their aborted engagement was suddenly a reality!

Only days later, though, Jonathan was on a train much like this one back to Phoenix, and for the rest of the war the sum of his relationship with his fiancé was comprised of the hundreds of letters they wrote to each other. No matter where Jonathan was, he and Francine faithfully wrote each other: finishing up his initial flight training at Thunderbird; going through advanced flight training at Luke Field, also just outside of Phoenix; over in England with the 8th Air Force, flying B-17 bombing missions over occupied Europe and then Germany itself; and then finally out in the Pacific, flying B-29s against the Japanese.

Almost every one of Francine's letters began with some variation of "My Dearest Jonathan, I received your latest letter and am so glad you are safe!" and ended with words like "I anxiously await your next letter and word that you are still safe and will soon be coming home to me." Once, two days after a particularly harrowing bombing run over occupied France in which more than a dozen B-17s were lost, Jonathan opened a just-received letter from Francine and read her usual salutation. Then he glanced at the handwritten date on the letter that indicated she had written the letter more than a month earlier. Jonathan thought to himself that while he had indeed been safe on the date she had written him, he might well have been shot down and dead by the time the letter arrived at the air base, and he never would have read her words.

Or, if not dead, then maybe Jonathan would have been settling into a Luftstalag as a prisoner of war, just as his brother Joseph had done. For nearly six months after word came that Joseph's B-24 had been shot down over southern Germany, the younger Coleman flyer had been listed as "Missing in Action" with no word of his fate. Jonathan knew that their mother in particular was a total wreck the whole time, and he would have given anything to have been stateside to be able to provide what little comfort he could as day after day passed without any further word beyond the terrible telegram his parents had received.

Finally, on an especially sunny morning in the middle of March, 1944, another telegram arrived at his parents' Polish Hill home bearing the news that the International Red Cross had confirmed that Captain Joseph Coleman was being held prisoner by the Luftwaffe at Stalag Luft III, about 100 miles outside of Berlin. They immediately wrote Jonathan to let him know…a letter he miraculously received only two weeks after it had been written! Jonathan knew that his parents breathed a collective sigh of great relief at word that their second son was alive after all. However Jonathan's own anxiety was only heightened when he attended a Top Secret briefing less than a month later in which they all learned that a massive escape of 76 P.O.W.s from that same camp had ended with the recapture of all but three of the escapees…and the execution of fifty of them at the hands of the Gestapo, according to intercepted communications. Initial reports were that the escape had come from the British compound in the camp, not the American side, but those reports were still not fully confirmed and therefore did nothing to ease Jonathan's worries about his brother's fate.

It wasn't until Jonathan himself received a letter from his brother in February of 1945 that Joseph had written back in May of 1944. The letter had been written nine months earlier, but still after the massive escape attempt and the repercussions. Finally, Jonathan knew then for certain his brother hadn't been among the escapees caught and executed by the Nazis, or who may have fallen victim to reprisals within the camp. The letter had taken so long to catch up with Jonathan since by that time the older brother had been reassigned to the Pacific. Jonathan imagined that single letter trailing him all over the world until it finally made its way to the island of Tinian.

In the letter, Joseph made a coded reference to the mass escape attempt and the frantic activity by the Luftwaffe and Gestapo in the immediate aftermath. Jonathan knew that as an American flying officer, Joseph was duty-bound to attempt to escape. He hoped and prayed that if his brother did make it outside the wire, he would either find his way to safety or at least be unharmed during his recapture.

Of course, Jonathan had no way of knowing at the time that he received the months-old letter that his brother was not even being held in Stalag Luft III any longer, but not because of him having escaped. Jonathan had heard that the Germans were frantically moving Allied prisoners en masse from camp to camp ahead of the allies closing in on the P.O.W. camps, but no official word had yet made its way to the Pacific that Stalag Luft III had been abandoned with the Soviets on its doorstep.

In early June, the official word that arrived of his brother's liberation by the American tanks more than a month earlier actually caused Jonathan to collapse to the ground in the middle of the pilots' ready room at North Field on Tinian, overcome by the release of all of the pent-up strain from more than a year and a half's worth of daily worry about Joseph's fate. Joseph wasn't home in the

States, and there was no word yet as to his health, but the news of his freedom brought such tremendous relief to Jonathan!

Now *he* had to survive however much longer he would be at war. Even though by June the American air superiority over Japan was overwhelming, many B-29 Superfortresses were still being downed by Japanese fighters or anti-aircraft guns. Many others simply crashed after running out of fuel or from succumbing to mechanical problems. So Jonathan was by no means out of danger yet; not with so many more bombing missions and the upcoming invasion ahead.

But survive he did. And now Major Jonathan Coleman – soon to be Jonathan Coleman, Civilian – was on his way home to Pittsburgh to see his family and his fiancé for the first time in more than three years; a visit that would culminate in his marriage to Francine.

❄ ❄ ❄

Marine Corps Private Thomas Coleman yawned for the second time, then the third, as he awoke as his train pulled into Richmond, Virginia. His uneasiness at being on board the *Sunland* with so many returning combat Marines had finally eased, at least a little bit. After all, it wasn't Private Coleman's doing that the war was now over. He had enlisted at the end of May, only a week after his high school graduation, while the Battle of Okinawa was still raging and the eventual invasion of Japan was all but a certainty. He had made it through the rigors of basic training at Parris Island and then infantry training at Camp Lejeune, and was as ready to fight as the next Marine. But because of those two super-bombs the war was suddenly, mercifully over. Consequently, Thomas Coleman wouldn't be invading any territory other than the many bars of Onslow County, North Carolina for one rip-roaring V-J Day celebration after another in the company of his fellow Marines.

So many of the Marines on board this northbound train had been on Saipan, Iwo Jima, Okinawa, Guadalcanal, and many of the other islands all over the Pacific. Thomas could tell by their battle ribbons and their war-weary faces, many of which still bore a distant, shell-shocked look. Thomas mostly kept to himself, not quite feeling the subdued esprit de corps of the hard-won victory that these men likely did. He might have been ready, willing, and able to go ashore during an amphibious landing or brave a banzai charge with steely nerves, but unlike many of these other men aboard he had not been afforded the opportunity.

That didn't matter, though. He would be home in Pittsburgh soon for furlough over the Christmas holidays, and then he would be on his way to Camp Pendleton, way out west in California. Thomas had no idea what awaited him after arriving, though. Maybe the post-war Marines would resemble the pre-war Corps, with sort of a low-key state of readiness and the overwhelming desire of trying to get stationed in Hawaii or some other exotic location as the chief "worry" most Marines faced.

Thomas would find out soon enough. For now, though, he couldn't wait to arrive at home and see his older brothers for the first time in years. He said another silent prayer of thanks that Joseph in particular had survived the war after being shot down and captured by the Nazis, then marched all over Europe from one Stalag to another as the Nazis tried to move their prisoners of war one step ahead of the allied forces who were closing in from all sides. Joseph would soon be home, as would Jonathan.

And also his sister, the movie star! The first time Thomas went to a movie during a weekend pass at Camp Lejeune, he and five of his buddies went to see Gene Kelly and Frank Sinatra in *Anchors Aweigh*. And even though Charlene – that is, Carla Colburn – only had a small supporting role, that was her third movie released during this summer of 1945 and she was already one of the most popular new starlets of the year. His very own sister!

Of course, it had been a little bit uncomfortable to walk into the barracks at Lejeune one afternoon and find the cover of *Photoplay* with his sister's smiling face pinned up over one of the other Marine's bunks. But at least it hadn't been one of those Betty Grable or Rita Hayworth sexy photos in a swimsuit or a negligee. Charlene's picture on that cover was that sort-of-wholesome "girl next door" photo, though her eyes did twinkle with that smallest touch of suggestiveness that apparently was part of the image the studio was building for her.

Thomas shook those thoughts out of his head, focusing instead on the opportunity to ask his sister how many movie stars she knew, and what they were really like.

❄ ❄ ❄

Irene Coleman found herself unable to stop repeatedly glancing at Lukas and Paulina Jaskolski, seated three rows in front of the one that she, her husband Gerald, and their youngest daughter Ruthie occupied this Sunday morning at Saint Michael's. The Kozlows were seated to the left of the Jaskolskis with the Pasternaks immediately to the right, and there were no open seats in their row. Yet there might as well have been – in fact, *should* have been – seats left empty in memory of both Damian and Sebastian Jaskolski. Christmas was now only a week and a half away, and whereas Irene's three sons would all soon converge on the Coleman house, the two Jaskolski boys would never be returning to their mother's home.

Irene glanced over at her husband and caught Gerald Coleman's vision traversing the exact same path that hers had a split second earlier. No doubt Gerald was thinking much the same thing that she herself had been considering.

Next Sunday; that's what Irene forced herself to focus on. Next Sunday, the entire Coleman clan would be gathered together for Sunday Mass at Saint Michael's for the first time in more than three years! The last time had been the very morning that Jonathan and Joseph had returned to Pittsburgh from Air Corps training at Thunderbird Field out in Arizona, and Irene had promptly marched the two older boys along with the rest of the family directly to Saint Michael's. November of 1942; that's when it had been. The Sunday before the first Thanksgiving of the war; the last Thanksgiving the entire family had been able to spend together. By the time the next Thanksgiving and Christmas had come around, Irene was all but certain that Joseph was dead. That terrible day in September of '43 that the Western Union man delivered the telegram was one that Irene was still certain had taken years off of her life, despite learning six months later that Joseph was indeed alive and being held prisoner by the Nazis.

But during Thanksgiving of '43, the Coleman family somberly gathered at their home for an occasion that felt far more like a wake than a holiday celebration.

For his part, Gerald Coleman was also thinking this morning of the tragic loss of the Jaskolski boys. Gerald was powerless to his mind's insistence on playing out a scenario from an alternate reality in which it wasn't Damian and Sebastian Jaskolski who would never come back from the war, but rather Jonathan and Joseph Coleman. In this nightmarish vision, all eyes were on poor Gerald and Irene Coleman, wondering just how the grieving parents would cope with the loss of their two beloved sons.

Finally, Gerald was able to drag his thoughts away from this horrible – but, thank God, imagined – scenario. Instead, he recalled one of the headlines in this morning's Sunday *Pittsburgh Press*: "End War, Truman Tells China." Truman had just sent General Marshall to China to personally deliver this message to Chiang Kai-shek and the National Government to cease their hostilities with the Chinese communists.

Wasn't the world sick of war by now? Along with China, the *Press'* editorial had called upon the British and the Dutch to halt the East Indies War in Java. This historic year of 1945, in which both Nazi Germany and Imperial Japan were finally defeated, was half a month away from its conclusion and war still simmered in China and the East Indies? Enough already! Even the official word in this morning's paper that the United States would be the capital for the new United Nations – the "world machinery designed to keep nations at peace," as the article proclaimed – seemed so hollow with fighting still raging in so many far-off corners of the world. Would this new organization, most likely headquartered in either

Boston or San Francisco according to the article, be able to enforce its mission of peace on those who seemed to believe – even after what they all had just gone through – that war was still the preferred instrument of both foreign policy and domestic one-upmanship?

Just when Gerald was questioning whether he should even bother reading the newspapers anymore, given the troubling news that was reported day after day, he finally was able to drag his thoughts to something more pleasant he had also read in this morning's *Pittsburgh Press*: the plans for glorious, city-wide Christmas celebrations to mark the homecoming of so many of Pittsburgh's returning soldiers, sailors, and airmen. The YWCA; the Salvation Army; the Home for the Friendless; the Evangeline Residence Friendship Club; and dozens more civic organizations had plans in the works for not only the returning servicemen (and servicewomen too) but also orphans and even youngsters in trouble at the Juvenile Detention Home.

Gerald Coleman's thoughts next shifted to the frigid cold that had settled onto Pittsburgh this Sunday. At this moment the mercury was resting at six degrees above zero…but at least it was above zero, considering that only two hours ago the temperature had been two degrees on the other side of zero! The coldest December 16th in Pittsburgh's history!

As miserable as those in Pittsburgh might be about their cold spell, however, further north in Buffalo the snow was coming down unabated! Pittsburghers wouldn't learn the full news until the next day's headlines, but forty-eight inches of snow – four whole feet! – would fall on Buffalo this day. As far west as Chicago and Indianapolis, snow and cold ruled the land.

Gerald thought about the various trains coming from the west carrying two of their four returning children. He said a rapid, silent prayer (he was in the proper place to do so, after all) that whatever snows there might be would not disrupt Jonathan's or Charlene's travel schedules, delaying their scheduled Tuesday arrivals at Pittsburgh's Penn Station by even an hour. Every bit as much as Irene, Gerald Coleman wanted his family back together for the first time in more than three years to celebrate this first Christmas after the end of the war.

1 – Sunday Evening, December 16, 1945

"Pittsburgh! Pennsylvania Station! Penn Station… Pittsburgh…"

Thomas Coleman was already out of his seat, holding his Marine Corps seabag with his left hand as he steadied himself on the seatback with his right hand, the train jerking to a stop almost precisely at 9:30 this Sunday evening. He was home!

Thomas crushed the remnants of his Chesterfield into the railroad car floor as he deferentially let a couple of G.I.'s and airmen from further back in the train car ease by his row while waiting to step out into the aisle himself. He could tell that these men were returning from one combat theater or another, and it only seemed right to him that they should get off this train and greet whomever was waiting for them before Thomas did. He searched the faces for any that might be familiar, but they were still pretty much the same men who had been on the train from at least Richmond. Nobody else on this train at least seemed to be from Polish Hill or any of the other neighborhoods that fed into Schenley High School.

"Go 'head, kid," Thomas heard a voice. He turned around and a Marine sergeant had paused so Thomas could step into the aisle. Thomas could feel the sergeant's eyes on him. The sergeant could of course tell that Private Thomas Coleman, USMC, might be returning home to Pittsburgh for the holidays but he was not doing so from out in the Pacific, or anywhere else where combat had raged for years. Thomas immediately began to feel self-conscious again, but he brushed the thoughts aside. I'm being overly sensitive, he told himself; I'm just a kid who had the luck of the draw to enlist in early '45 while guys like this sergeant here were finishing the job of winning the war before I had to join them in combat.

Thomas shook the thoughts from his head, nodded his thanks to the sergeant, and began heading down the aisle towards the door. More than six months had passed since he had last seen his parents and his little sister Ruthie. Thomas had last seen Charlene back in early '44…other than on the movie screen, of course. And for Jonathan and Joseph, it had been more than three years now!

Thomas had no way of knowing the order in which the Coleman boys and their sister would be arriving in Pittsburgh from their various points of origin, so he stepped off the train half-expecting to see at least one of his older brothers waiting on the platform for him. He was just beginning to scan the faces – and uniforms – in the crowded station when he heard his mother's voice:

"Tommy! Over here! Tommy! Over here!"

He looked to his left and there they were, about twenty yards away in the middle of the throng. He immediately picked out his father's face even before he could see his mother, but at first glance he saw neither Jonathan nor Joseph. He began to make his way through the crowd towards his family, being careful not to be too pushy yet at the same time, determined to make steady forward progress just as he had as a star Schenley High football halfback.

It was his sister Ruthie, however, who reached Thomas first. She had woven her way towards him as deftly as Thomas had ever done on the football field and he was still a good ten yards away from his parents when he felt the thud of his little sister colliding with him and hanging on in a tight welcoming embrace.

"Tommy!" the ten-year old girl said, greeting the next youngest in the family as if she hadn't seen him for the same three long years that Jonathan and Joseph had been away.

"Ruthie!" Thomas Coleman reached down, dropped his seabag, and easily lifted his sister so that she was face to face with him. "Gee, am I glad to see you!"

By that time Irene and Gerald Coleman had made their way to where Thomas and Ruthie were, and Irene leaned forward to give her son a huge hug even as he still held onto his sister.

"Ma!" Thomas said, surprisingly feeling his eyes begin to tear up just the slightest bit. "I'm glad to be home, let me tell you!"

Irene refused to release her embrace, reacting to the return of her youngest son as if he had been away at war rather than returned home to Pittsburgh courtesy of a holiday furlough. To Irene Coleman, the fact that Tommy had just made it out of training and that the years of war were finally over mattered not in the least; he was every bit the returning warrior that his older brothers would be when they would soon reprise this very scene. In fact, the enormity of Irene's welcome was at least in part because of her relief that the war had ended before Tommy had been forced to fight for his life in mortal combat.

Finally, realizing that Gerald also wanted to greet his son, she released Tommy. There would be plenty more times for embracing her son while he was home on Christmas furlough before he had to board that train to California shortly after New Year's Day.

"Hi, Pop," Tommy said as he lowered Ruthie to the ground and held out his right hand. Gerald hesitated for a moment and then stuck his own right hand forward to shake his son's hand; but he also, at the same time, reached forward with his left hand to give Thomas a fatherly squeeze on the boy's right shoulder as they shook hands.

"Welcome home, Private Coleman," Gerald said, his eyes appraising his son's forest green winter service uniform that Thomas had not been out of since leaving Camp Lejeune. As a private Thomas still had yet to earn any stripes, though he hoped to pin on Private First Class rank and that first stripe soon after getting to Camp Pendleton. Still, to his father, Thomas Coleman looked every bit the young Marine he was. Except, thank God, he wasn't returning home with either the hollow stare or jumpy eyes that some of the other young men on the Penn Station platform this very evening had brought home with them, courtesy of some horror of war or another.

Thomas was just beginning to reply to his father – he had uttered exactly half of "Thanks, Pop" – when he heard his sentence behind him finished by somebody else.

Private Thomas Coleman, USMC: "Thanks…"

Captain Joseph Coleman, USAAF: "Pop…"

Gerald's eyes flew open at the sight of his second son, and his mouth dropped. He was utterly speechless, as was Irene Coleman. Even Tommy seemed in shock at the sudden appearance of his brother. It was Ruthie who finally broke the silence.

"Joey!" she exclaimed, rushing forward to greet her brother Joseph in exactly the same way that she had greeted Thomas only moments earlier. For his part,

Joseph – who had last seen Ruthie when she was all of seven years old – seemed as much in shock as every other member of the family, though initially for him it was the sight of what those three long years had done to his baby sister.

Finally, Irene Coleman shook off the astonishment of the sudden appearance of her other son.

"Joseph!" she said as the tears instantly came, as she knew they would. "Joseph!"

She embraced Joseph, continuing to call his name over and over through the sobs that came along with the tears; unable to say anything else.

For his part, Gerald Coleman – ever the stoic one, always coolly collected even in the midst of an unfolding crisis – was utterly helpless against the appearance of his own tears as he patiently waited for Irene to allow him the opportunity to welcome his son home.

❋ ❋ ❋

Nearly fifteen minutes had passed before the Coleman family members that were gathered at Penn Station were ready to make their way out into the frigid Pittsburgh night. Both Thomas and Joseph had steeled themselves for the long, chilly walk home from the train depot, but Gerald Coleman had a surprise for both of his boys when he stopped directly behind a battleship gray Packard Six and opened the car's trunk lid, waiting for his sons to toss their service bags inside.

"What the hell is this?" Thomas Coleman blurted out, realizing his mistake before the sentence had finished passing through his lips.

"Thomas Coleman!" Irene Coleman shrieked.

"Tommy…" Gerald Coleman likewise chastised his son, albeit less harshly than the boy's mother.

"Sorry, Ma," Thomas replied sheepishly. "I was just surprised, that's all."

Thomas shot a glance towards Joseph, but he was getting no help there. Joseph just shrugged – so slightly that his mother wouldn't notice – and shot a look back at his younger brother that wordlessly said "You're not at Parris Island or Camp Lejeune, and when it comes to cursing you better think of Ma as tougher than any drill instructor you've encountered."

"Anyway," Thomas continued, turning his attention back to the Packard, "is this ours?"

"It is," Gerald nodded as he crunched through the crusty layer of now-grayish snow over to the back door on his driver's side to allow Ruthie to scramble into the car.

"When did you buy it?" Thomas wanted to know. When he had left for boot camp at the beginning of June, barely more than six months earlier, the Coleman family didn't own this Packard Six…or any other car. In fact, the Colemans had never owned an automobile, thanks to the Great Depression and then the wartime restrictions and rationing.

"Back at the beginning of October," Gerald replied. "It's a '38, and I bought it from a fellow over in East Liberty who was looking to sell it."

Gerald Coleman needn't have mentioned the Packard as being a 1938 model, at least for the benefit of Thomas. The boy may have grown up in a family that had never owned a car but he knew nearly every make and model of automobile on the road today, and dreamed of the day when he would make enough money to be able to buy a car of his own. Maybe not for the foreseeable future as a Marine private making all of fifty dollars a month, but down the road...

Ruthie had already scrambled over to the middle of the back seat, anxiously awaiting her brothers to climb inside on either side of her. The ride home might be a very short one, but to this little girl being in the company of her two brothers in uniform would be heaven!

Joseph tossed his duffel bag into the open trunk and then climbed into the back seat from the left side behind Ruthie, while Thomas likewise tossed his seabag into the trunk and then shut the lid before climbing into the back seat from the right side. He noticed a few rust spots on the back of the Packard and also on the right side before getting inside – not surprising with the car being a '38 model and having gone through so many Pittsburgh winters – but all in all, at least based on outward appearances the vehicle seemed sturdy enough. It might not be one of those upscale Packards like the rich people had driven even into the early years of the Depression, but it was a Coleman family car – the first one – nonetheless. Even though he didn't have a driver's license, Thomas Coleman's mind was already wandering to the prospect of borrowing the car once or twice while he was home on furlough, maybe in the company of some of his high school buddies, to drive around Pittsburgh to other neighborhoods.

During the drive home up Liberty Avenue, Joseph wordlessly looked outside the car; mostly through the back left window nearest to him, but occasionally out the front windshield or over across Ruthie and Thomas to the right of the car. The sights! The memories! So much of what had been tamped down into the deep recesses of his brain during his years as a prisoner of war was flooding back right now! Familiar buildings and business signs; the intersection at 16th Street, leading to the bridge across the Allegheny off to the left…all of it!

And then, making the turn off of Liberty Avenue for the last part of the drive home…Joseph couldn't help it, his thoughts again turned to those long-ago memories – far too brief memories – of Thanksgiving back in '42 and Abby Sobol, as the Packard crunched along the snow-crusted streets.

Thoughts of Abby had sustained him through those long months as a prisoner, even though the letters from her had stopped about a month before he was shot down. Ironically, whereas D-Day had been the beginning of the end for the Nazis it also meant the beginning of the end for mail delivered to the allied prisoners held by the Germans. German planes that had regularly flown in and out of Lisbon halted their shuttle efforts as the allies took France; and as the fighting moved closer to Switzerland, prisoners' mail through that other neutral country ceased as well.

It wasn't until Joseph was finally back in the United States, several weeks after his arrival at Syracuse Army Air Base, that word reached him via Tommy that Abby Sobol had gotten engaged that past April to some 4-F schmo who had spent the entire war working a desk job at one of the steel plants. As far as Joseph knew she wasn't married yet; but it was apparently only a matter of time.

And that was that.

❄ ❄ ❄

The Coleman house was a simple one without the luxury of a garage for the Packard, but the parking spot directly in front of their house was usually unoccupied as it was this evening. The brothers and their sister piled out of the back seat while their parents did likewise from the front of the car, and in less than one minute everyone was inside the house, basking in the warmth radiated by the coal stove in the basement.

Gerald noticed Joseph looking around the house as if he were seeing it for the first time ever; drinking in the sight of every piece of furniture, each framed picture, and every single knickknack as if each were a precious gift to be cherished to the utmost. Gerald looked over at Tommy and his youngest son who was also watching Joseph. Gerald's eyes traveled back to Joseph and in the light of the living room took in the details of his son's Army Air Forces uniform: the Ike jacket; the captain's bars; the two rows of battle ribbons; and most of all, the pilot's wings.

"I'll make hot chocolate," Irene's voice interrupted Gerald's thoughts. "We'll all sit in the living room and have hot chocolate and talk."

"Sounds great, Ma," Joseph said as he removed his officer's hat and sunk into what had once been his favorite chair, still looking around the living room as he reached into his Ike jacket pocket and extracted a Chesterfield. Joseph had taken up smoking Raleighs while a prisoner since the occasional Red Cross packages that made their way to Stalag Luft III almost always came with packs of Raleighs. As Joseph's barracks chief – a crusty Lieutenant Colonel from Iowa who had actually worked on the line at the Duesenberg auto plant during much of the Depression – proclaimed every time the parcels wound up being delivered and someone would inevitably remark about the ever-present Raleighs: "You smoke what you can get; we ain't on a rich man's vacation here with butler service, in case you boys ain't figured that out yet." Of course, a hefty share of the Raleighs were set aside to be used to bribe the Luftwaffe guards for small favors here and there, eventually resulting in a severe cigarette shortage until the next batch of Red Cross parcels would mercifully make their way to the Luftstalag. Those regular shortages, in turn, transformed every single Raleigh cigarette into much more of a preciously scarce commodity than it otherwise would have been to the imprisoned G.I.'s.

Raleighs had been alright, especially in the middle of a German winter and the red glow of a cigarette's lit end was just about the only warm thing around some days. But now, Joseph so much associated Raleigh cigarettes with his time as a prisoner that if he never smoked another one the rest of his life, that would be just fine with him. He held out a Chesterfield to his brother, who accepted, and another one to his father who did likewise.

Thomas was initially going to plop himself onto the chair closest to Joseph's, but he decided to leave that one for their father and instead walked over to the sofa and sat on the side closest to the good old Philco. Thomas instinctively reached to turn on the radio, and after the Philco warmed up he twirled the dial to look for music rather than a comedy or drama program. A little music in the background would be perfect for tonight as they welcomed Joseph home after such a long time.

Bing Crosby's baritone appeared, about halfway through *I Can't Begin to Tell You*. Thomas twiddled with the dial to wash out a touch of static, and then turned the volume down a couple of notches until Bing's rich voice was no longer dominating the cozy Coleman living room.

"I'll tell you," Joseph said, staring at the Philco, "I would've given my left arm to have that radio – or any radio for that matter – in the Luftstalag. We were starving for music. The Germans wouldn't even let us have a phonograph like they had in some of the other camps because they somehow got it into their heads that one of our guys, this B-24 radio engineer, was some kind of electronics genius who could take a record player apart and actually turn it into a radio transmitter."

Gerald carefully watched his son as Joseph mentioned, for the first time since his arrival, having been a prisoner of war. He had had no idea what to expect, and still had no idea how to respond. Having a son come back from war would be tough enough; he had realized that for a long while. Do you ask him about his bombing missions? About friends and comrades, many of whom no doubt had been lost forever in the skies over Europe? About what he did between missions when he wasn't flying?

All of that would be difficult enough with Jonathan when he arrived home. But with Joseph, there was also more than a year and a half as a prisoner of the German Luftwaffe. Would his son want to talk about what he had gone through? Would doing so help? Or would that terrible experience be one that Joseph would want to put behind him for the rest of his life and never, *ever* have the subject brought up in his presence?

Apparently, though, Joseph was willing to talk at least a little bit about what he had gone through. Gerald had so many questions! When Joseph had bailed out of his fatally shot-up B-24, did he think he would make it safely to the ground? What had gone through his mind the very moment he realized that he would be captured by the Germans? What was it like, day after day, living in a prisoner of war camp? Was he able to stay in reasonably good health as a prisoner? What had those first seconds of freedom been like when the American tanks rolled in and he realized that his long months as a prisoner of the Germans had just come to an end?

There would be time enough to ask his son these questions, and many more. At least Gerald thought so, but only if his son was willing to talk about it. Joseph was home on furlough for at least a month before the Air Corps would send him back somewhere until he accumulated enough points to be discharged in early '46. And then Joseph would be home for good, as his older brother would soon be.

Irene appeared in the doorway between the living room and the kitchen carrying a large tray filled with steaming cups of hot chocolate, with Ruthie trailing behind bearing a smaller tray just about overflowing with donuts. Irene walked over to the coffee table in front of the chairs where Joseph and Gerald were sitting and eased the tray downwards onto the table's surface, leaving room for Ruthie to do likewise with the tray of donuts.

Joseph couldn't help the grin.

"Just like the U.S.O.," he said as he reached forward to pick up a cup of hot chocolate with his right hand and, simultaneously, a glazed donut with his left hand. The donut was gone in three quick bites before Joseph even took a sip of his hot chocolate, or before anybody else was able to pick up a cup or a donut of their own. Irene was just about to instinctively scold her son for wolfing down the donut when she caught herself.

"Have another one," she said instead, reaching herself to retrieve another glazed donut and then handing the pastry to Joseph.

"Thanks Ma," Joseph said, still chewing the last remnants of the donut he had devoured so quickly. As if reading his mother's thoughts from a few seconds earlier, he added:

"Sorry, I don't mean to be…well, you know. I hadn't even seen a donut in years until making it back to the States, and ever since then I can't help myself when I get a chance to eat 'em."

"Even after you were liberated?" Thomas blurted out before realizing that he may well have inadvertently touched on a subject that Joseph had no desire to discuss.

His brother seemed to jolt a little bit at the question but fortunately didn't take any offense, at least outwardly.

"C-rations and K-rations for months," was Joseph's answer. "The camp was liberated right before V-E Day and let me tell you, all…" – he shot a look at his mother as he caught himself – "…heck broke loose, all over Europe. There was something like 100,000 of us in that last camp and after they pulled all of us Americans out from the rest of the prisoners they were rushing parcels in for us as quickly as they could. But it wasn't like there they had the Hollywood Canteen set up over there; nothing like that. Believe me, at least we were getting steady rations for the most part, which was better than the last four or five months or so in the camps after they started marching us from one to…"

Out of the corner of his eye Joseph caught his little sister closely watching him, captivated by the tale he was starting to tell. But this was no tale for a ten-year old girl; that was for sure. For his own part, Joseph was surprised at what was spurting forth from his mouth. For months he had wondered just what – if anything – he would tell his mother and father, and his sisters and even Tommy, about what he had endured since late '43 when he was shot down and captured. Telling Jonathan? That would be one thing, talking to a fellow Air Corps flyer every bit as much as talking to his brother. But the rest of his own family? Well, he may not have been sure but here he was, home for less than an hour, and already he was speaking matter-of-factly about the lack of a phonograph and living on those once-dreaded K-rations and C-rations after liberation.

Still, Joseph thought as he glanced over at Ruthie, some stories – in fact, many stories – were not for a little girl's ears.

"Anyway," Joseph said, changing the subject as he reached for yet a third donut, "I can't begin to tell you how much I've missed things like hot chocolate and donuts. Thanks Ma," he said, glancing at his mother, "you couldn't have chosen a better welcome-home for me."

Irene Coleman – always satisfied when one of her children expressed gratitude in response to her mealtime or snacking efforts – smiled appreciatively, but her mind couldn't get past the sight of her son finally sitting in her living room after all this time! And before too many more days had passed, Jonathan would be home as well; and in his case he would be home for good!

✵ ✵ ✵

Ruthie was shooed off to bed just before 11:30 that night; the latest the little girl had ever been allowed to stay up. She was already begging her mother not to have to go to school tomorrow, but Irene would have none of that. Ruthie may be extra-tired Monday morning but off to school it would be for her; and that would be that.

Sensing that Gerald wanted some time with just his two sons, Irene excused herself to bed about a half-hour after sending Ruthie upstairs. There would be plenty of time for her to talk with Joseph in the days ahead. Besides, Irene felt an overwhelming need for some private time of her own to give thanks for Joseph's safe return. Even after word of his liberation from that prisoner of war camp reached the Coleman household, very little further news followed. It wasn't until the end of August, not long after V-J Day, that a bundle of nearly two dozen letters Joseph had written as far back as early May made their way to the Coleman's mailbox. Irene had quickly devoured each and every word on each and every letter, and by the time an hour or so had passed Irene was finally convinced that her son was alive after all, and would soon be on his way home…hopefully in time for Christmas, based on what Joseph had communicated in the final letter that had been written only two weeks earlier.

Three more long months would pass until another bundle of letters arrived shortly after Thanksgiving. The most recent of those letters had been written during the first week of November just before Joseph had stepped onto a returning Liberty ship for a choppy, green-around-the-gills voyage back across the Atlantic. Upon his arrival at New York City, however, the Air Corps in its infinite wisdom decided that about a thousand returning prisoners of war – including Captain Joseph Coleman – would undergo at least a month's worth of additional debriefing and medical care up at the Syracuse Army Air Base before finally being allowed furlough in time for the holidays. Very little of the debriefing activity that took place in Syracuse was any different than the dozens of interview sessions Joseph participated in during the months in Europe following his liberation. But as the freed USAAF flyers told themselves and each other many times, "Well, you know the Army; everything in triplicate, or more!"

As it was, just before Joseph was granted holiday furlough he was sent from Syracuse to New York City for a ceremony honoring released prisoners of war. He would just as soon have skipped the ceremony – all he wanted to do at this point was get home to Pittsburgh – but orders were orders, and off to Manhattan he went.

All the while, Irene fretted for her son's safety. To her mind, until she saw with her own two eyes what she had witnessed downstairs this very evening – Joseph sitting in her living room, smoking a cigarette and enjoying a welcome-home snack – she would not believe or accept that he was indeed finally safe.

❄ ❄ ❄

Gerald stayed downstairs for another hour after Irene went upstairs. He had plenty of work in the morning but since he no longer worked at the war plant along with his own cobbler business, he no longer needed to rise early enough each day to guarantee at least a twelve-hour workday. So this morning he could sleep a little bit later than he usually did on a weekday and still be able to get his scheduled work done. Normally Gerald was up by 6:30 in the morning at the very latest; if he stayed asleep for an extra half-hour, he could squeeze in six hours of sleep…that is, if he could fall asleep right away.

As it was, though, Gerald Coleman remained awake until after 3:00 that morning, his thoughts churning over and over through Joseph's tale of the fifty-mile march through the freezing German winter at the end of this past January. Joseph had been among the group of prisoners chosen by their German guards to clear the snow from the road ahead of the main group of the remaining P.O.W.'s and their Luftwaffe "hosts." Gerald listened – horrified and fascinated at the same time – as Joseph confessed that after he had been selected for that work detail, for the first time since he had been shot down he had tremendous doubts that he would live to see another day. Tales had circulated throughout the Luftstalag about what might happen when someone was selected for a Nazi "work detail." So between the frigid weather and the constant fear of being "shot while trying to escape" – the same fate that had befallen fifty of the 76 prisoners who had made it out of Stalag Luft III through the tunnel ten months earlier – Joseph's expectations for his own survival were at their very lowest as that icy January of 1945 gave way to an even colder February. The guards assigned to march them from Sagan to Spremberg might be the same Luftwaffe enlisted men who could be occasionally bribed with American cigarettes and who seemed to yearn for an end to this war as much as their allied prisoners, but with the Third Reich crumbling all around them all bets were off as to whether these Luftwaffe men were really all that different than their fellow Nazis in the Gestapo and S.S.

Eventually, after the alarm clock ticked its way past three, Gerald finally slipped away into a restless sleep filled with dream snippets replaying some portion or another of his son's troubling tale.

❄ ❄ ❄

"I'm sorry about Abby," Thomas finally blurted out when the two brothers were alone, about five minutes after their father had trudged upstairs.

Joseph sighed.

"Yeah," he said, looking over at the Philco. That figured; Harry James and *It's Been a Long, Long Time* would have to be playing right now, wouldn't it? Talk about the wrong song to be on the radio for a returning warrior whose girl had gotten engaged to somebody else while he was surviving day to day in a Luftstalag.

"When did you know?" Joseph asked his brother. Tommy, in fact, had been the one to break the news about Abby to his brother by letter about two weeks after Joseph's arrival at the Syracuse Army Air Base.

Thomas took a deep breath and fidgeted on the sofa, obviously uncomfortable with the question.

"Come on, Tommy; I'm not going to take it out on you."

"Yeah, I know," Thomas quickly replied. "I mean, I felt terrible about having to tell you…"

"Yeah," Joseph interrupted. "It's not often you get a 'Dear John' letter written by your brother."

"I know," Thomas muttered, again looking away from his brother.

"So?" Joseph asked after about fifteen seconds of silence.

Realizing that his brother was not going to let the subject drop, Thomas Coleman finally looked back at Joseph.

"About a month before you were shot down," he eventually replied. "All the way back then. Not about being engaged – that was this past April like I wrote you – but about some other guy bein' in the picture. Francine came by *Weisberg's* when I was working after school, and said that Abby had told her that she had met this other guy and he had asked her to go steady with him, and…"

"Go steady?" Joseph interrupted.

"Well, you know," Thomas replied. "Whatever they call it when you're out of high school. 'Going with him' or something like that. Anyway, Francine said that Abby was going to write you a Dear John."

Thomas looked away from his brother for a couple of seconds, and then back at Joseph before continuing.

"I don't know what it was, Joey, but I had this bad feeling. I told her to tell Abby not to write you just then. I just…I don't know, I thought…"

Thomas couldn't put words to what he had felt at the time, but Joseph got the point.

"A premonition?"

"Yeah," Thomas nodded. "A premonition. I had a premonition that something was going to happen…you know, something like you getting shot down and captured, and I figured that the last thing you needed to know if the Krauts captured you and sent you to a P.O.W.

camp for the rest of the war was that Abby was seeing some other guy."

Thomas shrugged, then continued.

"I'm sorry, I shouldn't have…"

"No," Joseph interrupted, "you did the right thing; at least I think you did. The whole time I was in the Luftstalag, thinking about Abby kept me going. You know, having someone to come home to if I…I mean, after I got out of there."

Now it was Joseph's turn to look away, his thoughts miles away.

"It was stupid anyway," he said, his eyes gazing across the living room but actually staring back in time.

"I spent only a couple days with her before I had to go back to Thunderbird Field; what did I expect? Even though we wrote each other all the time we never saw each other again, and the whole time I kept wondering if…"

Joseph looked back towards his brother, not finishing his sentence.

"Anyway," he shrugged, "that's the way it goes, I guess."

He looked away again and then asked Thomas the question that had been on his mind for a while now, ever since learning that Jonathan would soon be home and that shortly afterwards he and Francine would be getting married.

"Do you know if she's coming to the wedding?"

"I don't know," Thomas replied after contemplating the question for a few seconds. "Francine never said anything about it, and I don't think she – I mean Abby – would come anyway if you're going to be…I mean…"

"Yeah," Joseph nodded, "I know what you mean."

As it was, precious little was known by either of the Coleman boys about their brother's upcoming wedding to Francine, other than that Joseph would be Jonathan's best man and Thomas would also stand up for his brother, as would their cousin Marty Walker. Marty had already been home from the Navy – discharged and everything – for more than two months, though for the wedding he planned to wear his Navy Dress Blues once again.

On Francine's side, though, other than her sister Julia serving as the matron of honor, the rest of the bride's wedding party was unknown. Irene Coleman was increasingly irritated with both Francine and her mother, Sally Donner, for what Irene perceived as being nearly totally excluded from the planning for the fast-approaching wedding. The affair would be the farthest thing from a big shindig; Jack Donner had put away enough money from his railroad yard job for a modest family event and not much more. But Irene was still the mother of the groom, and being so much in the dark about the plans for her son's big day was about as irksome as anything in the world might be. Sally Donner kept putting off the matter with "after Jonathan gets home we will all get together and finish up the planning" but Irene was far from mollified by the stalling on the part of Jonathan's future mother-in-law…especially with the wedding day approaching so quickly!

"Well," Joseph added, "if she does show up with her…" – he couldn't bring himself to utter the word "fiancé" – "…we should let Ma know that I won't make a big scene or anything like that."

"Francine too," Joseph added.

"Yeah," Thomas nodded, then looked back at his brother.

"How bad was it?"

For a moment Joseph thought that his brother was referring to Joseph hearing for the first time about Abby's engagement, but then he quickly realized what his brother meant.

"The first couple months were…I don't know, it was all really strange. They had just opened the American compound in the camp a little bit before I got there, and a lot of our guys who got transferred into there had been working on digging those escape tunnels out from the British side before they got moved. So I was getting settled in with a lot of other new prisoners, and the guys who had been there for a while were showing us the ropes, and all the while everyone was on edge knowing that this big escape from the British side was coming sometime in spring or summer."

He paused for a second and then added:

"If the Krauts didn't find the tunnels first, that is."

Joseph got up from his chair and started for the kitchen.

"You want a beer?" he asked Thomas.

"I'm not sure if Pop has any in the icebox," Thomas replied.

Joseph shrugged.

"Well, I'll go see," was his answer.

Sure enough, three bottles of Fort Pitt were resting on the top shelf of the icebox. Joseph grabbed two of them, flicked off the tops with the bottle opener, and then returned to the living room to hand one to his brother before plopping back down in his chair.

"It was strange," Joseph said again. "You really didn't do much from day to day. You couldn't go anywhere – obviously – but for the most part the Luftwaffe guards weren't too bad. Some of them you woulda liked to have gotten your hands on a pistol and put a bullet between their eyes, but most of them were guys just like us who had gotten stuck with being guards at a Stalag rather than flying missions on a Heinkel or a Junkers. Even a lot of the officers weren't too bad. They were flyers like we were, and by late '43 and '44 most of them were plenty happy not to be up in the sky anymore given how the war was starting to turn."

Joseph downed a little more of his beer before continuing.

"In some ways it was sort of like being in basic training back in the States – you know, at a military field and not being able to leave – but without having to do all the marching and training and other crap straight through for eighteen hours a day like in basic. We did have *Appel* – you know, roll call – twice a day for the Krauts to count us and see if anybody had escaped since the last one. And during the winter we would sometimes stand out there for hours, freezing our butts off, if some sergeant on their side kept messing up the count and had to start all over. But other than that, the winters were just…really cold."

The brothers continued talking until close to 4:30 that morning before exhaustion finally overtook both of them. Thomas mostly asked questions and listened to one story after another about his brother's prison camp experiences; however – in response to Joseph's question – he did tell his brother a little bit about the rigors of Marine Corps boot camp at Parris Island and then infantry training at Camp Lejeune. Joseph seemed to take pride at his younger brother's Marine Corps duty thus far. Air Corps basic training back in '42 hadn't exactly been a picnic, but Joseph knew that what Thomas had to succeed at as a Marine private was far tougher than what he and Jonathan had gone through out at Thunderbird Field before beginning flight training.

By 4:30 both boys were talked out. There would be plenty of time in the days ahead for more stories; for now their beds upstairs beckoned. Six months had passed since Thomas had last slept in his, but for Joseph it felt like a lifetime since Thanksgiving night back in '42 and the last time he had slept there.

Joseph paused at the bottom of the stairs and then turned back towards his brother, who had just finished shutting off the Philco and the table lamps before starting towards the stairs.

"I'm glad to be back," Joseph said, reaching forward at first with his left arm to give his brother a squeeze on the right shoulder – the same gesture Gerald had made towards Thomas at Penn Station earlier this evening, moments before Joseph's sudden appearance – but in response Thomas stepped forward to embrace his brother.

"We were all so worried about you," he said, feeling the tears filling his eyes but determined that his voice wouldn't quiver with sobs. "Ma especially, but everyone, including me. Jonathan too; every letter we would get from him all the way through the end of the war would ask if we had heard anything. Back in March or April when we got that letter from him saying that he had gotten yours from the camp that you had written something like nine months earlier, he was so relieved to hear that you were alright."

Thomas released the hug and wiped away his tears with the sleeve of his dress uniform.

"Anyway, that's all over. You're here, and Jonathan will be home soon. Charlene too. We're all going to be together, at least over the holidays until you and me ship out again."

Joseph nodded. Surprisingly, his own emotions were well within check. He wondered about that. For months now, he had wondered if, when he finally set foot back into the Coleman house, he might well dissolve into a helpless blubbering mess. But nothing like that had happened, even when painfully discussing Abby Sobol with his brother after their parents had gone upstairs.

Oh well, Joseph thought; no sense in giving the matter any further thought. Apparently he was just fine, despite all that he had gone through.

That night, though, the nightmares of a liberation gone terribly wrong were again waiting for Captain Joseph Coleman as soon as he surrendered to sleep.

2 – Monday, December 17, 1945

Ruthie Coleman's first thought this Monday morning, upon being woken by her mother, was that her brothers were home! Well, not all three; but two of the three, with Jonathan soon to follow. And Charlene too; just about the same time that Jonathan would arrive, according to Momma.

Like most young girls, Ruthie's memories of her even younger years were flimsy and sporadic at best. She had been six years old back when Pearl Harbor was attacked and America quickly went to war. Ruthie had vague memories of that year's Christmas only weeks later being an especially angst-filled one, and not just because of the new war. She remembered there had been some trouble with Jonathan and Francine, and she remembered angry words being passed back and forth between Charlene and her mother about…well, something to do with Charlene's boyfriend, she vaguely recalled. But six-year olds are often sheltered from such family controversies so even if Ruthie's powers of memory retention had been stronger than those of the typical very young girl, she almost certainly would not have any clearer of a recollection of that long-ago Christmas than she actually did.

A year later, Christmas had been a somber affair. Jonathan and Joseph had come and gone so quickly for their short Thanksgiving furlough, and Charlene was leaving the next day for New York City. Even seven-year old Ruthie was well aware of the strains throughout the household and the iciness that lay between Charlene and her mother.

A little girl's awareness increases year by year, and by Christmas of '43 with Joseph's fate so uncertain; Jonathan away at war; and Charlene out in Hollywood, the holiday had been a terrible one, even for her. Gerald and Irene Coleman had gone out of their way to make the holidays as cozy as possible for their youngest child despite their own crushing worries. However no amount of parental veneer could totally shield Ruthie from the terrible burdens that her parents – and even her brother Tommy – were forced to endure throughout that somber Christmas season two years ago.

Last year had been better…somewhat. But war still raged; Joseph was still a prisoner; and Charlene was still gone. By this time, the nine-year old girl was yearning for a return to a Christmas from the old days. Wispy, fragmented memories notwithstanding, Ruthie ardently remembered that first Christmas of the war as the last true Christmas the Coleman household had celebrated.

Until now.

Despite missing her brothers and sister so much, Ruthie had become accustomed to being the only child around for Irene Coleman to dote on. Ever since the summer of '43 it had just been Thomas and Ruthie at home, other than when Charlene returned for a couple of very short visits. And then, for the past six months, just Ruthie. But even before Tommy headed off for the Marines soon after graduating from high school, between school and sports and his job lugging produce boxes at *J Weisberg & Sons* – the same job Jonathan had held before leaving for the Air Corps – he was rarely at home other than for supper most nights. Irene had channeled most of her angst for the welfare of her absent first three children – and then four – into more motherly attention for Ruthie than the little girl had ever realized possible.

Would that single-minded motherly attention come to an end now with the house suddenly about to once again be filled with all five of Irene's children? Ruthie wondered about that prospect every so often, and did so again this very morning that saw two of her brothers once again sleeping in their old beds down the hall from her own bedroom.

Ruthie Coleman's thoughts were interrupted by Irene's motherly bellow from the kitchen – "Breakfast, Ruthie; hurry down now!" Ruthie wondered if her mother's loud cry would wake her brothers – or maybe they were already awake and downstairs, waiting for breakfast – but when she passed each of their rooms in the upstairs hallway, both doors were still shut.

And from Joseph's room, behind that closed door, Ruthie could hear what sounded like her brother crying out "No! No!" in a voice that might have been muffled but still carried notes of recognizable terror.

❄ ❄ ❄

Tommy Coleman came downstairs around 8:30. He was wearing civilian clothes for the first time in more than six months. In fact, the last time that Tommy Coleman had worn dungarees and a flannel shirt and penny loafers had been when he stepped off of the bus at Parris Island and almost immediately was brusquely shoved by a Marine Drill Instructor into the line to receive his uniforms and gear. The civies were traded in for a utility uniform about 45 minutes later, and from that point until this very moment it was one uniform or another, and nothing else, for Private Thomas Coleman.

His dungarees were a touch loose on him yet the flannel shirt felt a bit tight. Tommy figured that he had lost about ten pounds during boot camp and infantry training, but even a star high school football player like himself couldn't help putting on a little bit more muscle from all of the tough physical activities he endured day after day. But the clothes resting in his dresser drawer and closet still fit, and he relished the feel of them. For most of his junior and senior years in high school he couldn't wait until he was able to put on a military uniform like his two older brothers; now, though, dungarees and a flannel shirt were just fine with Private Thomas Coleman, thank you sir!

Ruthie had already been sent off to school, the thermometer resting at nine degrees notwithstanding. Gerald had already headed over to his little shop several blocks away where he spent his days both repairing shoes – heels, soles, stitching, and even leather repair if it could be done to Gerald's high standards – as well as making brand new shoes for those who felt the time had come for a new pair. Gerald usually returned home for lunch so Tommy figured that he would see his father sometime around noon, though he figured he might trek on over to the shop with Joey before then.

"Is Joey up yet?" Tommy asked his mother who, upon hearing her son's footsteps on the stairs, had already cracked three eggs into a frying pan and had slid two slices of bread into the toaster.

"Not yet," Irene answered without looking up at first, but then she caught herself. This wasn't an ordinary morning from earlier this year, with Tommy coming down the stairs for a quick breakfast before he headed off to Schenley High School. She turned around, noticed her son wearing the same kind of clothes she had always seen him in – before last night, that is – and smiled.

"How did you sleep?" she asked.

"Great," Tommy replied as he walked over to the three-quarters full coffee pot to pour himself a cup. He was actually still tired after only four hours of sleep following the draining train ride, but he wasn't going to complain to his mother about that. Instead, a little idle chit-chat about sleeping conditions for stateside Marines in training was called for, he figured.

"Once the war was over they started letting us sleep in on Sundays but most of the guys still got up pretty early anyway." He wanted to add "…if they weren't in really bad shape from Saturday night, that is" but figured that particular sentiment would be better saved for his father or brother, and not shared with his mother.

"Sit," Irene Coleman nodded towards the kitchen table as she kept an eye on the frying eggs. Tommy complied, placing his steaming cup of coffee in front of where he had sat for years and then easing himself into the kitchen chair.

"Anyway, I don't remember the last time I slept until after eight. I hope I don't get too used to it; you know, for when I get out to Camp Pendleton. I'm sure they will have us up early every morning for calisthenics and all that."

"Well," Irene Coleman replied as she scooped the fried eggs onto a breakfast plate that was already more than half-filled with potatoes and sausage, "that's for after you get there. For now, you should get as much rest as you can to catch up on all the sleep you lost."

"I know, Ma," Thomas nodded as his mother quickly buttered the toast and placed the overflowing breakfast plate in front of him. The truth was, Thomas had only so much time here in Pittsburgh until it was time to head west, and he didn't want to waste too much of those precious hours sleeping away one morning after another. As soon as Joey got up Thomas would discuss with his brother what they should do this first day home. Maybe go over to Schenley High and visit, or perhaps go see a movie this afternoon; or maybe even both. The temperatures were supposed to get close to twenty degrees by this afternoon which was still pretty cold, and Thomas was already scheming for how to ask his father for use of the Packard so that he and Joseph didn't have to spend hours outside walking all about the city in the frigid weather. At least Pittsburgh didn't get blasted with the four feet of snow that Buffalo had gotten, but it was still bitterly cold outside. For someone who had spent the past six months down south, including those steamy months at boot camp in South Carolina, Tommy Coleman wasn't quite ready for the shock of day after day being filled with dreary cold and frequent snowfalls. Still, he wasn't about to complain about the temperatures any more than grabbing only a few hours of sleep. Enduring this inhospitable weather was a reasonable price to be paid for being home for Christmas.

Thomas began eating with a frenzy that caused Irene's thoughts to travel back in time more than three years when Jonathan had done exactly the same thing at this very breakfast table when they were home on furlough from Thunderbird Air Field. Irene had understood the reason – the need for her oldest son to eat as quickly as possible while at Air Corps training before being rushed on to whatever was scheduled next – but the sight had made her incredibly sad with the recognition that her first-born was no longer a little boy.

Now, watching her youngest son do the exact same thing, and knowing that her little Tommy had already successfully endured Marine boot camp and infantry training; well, the sight brought a fresh wave of bittersweet sadness to Irene. She was every bit as proud of Tommy as she was of her other sons. But watching him wolf down his breakfast out of habit forced her to acknowledge that just like his older brothers, Tommy was no longer a young boy. He might be sitting at her table wearing the same dungarees and flannel shirt that he had worn last winter while still at Schenley High, but Thomas Coleman had changed forever.

Thomas was about halfway done with his breakfast when both he and his mother heard footsteps on the stairs. He paused and a few seconds later, Joseph appeared in the doorway of the kitchen, dressed the same as his brother after rummaging through the closet in his old room that had remained untouched during his absence.

"Morning, Ma," Joseph said before adding, "Morning, Tommy."

"Good morning," Irene replied, already busy cracking three more eggs into the frying pan and popping two more pieces of bread into the toaster.

"How did you sleep?" she added.

"Fine, I guess," Joseph said in even tones, looking away from both his mother and brother as he replied. He spotted the coffee pot – just where it had always been, Joseph thought – and walked over to pour himself a cup.

"Joey, what do you want to do today?" Thomas asked. He had already paused his frontal attack on the breakfast plate, deciding to wait for his brother's plate to arrive and then he would continue eating along with Joseph. To kill the time, he lit a Chesterfield and offered one to his brother, who accepted. Irene thought about asking her sons to wait until after breakfast to smoke their cigarettes, but decided against doing so. Her sons were young men now and if Air Corps pilots and Marines smoked while they ate breakfast, then Irene Coleman could tolerate her boys doing just that.

"I dunno," Joseph replied. "See a movie maybe?"

"I was thinking that," Thomas nodded. "Maybe also go over to Schenley?"

Joseph shrugged as he traded off the cigarette for a long drink of coffee. He could see where Tommy, only months removed from Schenley, would want to go visit his old high school and see friends who had only been a year or two behind him. For Joseph, though, it would be different. Thomas had been a freshman when Joseph had graduated back in '42 so the school would be filled with kids who were strangers to Joseph.

Still though, Joseph contemplated as his mother placed the overflowing breakfast plate in front of him and as he crushed out his Chesterfield, there were a few teachers Joseph wouldn't mind saying hello to. He had been an average student but a likeable one, and nearly every teacher at Schenley had fond enough memories of Joey Coleman. They would no doubt be happy to see him, especially since word of Joseph's prisoner of war status had been known to so many people throughout Polish Hill, Oakland, and the surrounding neighborhoods.

Tommy's previously frenzied attack on his breakfast plate instinctively slowed as Joseph began to eat. He didn't want his head start to mean that he would finish long before his brother, so he began eating much more slowly than he had earlier…though still unaware that his boot camp and infantry training mealtime habits had carried over to his mother's breakfast table.

Joseph, for his part, relished the tastes of his first breakfast meal at home in so many years. Even after finally making it stateside and being sent up to the Syracuse Army Air Base, chow time wasn't all that different than it had been out at Thunderbird or later at Luke Field for advanced flight training: the typical mush of creamed chipped beef on top of soggy toast – the notorious S.O.S. – accompanied by rock hard potatoes and occasionally a couple of suspect sausages.

His mother's breakfast, however, was heaven to Joseph Coleman, and he luxuriated in every bite. Thomas, now eating at a far more relaxed pace, finally was cognizant of the marked difference between his mother's cooking and that of the cooks at Parris Island and Camp Lejeune.

"This is fantastic, Ma," Thomas offered. "Best breakfast I've had in months!"

"Same here," Joseph said, then added: "Years, for me."

Thomas still managed to finish his food before his brother did, but just as he did two more eggs, another pile of potatoes, and three more sausages slid onto his just-emptied plate from the frying pan held by Irene Coleman.

"There's more for you too, Joseph," Irene Coleman said. Joseph just nodded in response, feeling that the eggs and potatoes and sausages and toast could keep coming for the rest of the day and he would be up to the task of eating every bite.

❄ ❄ ❄

"Hi Pop!" Joseph and Thomas Coleman said nearly simultaneously as they hurried inside Gerald Coleman's shoe repair shop, quickly shutting the door as soon as they were inside. Just the couple of blocks from home to the shop had been bone-chilling. Joseph was wearing civilian clothes: dungarees and a flannel shirt just like Tommy, though both brothers had switched from penny loafers to boots. Still, because of the frigid day, Joseph was also wearing his B-3 flying jacket. The thick white wool collar had grayed significantly during Joseph's time in the Luftstalag but it was the warmest jacket he had…not to mention it instantly identified Joseph as an Army Air Force flyer even from a distance. Even though he wasn't in uniform, Joseph was also wearing his officer's hat to keep his head warm. Tommy, for his part, was wearing his civilian wool-lined corduroy jacket because the coats from his various Marine uniforms brought home in his seabag were totally unsatisfactory for the frigid Pittsburgh cold this morning, just like the uniforms themselves.

"Hello, boys," Gerald said. Both of his sons – Jonathan also – had loved to hang around Gerald's shop when they were young boys, though as each got older and entered high school the visits became far less frequent.

"It's freezing out there!" Thomas said. "I'm not used to this, that's for sure!"

The clock had ticked just past ten as they stepped inside the shop. Earlier after breakfast Joseph and Thomas had remained seated at the kitchen table, smoking several more cigarettes apiece, while talking with their mother. Most of the conversation was centered around their fragments of knowledge about Jonathan's upcoming wedding…and, of course, Irene Coleman's irritation with the entire Donner family but especially Francine's mother.

"Ma's really steamed about the wedding arrangements, huh?" Thomas asked his father as he removed his gloves and reached into his jacket pocket for his cigarette pack. He offered one to his brother and another to his father, and then produced a pack of matches but was barely able to strike one of them because of how numb his fingers were despite the wool-lined gloves he had been wearing.

Gerald let out a sigh.

"I don't get involved with that business," he shrugged as he waited for Thomas to pass the matchbook to him. "I figure it's Jonathan's and Francine's doing most of all, and the rest of it isn't all that important. But you know your mother…"

Two sets of raised eyebrows acknowledged Gerald's sentiment; they indeed did know their mother and like most mothers, being all but excluded from a son's wedding plans by the bride's family was as irksome as anything in the world might be.

"So I still haven't gotten all the details on how they decided to get married so soon," Joseph said, realizing that last evening's late-night conversation between Gerald and his sons hadn't even touched on his older brother or the rapidly approaching wedding. "The last letter I got from Jonathan was back in September and he still wasn't sure that he was going to be home, or if he was going to be discharged."

"I don't know much either," Thomas added, "since I was still at training."

"Well," Gerald said, plopping down his cutting shears that he had picked up after lighting his cigarette, "he got word right around the second week of October, I think it was, that he had enough points and would be discharged sometime around New Year's, and that he would be able to get a spot on a ship coming back to San Francisco…"

"Where was he?" Joseph interrupted. "Still all the way out on Tinian? That's where he was last time he wrote me."

"No," Gerald shook his head, "he was back in Hawaii by that time. I think he got to Hickam Field at the beginning of October; something like that. Anyway, as soon as he got his discharge number and was fairly sure he had a transport back home, he wrote Francine to ask her about getting married right after Christmas. She came over to the house as soon as she got the letter to tell us; this was right before Thanksgiving."

"How did Ma take the news?" Joseph asked.

Gerald shrugged.

"She was happy for them, but you know your mother. I know you boys won't say anything to her, but don't tell Jonathan either. If it were up to your mother she would rather see them get married sometime next spring."

"Did Ma actually say that?" Thomas asked.

"I can understand why Jonathan and Francine are doing it, with him being gone for so long and losing all that time," Gerald offered instead of a direct answer, "and hopefully after a while your mother will also." The latter part of Gerald's sentence was all the answer the boys needed to Tommy's question.

"Yeah, think about it," Thomas said in response to his father's mention of "losing all that time." "He and

Francine are about to get married yet ever since that Christmas right after Pearl Harbor, they've spent only a couple days together. Isn't that strange?"

Too late Thomas realized that his words were so very much like Joseph's from last night, musing about his own doomed-from-the-start romance with Abby Sobol.

"Sorry…" Thomas said awkwardly, looking over at his brother.

Joseph just replied with one of those "don't worry about it" waves of his right hand.

Gerald Coleman seemed to contemplate his son's musing but no doubt had spent a great deal of time considering the very same question himself.

"I'm sure it will all work out," was all he said.

❄ ❄ ❄

Thomas Coleman was indeed successful in his efforts to convince his father that he should be entrusted with the keys to the Packard, absence of a driver's license notwithstanding. Gerald Coleman figured that if they somehow got pulled over by a Pittsburgh policeman for some minor traffic infraction, they would likely get off with just a warning because of being servicemen who had just returned home.

"Just watch for ice on the roads," was Gerald's only caution to his son as the boys zipped up their jackets and put their gloves back on before heading back home to grab the car keys.

"We'll see you for dinner, Pop," Joseph said, following Tommy out the door.

The exhilaration of winning unrestricted access to the Packard seemed to negate much of the winter chill during the walk back home. Still, the brothers remained inside the house for about ten minutes to warm themselves before telling their mother that they were leaving and would be back later that afternoon.

"You can drive if you want," Thomas said to his brother as they headed out of the front door onto the porch.

"That's okay," Joseph declined. "I drove a Jeep a few times in England after getting there, but that was a couple years ago now. Up in Syracuse I didn't have a chance to drive anything, so I'm pretty rusty. Plus just like you, I don't have a license anyway."

"Well, I did drive one of the motor pool Jeeps pretty regularly all around Lejeune," Thomas replied, "so I should be just fine."

Joseph shot his brother a look that indicated "should be just fine" wouldn't do it if something happened to the Packard.

"Yeah, I know," Thomas nodded, understanding perfectly well what his brother was wordlessly telling him.

Their first stop was Schenley High School. The drive from the Coleman home was less than a mile and a half, a journey that each of them had made on foot hundreds of times in either direction, often in wintertime weather even worse than today. Neither brother would have wanted to make that trek today, though, with the Packard just sitting there so temptingly. The short drive was uneventful and

Thomas expertly glided the car to a stop along the curb in front of the high school.

"It seems like forever since I've been here," Thomas said after stepping onto the sidewalk. He then turned to Joseph and said:

"I can imagine what it's like for you, huh?"

Joseph was just standing next to his brother, staring at the building but also – just as last night during the drive home from Penn Station – gazing across time. Finally he took a step forward and began walking towards the stairs leading to the high school's front doors. Thomas fell in behind his brother, and was almost immediately aware that his feet were instinctively keeping the same cadence as Joseph's: left, right; your left; your left; your left, right, left…

Inside the front doors of the school, Joseph removed his officer's cap and unzipped his flight jacket, and Thomas did likewise with his jacket. The Schenley furnaces were blazing away and if anything, the inside hallway was too warm. Joseph felt the beads of perspiration break out on his forehead, but wondered how much of that was from the inside warmth and how much might be from anxiety.

The boys began walking down the deserted center hallway – classes were running so the high school kids were all in various classrooms at the moment – but it was less than a minute until Joseph and Thomas were recognized. A teacher was headed towards them, his eyes cast down at the top sheet of a stack of papers in his hands, but when he was about fifteen feet away he happened to look up, directly at the Coleman brothers. The very first thing the teacher noticed was the Air Corps flight jacket on one of the strangers, and his eyes traveled upwards and he immediately recognized the face.

"Joey Coleman!" the teacher's mouth dropped.

"Mister Sadowski," Joseph immediately responded.

"Oh my Lord!" Stan Sadowski, Joseph's 11th-grade history teacher, responded, frozen in place. A few seconds later he looked at the other visitor.

"Tommy Coleman!"

"Hello, Mister Sadowski," Thomas reprised his brother's greeting. Like Joseph, Thomas had taken 11th-grade history from Stan Sadowski. However by the time Thomas was in Mister Sadowski's class, both of his brothers were off at war. In fact, Thomas had been sitting in Mister Sadowski's class that terrible day back in September of '43 when the classroom door opened and an ashen-faced Gerald Coleman stepped into the room, his eyes searching for Thomas to break the news that his brother's plane had been shot down and that Joseph's fate was, at the moment, unknown.

The entire stack of papers slid from Stan Sadowski's hands, but he appeared not to notice as he stepped forward to grab Joseph Coleman's hand and nearly – but not quite – give Joseph a welcome-home embrace.

"You're home!" the teacher said.

"Yeah," Joseph replied. "Just got in last night. Tommy too," he added, nodding his head towards his brother.

"Oh, my Lord," the teacher repeated. "I am so glad to see you! Both of you!"

Thomas was already crouching down, gathering up the papers that Mister Sadowski had dropped. Graded exams, Thomas could see. Thomas couldn't help but grin when he noticed the pronounced, almost exaggerated red pencil scribbling – Mister Sadowski's trademark, as every student at Schenley for the past fifteen years knew very well – and he took in plenty of C's and a few D's among the grades written in the upper right hand corners of those exams. Thomas had actually done okay in Sadowski's class – B's on most of his exams and homework, and a B overall at the end of his junior year – and he recalled Joseph doing about the same a couple of years earlier. Jonathan, of course, had gotten A's from Sadowski, as he had from pretty much every other teacher at Schenley.

"Thank you, Tommy," Stan said as Thomas handed him the regrouped stack of exams. "Come on, both of you; let's go to the teachers' lounge and talk for a few minutes until the next period starts."

Neither Joseph nor Tommy had ever been invited to the Schenley High teachers' lounge before and they both followed Mister Sadowski back towards the front door but then to the right side, entering through a door next to the Principal's office. Unlike the teachers' lounge, both of the Colemans had indeed made a few visits to the Principal's office over the years, usually for some minor cutting up in class. Given that both of them were pretty fair Schenley athletes and decent enough students, though, the visits to the Principal's office rarely ended up with anything other than a mild scolding...often followed by something along the lines of "we're going to beat Peabody Friday afternoon, right?"

No other teachers were in the lounge and Mister Sadowski nodded towards a threadbare bluish sofa. Joseph and Thomas sat there while their former history teacher took a seat in a chair directly across from the sofa.

"Is your brother…" Stan Sadowski began, then abruptly halted. He was about to ask if Jonathan Coleman was also home, but then he realized that he hadn't heard any recent news about Jonathan's fate. Perhaps Jonathan Coleman was…

"He'll be home tomorrow afternoon," Thomas answered. "At least that's what we hear. He's coming from San Francisco; he was out in the Pacific and made it stateside a little bit ago."

"Wonderful!" Mister Sadowski proclaimed, and indeed he was truly grateful to hear the news that another one of Schenley High's boys was making it back safely to Pittsburgh.

"You hear he's getting married right after Christmas? To Francine Donner?" Joseph added.

"They are? That is just wonderful! I remember the two of them going together in high school! Though when they were in my history class she was going with Donnie Yablonski, I think it was."

Both Joseph and Thomas winced at hearing that name for the first time in years.

"Has anybody had any word about Donnie?" Stan Sadowski asked.

Joseph started to offer an opinion on the question, but quickly decided his old teacher didn't need to get dragged into a Coleman family controversy.

"None," was what Joseph answered instead.

"You boys heard about Tommy Bonnaverte, right?" Mister Sadowski said as he pursed his lips together.

"Uh-huh," Joseph said somberly. Tommy Bonnaverte had been in the same grade as Joseph, and had enlisted in the Navy right after graduation, two days after Joseph had signed up for the Army Air Forces. His ship had taken a direct hit from a kamikaze plane off of Okinawa at the end of April – ironically on the exact same day as Joseph's liberation from Stalag VII-A – and Tommy Bonnaverte was killed in the attack.

Mister Sadowski spent the next few minutes offering up what he knew about Joseph's classmates, and those a year or two ahead as well as those slightly behind. Most had made it back from the war, or – like Jonathan – were known to have survived and would soon be home. A few, like Damian and Sebastian Jaskolski – and Tommy Bonnaverte – didn't make it back, and Stan Sadowski seemed to be in the know about so many of Schenley's boys who had gone to war and what the fate of each of them had been.

The school bell clanged, indicating that the current period had just ended and that the high schoolers – and their teachers – had ten minutes to make it to their next classroom. Mister Sadowski made Joseph and Thomas promise to bring Jonathan by after he got home, and the Colemans agreed. After Stan Sadowski left for his class, Joseph and Thomas headed over to the school gym, hoping to run into any of their old coaches. However, because it was early enough in the school day all of the coaches were otherwise engaged in teaching English or math or history, and none could be found in or around the gym. Thomas suggested that rather than wait another entire period for classrooms to empty so friends and former teachers could be found, they leave now so they could grab lunch and make an afternoon movie. For some reason this single reunion with Stan Sadowski was suddenly as much as Tommy could bear for this first morning home, and Joseph was in total agreement.

The brothers left Schenley, each of them immediately feeling less edgy as the winter chill enveloped them, and walked back to the Packard.

"Sadowski looked at me like I was a ghost or something," Joseph mused as he zipped up his jacket.

"Yeah, I know," Thomas agreed. "I guess he was really surprised to see you. You know I was in his class when Pop came in with the news about you…"

Tommy's voice trailed off, but he didn't need to finish the sentence.

"Maybe that's it," Joseph said. "You figure if he was right there and heard Pop tell you that I got shot down and nobody knew anything, I guess in his mind I was a goner even if he heard later that I was in a Luftstalag. Anyway, he was nice enough but it's a little bit creepy knowing so much about what happened to everyone, you know?"

As Thomas gunned the Packard to life and pulled out into traffic, he thought about what Joseph had just said.

"I don't know," Thomas said. "Maybe it's because you were away but during the war, everyone around here pretty much knew everything about everybody. Ma would walk into the butcher shop and Mister Rosenbaum would tell her what he had heard about all the guys who were in Europe or the Pacific or still stateside, and then he would even tell Ma what he had heard from Francine's mother about what Jonathan had written to Francine; maybe something that Ma didn't even know because she hadn't gotten a letter in a little while. It was the same with news about you, until…you know…"

Thomas eased the Packard to a stop at a red light, then continued.

"Everybody just knew everything; like we were all in this together. Any news that came from the war was…I don't know, it was news for everyone. Does that make any sense?"

Joseph shrugged.

"Yeah, I guess," he answered.

"Anyway," Thomas offered, "that probably will all come to an end after everybody gets home. But for a couple of years there, probably starting right after Christmas of '42 and going all the way up until I left and then probably even afterwards, you could ask almost anybody and find out all kinds of news about lots of guys from all over Pittsburgh."

"You know," Joseph said, staring out the passenger side window as his brother drove along, "Sadowski talking about Tommy Bonnaverte reminded me of when we were in the sixth grade, and me and Tommy had this big showdown fight that was about a week in the making. We went over to the baseball field after school and just pounded the living hell out of each other. You remember that?"

"Yeah, sort of," Thomas replied. "I was in third grade then and I remember you got in a big fight with someone, but I didn't remember it being Bonnaverte, or who won."

"Nobody won," was Joseph's response. "It was a flat-out draw after about ten straight minutes. But the strange thing was that afterwards me and him were best friends for about three years, until we got to Schenley and started hanging out with different groups of guys. But until then…remember he was over the house a lot?"

"Yeah, that's right," Thomas nodded, fragments of long-forgotten memories coming to life. "Didn't he like Charlene for a while?"

"Wow, I forgot all about that!" Joseph chuckled. "I think that was when me and him were in eighth grade and Charlene was in seventh, and he used to always suggest that we should go over to my house after school. And when we got there he would ask if Charlene was home, or when she would be getting home. He wasn't really smooth about it, ya know? And Charlene thought he was a creep, but deep down I think she liked all the attention from a guy who was a year older."

Both of the brothers were laughing at the recollections, until all of a sudden it hit Joseph: Tommy Bonnaverte was gone forever; he was dead.

"Let's go get some lunch," Joseph said, his voice somber, not wanting to say or hear another word about his dead childhood friend.

❄ ❄ ❄

"Sorry, Major. I don't know when the trains will be getting underway. There's a big snowstorm this side of Indianapolis and all train traffic headed east is being held up here."

Jonathan Coleman stood at the ticket window inside the St. Louis Union Station, determined to keep his cool. It wasn't this ticket clerk's doing that his train had yet to leave St. Louis, more than an hour after its scheduled departure. Still, the lack of anything even approaching precise information had him seething. Rumors were sweeping the station that it might not be until tomorrow until eastbound train traffic out of St. Louis resumed. Jonathan hoped not, but he was mostly frustrated that he couldn't get a straight answer from anybody about the situation.

The *Golden State* had rolled into St. Louis on schedule but the train he was scheduled to board next – the Pennsylvania Railroad's *Jeffersonian* – was among the eastbound traffic halted here in St. Louis. Eventually he would be underway again; hopefully before too much more time had passed. For now, Jonathan figured he might as well make himself comfortable. At least he was stuck in one of the largest and busiest train stations in the country, rather than some single-platform Podunk town with a population of about two hundred. He would keep an eye on the traffic board and just to be safe, head back to the ticket window every hour or so to see if there were any updates. He was far from the only man in uniform traveling through Union Station at the moment, but being an Army Air Forces major did have its privileges, at least when it came to being treated with respect by the ticket clerks rather than having his questions dismissively brushed aside.

First, though, he would try to let his parents and Francine know that he had been delayed. Jonathan reached into his duffel bag and extracted a generous handful of quarters, dimes, and nickels. When he finally located a vacant telephone booth, he stepped inside and dialed "0" for the operator as he shut the door. After a few seconds the operator came onto the line and Jonathan recited the Coleman house's telephone number to her. Upon hearing the required amount - $4.45 for the first three minutes – Jonathan began feeding change into the phone's coin slot. Finally, enough coins having made their way into the telephone, he waited a few seconds until he heard the tones indicating that the phone in the Coleman house was ringing. Alas, no luck; he counted twenty-five rings and after nobody picked up, he hung up the phone and waited for his coins to be returned. He then tried Francine's house but wound up with the same result. Letting out a deep sigh, he gathered up his change and slid it all back into his duffel bag. He would try again a little bit later, he thought to himself as he yielded the phone booth to another Army Air Forces flyer – a captain – who had lined up to use the phone shortly after Jonathan had stepped inside. Jonathan nodded to the captain as he passed him and the other flyer did likewise as Jonathan said:

"Hope you have better luck than I did; nobody home."

"Sorry to hear that," the captain replied. "Where you headed, Major?"

"Home to Pittsburgh," Jonathan answered. "How about you?"

"Brooklyn," was the captain's response, his distinctive accent now definitely recognizable. "If I get out of St. Louis, that is. Where you comin' from?"

"San Francisco on the train, but from Tinian via Hawaii."

"B-29s?" the captain asked.

"Yeah," Jonathan nodded, "and B-17s in Europe before that."

"B-24s in the C.B.I. for me," the captain offered, referring to the China-Burma-India theater of the war that was less well-known back home than Europe or the Pacific. "Made it stateside to L.A. and headin' home from there."

"Oh yeah? My brother flew B-24s out of England and then North Africa until he was shot down in '43. He made it down okay and spent the rest of the war in a Luftstalag. He's on his way to Pittsburgh from Syracuse Air Base, and in fact might even be home by now."

"That's great," the captain responded. "Bet you can't wait to get home and see him, huh?"

"That's for sure," Jonathan nodded. "My fiancé too; we're getting married right after Christmas."

"That's great," the captain repeated. "My sister is gettin' married too; they held off the wedding so I could make it home to be there."

"Well, good luck," Jonathan offered.

"Yeah, you too, Major, and same to your brother," the other flyer answered as he stepped into the booth and shut the door.

Jonathan reflected on the brief one-minute exchange as he walked away from the telephone booth. Before the war, if for whatever reason he might have happened to be in the Union Station in St. Louis, chances are that he and this stranger from Brooklyn – both dressed in civies – wouldn't have said a word to each other. As it was, the few sentences they did pass back and forth were little more than pleasantries between two men who not only didn't know each other but most likely would never see each other again. Or, if they did cross paths some day in the future, almost certainly neither Jonathan nor this other guy would make the connection to this brief, just-concluded conversation because both would be wearing civilian clothes, not Army Air Forces uniforms.

But at this particular moment in history, solely because both Jonathan and the other man had been wearing their respective uniforms, Jonathan had felt the need to engage in at least a brief conversation with this other man; and Jonathan had no doubt the other guy had felt exactly the same. True, the other guy might have felt obligated to respond to Jonathan's overture simply out of politeness or because Jonathan outranked him. But Jonathan had been party to probably two hundred such exchanges during the past week since his arrival in San Francisco, with just as many initiated by someone other than Jonathan – men of all ranks, officer and enlisted alike, but mostly Air Corps – as by Jonathan himself.

These men had all been through similar experiences that would mark their lives forever, and that shared experience of fighting together for victory in this all-consuming global conflagration had created bonds among strangers that would never have existed otherwise. The uniforms that they all were still wearing, though probably not for much longer, were the instant visual signals to Jonathan that a total stranger had something in common with him.

Jonathan decided to head over to one of the station's restaurants to grab a quick lunch, even though it was already 2:30 St. Louis time. He had eaten breakfast on the train around 8:00 that morning and even though the train had pulled into St. Louis around 1:00 for its scheduled half-hour stop, Jonathan was too focused on finding out the latest news about the delay to worry about eating. Now, however, he was famished and figured he could eat something quick and make it back to see if there were any updates.

As Jonathan walked across the center hall of the station he noticed a commotion off to his right, about thirty or forty yards away. A fairly large group of people, many of them servicemen, were clustered in a circle;

probably surrounding someone, but Jonathan couldn't tell for sure. The commotion didn't appear to be a troublesome one; more like someone famous might be in the middle of the crowd, and everyone might be trying to get a better look at whomever it was or maybe even get an autograph.

Curious, Jonathan changed direction to head towards the crowd. Maybe it was a famous baseball player on his way back from wartime service just like Jonathan himself was. Or maybe it was some movie star who had also gone to war; could it be Jimmy Stewart or Clark Gable, somebody like that?

As he approached the outer ring of the crowd, Jonathan still couldn't get a good look at who was the center of attention. He eased his way into the crowd…just a little bit, not wanting to be too pushy. When his forward progress had come to an end, Jonathan turned to a nearby Marine – a sergeant wearing the shoulder patch of the 3rd Marine Division, indicating that he had probably fought on Iwo Jima – and asked:

"Any idea what the big attraction is, Sarge?"

The Marine looked over, his eyes catching Jonathan's gold Major's oak leaf, and said:

"Movie star, Major. That actress Carla Colburn."

It took a good five seconds for the significance of that name to register with Jonathan Coleman.

❄ ❄ ❄

Jonathan Coleman wasn't normally the mischievous type, but as soon as his brain finally equated "Carla

Colburn" with "Charlene Coleman" he instantly had an idea. Jonathan steadily eased his way forward as many of those in the crowd (more than three-quarters of them servicemen, Jonathan now estimated) waited in turn for a few brief seconds to secure the starlet's autograph and maybe exchange a couple of words. Five or six minutes passed until Jonathan was within a couple feet of his sister, right behind that same Marine sergeant. As soon as the Marine got his autograph – and a smile – from the actress and then stepped aside, Jonathan took a step forward and held out a fountain pen and a scrap of paper he had fished out of his uniform jacket.

Jonathan had noticed that Charlene – Carla – was signing autographs so rapidly that for nearly everyone she would take the offered pen and paper without looking up first, sign her name, and only then gaze up at that person to lock eyes and smile as she handed back the pen and whatever it was that she had just signed. Sure enough, the pattern held with Jonathan.

"You're my favorite movie star ever, Miss Colburn," he said, deliberately disguising his voice.

"I've loved every single movie you've ever done," he continued as she accepted the offered paper scrap and pen. "I really mean it! I think you're better than Betty Grable and Marlene Dietrich and Rita Hayworth all together!"

Charlene just had to glance up and take a look at this fawning G.I. even before she signed the piece of paper. It took just as long as it had taken Jonathan for her stage name to register with him – about five full seconds – until the anonymous war-weary face of yet another Air Force flyer transformed into one that Charlene had known all her life.

"Jonathan!" she screamed as she hurled herself forward and fiercely embraced her brother. "Oh my God, Jonathan!"

Tears of joyous relief at the first sight of her brother in more than three years sprung to her eyes. The servicemen still waiting in line wondered just who this flyboy was and how he rated a giant hug from Carla Colburn. She obviously knew him since she had screamed out the guy's name. Maybe this flyer was a movie star himself who had gone to war; many of those in the crowd now tried to get a good look at the major's face to see if it was a recognizable one.

"Everyone, this is my brother!" Charlene cried out when she finally released her embrace. "Jonathan Coleman! *Major* Jonathan Coleman of the Army Air Forces! I haven't seen him in three years and he's finally on his way home!"

With those words Charlene once again embraced her brother, her tears now flowing freely. A flashbulb popped; no doubt a newspaper or magazine photographer had made his way into the crowd, and he immediately recognized the epic photo opportunity right before his eyes. "Carla Colburn at St. Louis Union Station, surprised by Air Corps brother she hasn't seen in three years," the caption would read.

"Let me finish signing these, okay?" Charlene pleaded with her brother. "Don't go anywhere!"

Intrigued – and even a touch amused – at the sight of his pesty younger sister transformed into a popular movie star, signing autographs for G.I.'s and sailors and marines like she had just finished performing in a war zone U.S.O. show, Jonathan stepped aside and lit a Lucky Strike...and watched. He wondered what their mother would think if she could witness this scene! Jonathan's mind wandered back to that big brouhaha back during Thanksgiving of '42 when Irene Coleman had forbidden her daughter to pursue anything related to the entertainment business. If it hadn't been for the war, and the uncertain fate that Jonathan himself and Joseph were facing, Irene would have won out and Charlene's dreams of stardom would have been dashed then and there. As it was, Gerald Coleman stepped in and gently – but firmly – countermanded his wife and gave Charlene the opportunity to follow her dream, beginning with the War Bond Tour headlined by Dorothy Lamour during those very same holidays.

And now, look at her! The girl Jonathan had last seen as a seventeen-year old not even finished with high school was now signing autographs for admiring servicemen the same as Betty Grable would do if she were here in place of Charlene. Jonathan shook his head at this surreal scene that drove home how much had changed – and so dramatically – during the years he had been away.

The crowd finally dispersed and Charlene walked over to where Jonathan had been waiting, shaking her right hand that was balled up into a loose fist.

"Writer's cramp?" Jonathan smirked, looking at Charlene's hand and then up at her face.

She laughed lightly.

"You know it," she said. "Signing an autograph or two at a time is one thing, but every so often you get a crowd of G.I.'s like that and before you know it, a half-hour has gone by and I've signed my name a hundred times."

"I can't get over it," Jonathan verbalized what he had been thinking earlier. "My little sister the movie star!"

"Don't," Charlene said, more tersely than Jonathan would have thought. "Just don't."

"Don't what?" he asked, puzzled.

"Call me a 'movie star,'" she answered, her voice still a touch edgy. "Don't start with the whole 'move star' thing. One of the nice things about going home is that for a little while I can be just plain old Charlene Coleman, not 'Carla Colburn, Starlet.'"

"Okayyyy," Jonathan drew out his two-syllable response, indicating his surprise over what he was hearing yet at the same time, letting his sister know that he would indeed comply with her wishes.

"I'm starving!" Charlene said. "Let's get something to eat, okay?"

"That's where I was headed when I saw the crowd," Jonathan replied. "Me too; I haven't eaten since breakfast."

"Let's check the board once more, though," Charlene suggested. "Maybe they've cleared up the delay in Indianapolis by now."

"Well, they hadn't about a half-hour ago," Jonathan said, "but you're right; let's see if there's anything new."

Sure enough, just as brother and sister were nearing the ticket counter they heard the overhead announcement:

"Attention in the terminal; attention in the terminal. Pennsylvania Railroad *Spirit of St. Louis* with delayed service to Indianapolis continuing to Dayton is now boarding for a 3:20 P.M. departure from Union Station. Pennsylvania Railroad *Spirit of St. Louis* with delayed service to Indianapolis..."

"That's my train!" Charlene exclaimed. "Come on, let's go!"

Jonathan glanced up at the board. Charlene's train might soon be getting underway, but his own – the *Jeffersonian* – was still showing a delayed status, with no departure time indicated.

"Looks like I'm still delayed," Jonathan said, then added: "unless the board hasn't been updated. Hang on a second, I'm going to ask the ticket guy."

Only one passenger – an elderly man in a business suit – was ahead of Jonathan in line, and whatever his business had been it was quickly concluded. Jonathan stepped forward and sure enough, he learned that even though some of the eastbound traffic out of St. Louis had been released, not every train would be getting underway. And of course, the *Jeffersonian* was among the still-in-limbo trains.

"Just come on my train," Charlene interjected. She was standing off to the side of the ticket window so the clerk couldn't get a good look at the woman standing next to this Army Air Forces major, even though he could hear what she was saying.

"What about that?" Jonathan asked the same clerk whose window he had been at fifteen minutes earlier. "How 'bout me hopping onto the *Spirit of St. Louis* instead?"

"Sorry, Major," the clerk replied, shaking his head. "It's all full. Just wait and sooner or later the *Jeffersonian* will get underway, okay?"

The clerk was already looking past Jonathan to the next passenger queued up behind him. Jonathan was contemplating how big of a stink to make about the clerk's denial when he felt his sister nudge into him as she stepped into the line of sight of the clerk.

"Excuse me," Charlene said sweetly, her smile lighting up as she spoke. "This is my brother, Major Jonathan Coleman, and I'm..."

"Carla Colburn!" the clerk finished her sentence. "The movie star!"

"I am," Charlene said, her smile broadening even more. "I just ran into my brother here while we were both delayed, and we are both headed home to Pittsburgh for Christmas. My brother has been away fighting in the war for three years, and it would mean so much to me" – her eyes instantly flashed her trademark wholesome yet seductive look at the clerk – "if he could come on my train with me and we could talk to each other the whole ride home. Please..."

Jonathan struggled to refrain from bursting out laughing. Surely his sister's little "movie star flirting with the railroad ticket clerk" act wasn't going to get them anywhere...would it?

"Well...." the ticket clerk hesitated, obviously captivated by this totally unexpected display of attention from the starlet Carla Colburn, "I'm not supposed to...I mean..."

"Please...." Charlene repeated. "It *really* would mean *so much* to me..." Charlene reached forward through the opening at the bottom of the ticket window and was just able to reach to gently grasp the clerk's left hand with her right one.

The ticket clerk blew out a breath; an exhale of surrender.

"Okay, Miss Colburn," he said in a lowered voice, and then looked over at Jonathan. "Gimme your ticket, Major."

As astonished as Jonathan was, he instantly reached inside his service uniform jacket to the inside pocket and withdrew his Pennsylvania Railroad ticket, and slid it through the window towards the clerk. The clerk – reluctantly withdrawing his left hand from the sweet clasp of the one and only Carla Colburn – punched a few buttons on his ticket machine and in a few seconds, a new ticket popped out that he then slid back through the window where Jonathan could reach it.

"Thanks a million," Jonathan said.

"Thank you so much," Charlene added, her seductively sweet smile still firmly in place, again locking eyes with the smitten ticket clerk.

"Of course, Miss Colburn. I'll be watching for your next picture."

"Thank you again and Merry Christmas," Charlene said in her syrupy voice one final time as she and Jonathan stepped away from the window and then picked up the pace on their way to the platform.

"I thought you said you didn't want to be Miss Movie Star for a while," Jonathan gently teased his sister and they hurried along.

Charlene looked over at her brother and couldn't help giggling.

"Well, it does have its advantages sometimes, huh?"

She smiled – her normal "Charlene Coleman of Pittsburgh's Polish Hill" smile, not her "Carla Colburn, Movie Star" smile – and added:

"Come on, let's go home."

❉ ❉ ❉

"Hey Joey; did you read this?"

Thomas, Joseph, and Gerald were all seated in the Coleman living room after supper, and Thomas was skimming the evening's edition of *The Pittsburgh Press.* Irene was in the kitchen doing the dinner dishes, assisted by Ruthie. A modest feast of roast turkey, stuffing, potatoes, green beans – a belated Thanksgiving dinner, in a way – had been tonight's meal, though a *real* feast was in the works for tomorrow night after Charlene and Jonathan were home as well.

"What's that?" Joseph asked.

"A train wreck down in South Carolina," Thomas said. "Two trains collided and six people were killed and 62 hurt."

He paused for a few seconds and then muttered: "Oh man…"

"What?" Joseph asked.

"This sergeant from Gibsonia was killed." Gibsonia was a small community of a couple thousand people, about fifteen miles north of Pittsburgh. "A couple of sailors too."

"Oh man," Thomas repeated. "It says this sergeant was out of the Army for only one day after five years of being enlisted, and was on his way home."

"Don't ready any more of that," Joseph snapped. "At least out loud. If you want to read about guys dying on their way home just keep it to yourself."

Gerald looked over at Joseph, and then back at Thomas.

"Sorry," Thomas said. He understood how that particular topic could hit home. That could have been his own northbound train a day or two earlier, or Joseph's westbound train out of New York; but Joseph was especially prickly tonight. He had been quiet during lunch after their visit to Schenley this morning, and then when they went to see *And Then There Were None* at the Senator he seemed especially moody. During the drive back home after the movie Joseph didn't say much, staring out the window most of the time. And then during supper every time their mother tried to bring him into the lively dinnertime conversation, Joseph would only offer a superficial comment or two; nothing more.

Gerald had noticed Joseph's moodiness as well, but wasn't going to say anything to his son about it. He figured that after the euphoria and relief of finally making it back to Pittsburgh, a touch of…well, something troubling would likely begin to set in on Joseph's demeanor. It probably wouldn't last too long – hopefully – but he wasn't surprised at all by his son's quiet edginess.

"I'm goin' for a short walk," Joseph proclaimed suddenly, rising from the easy chair.

"It's freezing out there!" Thomas blurted out. The temperature had settled in the low 20s for most of the late afternoon but now, as the clock ticked past 7:00 this Monday evening, the winter cold was easing back down into the mid-teens.

"Just around the block," Joseph said as he walked to the hall closet to retrieve his flying jacket. "I just want to get some air for a little bit."

Thomas looked over at his father, whose facial expression wordlessly signaled his youngest son to just let his brother be. Thomas shrugged and turned back to the *Pittsburgh Press*.

Joseph opened the front door to walk out into the frigid Pittsburgh darkness. The iciness hit him immediately but the sensation was actually a welcome one. He had spent the afternoon brooding about the death of his childhood friend Tommy Bonnaverte during the Battle of Okinawa. He had known about Tommy's death for more than a month now, ever since a letter from his father that had been written shortly after Joseph arrived stateside had broken the sad news. But Bonnaverte's death didn't really hit home until reminiscing about him with his brother Thomas as the Packard headed from Schenley over to Oakland, in search of a place to eat lunch. The route that they took passed so many places that brought back so many memories; not just of Tommy Bonnaverte but also the Jaskolski brothers and others who hadn't survived the war.

But it wasn't just the guys who didn't make it back; it was the overall memories of those long-ago years that really weren't all that long ago, if Joseph stopped to think about it. Less than four years had passed since Joseph had been a high school kid himself; why did that seem like a lifetime ago?

Joseph's mood wasn't helped by this afternoon's movie the brothers decided to go see after lunch. *And Then There Were None* was a good enough flick; that wasn't the problem. The problem was *where* the boys had decided to go to spend the afternoon at the movies. Too late, after they had already parked the Packard, Joseph remembered that this theater – the Senator – was where his first date with Abby Sobol had been. What a strange and wonderful evening, both at the same time! Not only was he unexpectedly going to the movies with this girl who had enraptured him almost instantly, but that first movie – *Thunder Birds* – was one in which Joseph and his brother actually appeared! The movie about Air Corps flight training had been filmed at Thunderbird Field shortly after the brothers had arrived, and there he was – Flying Cadet Joseph Coleman, United States Army Air Forces – right up there on the screen in several group scenes, as he proudly pointed out to Abby Sobol moments before he kissed her.

All those memories came flooding back to Joseph as he sat there in the Senator watching the afternoon's movie. He tried to concentrate on *And Then There Were None* but his eyes insisted on interspersing omniscient scenes of himself and Abby Sobol kissing each other as if they were longtime sweethearts rather than on their first date while *Thunder Birds* played in the background. By the time *And Then There Were None* had finished, Joseph was feeling as down as he had in a long time…maybe even as far back as those days this past winter and spring when his hopes for surviving the war were at their lowest.

Half an hour passed until Joseph couldn't stand the outside cold any longer. He had been walking around the blocks of Polish Hill so he wasn't too far from the Coleman house, so within five more minutes he was walking back through the front door into the warmth of the living room. The *Pittsburgh Press* had been passed from Thomas to Gerald by this point, and Gerald was reading the sports pages.

"It says here that the Cleveland Rams are going to play the Redskins next September way out in Los Angeles," Gerald said, attempting to engage Joseph in conversation after his head-clearing walk. A day earlier the Cleveland team had defeated Sammy Baugh and the Washington Redskins for the professional football league title. The side story in the *Press* noted that more than 35,000 people had attended the game at Cleveland's Municipal Stadium, and the money brought in from the event – more than $164,000 – was the highest gross in the thirteen years that the pro league had been holding a championship game. Another sign of America slowly getting back to some semblance of normalcy after the years of war, Gerald thought.

Unbeknownst to Gerald or his sons, less than a month following this very evening the Cleveland Rams would surprisingly announce that they were moving to Los Angeles…the first hints of America's burgeoning westward migration that someday would come to include much of the Coleman family.

❄ ❄ ❄

Just after 9:00 that night, the telephone in the Coleman living room rang. Irene and Ruthie had joined the others by then, and they were all listening to the radio. *Cavalcade of America* had concluded and there was a half-hour break until the *Information Please* quiz show began at 9:30. Thomas was again twirling the Philco's dial, as if he missed fiddling with the radio as much as anything during his months away at Marine Corps training.

Irene hurried over to the telephone. She had a hunch that the voice on the other end of the line would be either

Jonathan's or Charlene's, conveying a quick long-distance confirmation of an arrival time tomorrow at Penn Station. Charlene was scheduled to arrive at 11:30 in the morning, and Jonathan at 3:00 tomorrow afternoon.

Through the telephone line's static Irene was surprised to hear both of her children's voices; Charlene's first, then a second later Jonathan's.

"Hi, Ma!" each one said in rapid succession, with Charlene then hollering:

"I saw Jonathan in St. Louis! He's on the same train as me now…Ma, can you hear me?"

"I can," Irene Coleman shouted back. The static on the long-distance lines was especially bothersome tonight, no doubt because servicemen all over the country were making quick telephone calls to their homes with similar updated information. Having that many calls on the lines at the same time was definitely affecting the sound quality of the calls that could actually get through.

"We were late getting out of St. Louis but now we're in Indianapolis," Charlene said. "We're now scheduled to get into Penn Station tomorrow night at 7:00. That's tomorrow *night*, not tomorrow *morning*. The train is going extra slow because of all the bad weather. We'll call you from Dayton if we're going to be any later than that."

"Charlene and Jonathan are together on the train," Irene cupped her hand over the bottom of the telephone as she relayed this new information to her husband and her sons. "They will arrive at Penn Station tomorrow night at 7:00."

"Ma?" Charlene again.

"I'm here, I was just telling your father and your brothers what you just told me."

On the other end of the line, the word "brothers" immediately registered with Charlene.

"Both Tommy and Joey are home?" she eagerly asked.

"Uh-huh," Irene replied. "They made it in on schedule last night, and Joseph's train was actually a half-hour early. He surprised us while we were still saying hello to Thomas."

"Joey's home!" Irene could hear Charlene's fainter voice, no doubt relaying the wonderful news to Jonathan.

"Hang on, Ma, Jonathan wants to talk to you."

A couple of seconds later:

"Hi, Ma!"

Irene Coleman couldn't help it. For the second night in a row, the tears started flowing.

"Jonathan! Jonathan!" her voice quivered into the phone.

"We're almost home, Ma," Jonathan said. "Before the time runs out, can you put Joey on the line?"

Sniffling, Irene turned towards the others in the living room.

"Jonathan wants to talk to you," she said, holding the telephone handset in the direction of Joseph. "Hurry, I don't know how much time is left on the call."

Joseph rose quickly and hurried across the room to take the phone from his mother.

"Jonathan?" he said.

"Joey?" came the reply.

"Yeah, it's me."

"Joey! You made it!"

"I did," came the reply. "Been hanging out with Tommy all day. We went over to Schenley and talked with Sadowski for a while, and he asked about you."

"Say again?" was Jonathan's reply, however, unable to clearly hear his brother's words over the static that had worsened a few seconds earlier.

"We went to Schenley today; Tommy and me."

"Got it," came the response. "Tell me all about it tomorrow night when we get home. I can't wait to get there. We're in Indianapolis right now, I ran into Charlene in St. Louis. You shoulda seen her, she was…"

The line suddenly went dead. No doubt the time had been used up. Joseph wondered if Jonathan and Charlene would plop another four or five dollars of change into the payphone, but he figured if they were making a quick call from the Indianapolis Union Station they probably didn't have too much more time until they had to re-board their train. They would both be home soon enough; stories could wait until then.

Hearing his brother's voice, even for less than a minute, did put Joseph in a better mood than he had been in for much of the day. When his mother returned from the kitchen a few minutes later bearing a reprise of last night's donuts and hot chocolate (having taken the time to compose herself), Joseph quickly scarfed down two of the pastries as he talked sports with his father and brother. The local Pittsburgh Hornets hockey team had played to a six-to-six tie last night up in Connecticut against the New Haven Eagles.

"Let's go see a game after Jonathan gets home," Thomas suggested. Back before the war the brothers would occasionally go see a game at the Duquesne Gardens when they could scrape together enough money. None of the Coleman boys was that much of a hockey fan; but in wintertime when the Pirates weren't playing, pretty much any kind of local sporting event would catch their attentions.

"Yeah, sounds good," Joseph replied as Thomas checked the time on the grandfather clock. With less than two minutes until the start of *Information Please* he turned up the volume on the Philco as they all settled in to listen to the program.

Both Irene and Gerald, each one having taken notice of Joseph's gloomy mood during and after dinner but now noticing his improved disposition after his brief exchange of words with his older brother, were glad to see him play along with the radio quiz show. Considering that Joseph had spent a year and a half in a Nazi prisoner of war camp and had been overseas since early '43, he surprisingly knew many of the correct answers to the questions offered to the program's panelists. Gerald recalled, though, that last night Joseph had mentioned the American P.O.W.s getting their hands on dozens of copies dating back several years of *Life* and *Look* and *Collier's* after being freed from the prison camps. The stories and advertisement pages in each issue had been devoured, cover to cover, by as many of the formerly imprisoned and news-starved flyers as possible – Joseph included – as the magazines were passed around. When he made it stateside Joseph was surprised to realize that he was no longer totally out of touch with what had happened outside of the war during the past three years. That must be it, Gerald thought.

After the program's conclusion, another half-hour programming break occurred until *Dr. I.Q.* would come on at 10:30. Again, Thomas fiddled with the Philco's dial with the expertise of a B-24 radioman, Joseph mused. He settled on one of the local music stations and for another thirty minutes, the Coleman family enjoyed another round of donuts and hot chocolate as they listened to Ella Fitzgerald, Nat King Cole, Harry James, Benny Goodman…though when the station began playing *In the Mood* the collective disposition in the living room darkened at the reminder of Glenn Miller's death last December. Two days earlier, many of the Saturday night radio programs had played an abundance of Glenn Miller recordings to mark the one-year anniversary of the bandleader's disappearance over the English Channel. Gerald had listened to the radio that night, alone, somberly thinking of not only the great bandleader but also his own two sons and their many hours of flying through the dangerous skies over Europe.

As with the earlier quiz program, Joseph played along and again correctly answered more of the questions than he missed. This time, Thomas joined in and the two brothers engaged in a friendly rivalry of their own alongside that of the program's audience members who had been chosen to answer the questions. Finally, as the eleven o'clock hour arrived, everyone in the household still awake (Ruthie had been sent upstairs an hour and a half earlier) agreed that bedtime had approached.

Joseph took more than an hour to fall asleep, his mind churning through a mélange of jumbled thoughts about Tommy Bonnaverte, Schenley High School, his brother Jonathan, Abby Sobol, the radio quiz shows, flight training at Thunderbird Field, Glenn Miller…

That night, when he finally did fall asleep, the nightmares were there waiting for him once again. This time, however, the German Panzers and the S.S. thugs weren't rolling into Stalag VII-A to commence with their killing; they were approaching Schenley High School right here in Pittsburgh, Pennsylvania. Inside the school's main hallway Joseph, his entire family, and hundreds of others (including Tommy Bonnaverte) were attending Abby Sobol's wedding. Suddenly aware of the approaching Nazi killers in the middle of the ceremony, the Schenley High halls of this nightmare were now filled with those trapped inside, helplessly awaiting imminent death.

3 – Tuesday, December 18, 1945

Francine Donner awoke to the instant realization that today was finally The Day: Jonathan was finally coming home! At 3:00 this afternoon she would be waiting for him – along with his family, of course – at Penn Station, and she would rush into his arms and greet her returning fiancé with the biggest kiss imaginable. It would all be so glorious! Just like in the movies!

A bit of cold water was thrown on her morning, though, when less than two minutes after she had awoken her bedroom door opened and in walked her mother.

"Irene Coleman just called," Sally Donner said. "Jonathan…"

Immediately, Francine's mind started racing. Jonathan wasn't coming home, after all! His furlough had been revoked and he was being sent back to Hawaii! Or perhaps he lost his space on the train, and with the terrible weather all over the northern part of the country he was unable to secure passage on another one! Or maybe something awful and terrible had happened to him!

"…will be four hours later than planned," Francine's mother continued, unaware of the whirlwind of ominous thoughts that had flown through her daughter's mind in less than one second. "There was a delay in St. Louis because of snow in Indianapolis, I think it was, but he's underway again. He's supposed to call from Dayton if he will be later than that, but if they don't hear from him, expect him at seven."

Francine let out a deep sigh of immense relief. The war was over; why was she still reacting like a scared rabbit at every single mention of Jonathan's name, with her mind instantly fixating on the worst possible scenario until she actually heard words to the contrary?

Much like Irene Coleman, she wouldn't be at ease until she actually set eyes on Jonathan Coleman, right here in Pittsburgh, Pennsylvania. Francine of course would never have such a conversation with Jonathan's mother; the woman was…well, if not cold towards her future daughter-in-law, then pretty darn close to it. Francine was well aware that if Irene Coleman had her druthers, she and Jonathan would not be getting married one week from this coming Saturday. She knew that Irene had nothing against her personally; it was a matter of timing and nothing more.

Ironically, when it came to this particular matter, Irene Coleman and Sally Donner were very much of the same mind, even though the frostiness between the two mothers thankfully prevented them from forming an alliance against the fast-approaching wedding. Both mothers were firmly of the mind that Francine and Jonathan were rushing into marriage far too quickly; Sally Donner had bluntly told her daughter as much less than two minutes after Francine excitedly told her mother about Jonathan's letter.

There was no way on this earth, however, that Francine would turn down Jonathan's idea of a quick wedding with a counter-offer of waiting until this coming April or May to get married. Maybe this all wasn't "normal" by traditional measures from her mother's own younger years, but the war had changed everything. Francine was 23 years old now – the same age as Jonathan – and it was time for them to get married and begin their family, the handful of days they had spent together during the past four years notwithstanding. Wait until the Spring of '46? Nothing doing!

"I'll be right down," Francine told her mother, and Sally Donner exited her daughter's room to head back downstairs and make breakfast for Francine. Her sister Julia – two years younger than Francine – was long gone from the Donner home, having gotten married nearly two years earlier. Francine's brother Albert, a sophomore at Schenley High, had already been sent off to school this morning. Soon – very soon – Albert would be the only one at home. Francine and Jonathan would buy a cute little house; possibly here in Polish Hill, but more likely in a close-but-not-too-close neighborhood such as Bloomfield or Lawrenceville. Jonathan and Francine would be starting a new life together, and a little space between them and her parents – and *definitely* his – would be a good thing.

Once again, the home movie in her imagination flickered to life and she saw her business suit-dressed husband come down the staircase of this imagined house, kiss Francine in their cozy kitchen as their three children – two boys and a girl – sat politely around the table, each one quietly eating breakfast. Jonathan walked around to each one, tussling the hair of each son and then giving his daughter – four-year old Louise, that's what she and Jonathan had named her – a kiss on the top of her golden blonde hair.

It would all be so magnificently perfect! Francine reluctantly got out of bed and braved the cold wooden floor to fish for her bedroom slippers in the still darkened room. She would rather remain in bed for another hour or so, continuing to dream about the wonderful life that was just ahead of her, but today was a big day for her.

Jonathan's arrival might be delayed for four hours or so, but it was still going to be today!

Today!

The *Spirit of St. Louis* was still two hours outside Dayton, Ohio and its scheduled 45-minute stop there. As long as the train's departure from Dayton remained as scheduled, no further long-distance call to the Coleman home would be necessary.

Jonathan had been so glad to hear his brother's voice that he neglected to ask Joseph – or his mother – to let Francine know about the four-hour delay, but he was certain that someone would indeed call her to let her know.

"I still can't believe you're getting married in eleven days," Charlene said to her brother as if reading his thoughts. "I'm so glad for you that everything worked out with Francine."

His sister's use of the phrase "worked out" instantly brought forth a wave of irritation but Jonathan was quick enough not to say anything in response. He knew what Charlene meant, and more than a few times he had entertained pretty much the same thoughts. The very night that he had received Francine's letter agreeing to his proposed wedding date, Jonathan had a terrible dream that just after he read his just-received letter he walked down to the beach at dusk and there they were – Francine and Donnie Yablonski – passionately kissing one another with the glorious Honolulu sunset as the perfect backdrop for this little scene. Jonathan awoke in a cold sweat and for the next three hours tossed and turned, wondering if he had done the right thing asking Francine to walk down the aisle at Saint Michael's so soon after he would see her for the first time in three years.

Riding along on the Pennsylvania Railroad train, Jonathan focused his thoughts on the same thing he had told himself perhaps a hundred times by now: just like a bombing mission, once you're underway the time for regrets and second-guessing and worst-case scenarios had passed, and only a fool thinks of anything other than a successful outcome.

❄ ❄ ❄

"We start filming January 15th," Charlene said in response to Jonathan's question about when her next picture would start shooting. "It's with Robert Taylor; I'm not sure yet who else will be in the cast."

"Wow, Robert Taylor!" Jonathan was indeed impressed. Jonathan had seen the famous actor in *Bataan* and despite the tragic outcome of the actual battle portrayed in the movie, the tale of heroic sacrifice had been popular among the Air Corps pilots when prints of the film were sent over to the air bases in England. Jonathan was quick to recognize the film for what it largely was…propaganda designed to keep American fighting men, as well as those back on the Home Front, intensely determined to stay the course through the tough years of war still ahead. Still, any movie – even a propaganda-style war flick – was a welcome distraction for Joseph and his fellow flyers between bombing missions.

Her brother might be awestruck to hear that his sister would soon be filming a movie with Robert Taylor, but to Charlene that piece of news was far less impressive. The truth was that Charlene was incredibly worried that her career had somehow taken a turn in the wrong direction. Not only hadn't the studio assigned her to a project with that long-awaited leading actress role, in this next movie Charlene would have all of five lines. Five! And two of those lines were only two words apiece: "I know" and "Of course."

Charlene had a theory, and it was a worrisome one. The image that the studio had cultivated for her was that of the sweet – yet slightly seductive – girl next door. They had arranged a couple of *Modern Screen* and *Photoplay* covers for her, and each of those cover photographs had been carefully shot and polished to convey that precise image. She was regularly coached before her U.S.O. and War Bond Tours or any other studio-arranged photo shoots about how she should present herself and how she should smile and what she should say, and the theme never varied.

The more Charlene thought about it, the more she became convinced that it was this specific image every bit as much as her acting and singing – maybe even more so – that was integral to Carla Colburn's role in the great big wartime Hollywood machine. Something like: "Listen up, you G.I.'s and sailors and Marines: you're not only fighting to win the war, you're fighting to come home to *this girl* who lives right there in your neighborhood just down the street, and she's waiting for you! So go win the war and then come home to claim your prize!"

Now, with the war won and millions of servicemen already home or on their way back, perhaps the studios no longer needed that image in their arsenal as they geared up for whatever awaited Hollywood and the movie industry during the rest of the 1940s. At least that's the way it seemed to Charlene. Nobody had said as much, of course, and even as recently as this past October and November Charlene had been part of the final big War Bond Tour. But beyond her many public appearances, news from the studio about upcoming films and roles for Charlene was depressingly sparse.

The servicemen she came in contact with – those G.I.'s from Cleveland back on the Southern Pacific train, or the dozens for whom she had signed autographs yesterday afternoon at the St. Louis Union Station – seemed to have a different opinion about the post-war desirability of Carla Colburn than her studio bosses did. But when it came to whatever movie roles that Carla Colburn would be given in 1946 and – hopefully! – beyond, unfortunately the opinions of soldiers and sailors and Marines were trumped by whatever was in the works out in Hollywood. And right now, Charlene Coleman was totally in the dark about whatever that might be…but the hints she was picking up were far from comforting.

It wasn't just Charlene who seemed caught in some sort of Hollywood Purgatory, either. Wayne Morris, the well-known Warner Brothers actor who had appeared in *Flight Angels* back in 1940 and then became a real-life Navy flying ace during the war, had yet to be assigned to a new film. One would think that with the flood of new war movies planned in the aftermath of victory, an actor who had shot down seven Japanese planes and earned four Distinguished Flying Crosses would be at the top of the list for starring roles and scheduled almost non-stop for the next two or three years. Charlene had met him at a Hollywood War Bond gathering two months ago, and he seemed like a nice enough fellow. In an unguarded moment, talking offstage with Charlene and several other actors and actresses while they waited for their respective turns to speak or perform, Morris had expressed many of the same frustrations that Charlene and several others in that group also felt. Maybe his appearance on Bob Hope's Christmas radio show tonight will remind the studio that he was actually back from the war, Charlene thought.

Charlene heard a snort and then a gasp as Jonathan abruptly awoke.

"I fell asleep, huh?" he asked his sister.

"About fifteen minutes ago," Charlene replied, realizing that she had been alone in her own thoughts. "We're still about two hours from Dayton. I can't believe how slow this train is going!"

"Yeah," Jonathan said, rubbing his eyes and yawning. "But it could be worse; we could still be sitting in St. Louis. This time of year a blizzard could come out of nowhere and shut down the whole system, and then you never know when we would get going again."

"I know," Charlene answered. "I'm just anxious to get home already."

She looked over at her brother again.

"But I'm sure you're even more excited than I am, with Francine waiting for you...right?"

Jonathan smiled and nodded.

"Yep," was his response.

Last night's conversation aboard the train had been filled with stories about some of Jonathan's missions and Charlene's adventures in Hollywood and on U.S.O. and War Bond Tours, and how each of them had celebrated on V-E Day and V-J Day. More somberly, Charlene confessed the immense sadness she felt – and of course had to hide – at every U.S.O. show realizing that so many of the boys and men in the audience at any given show would soon be wounded or dead. Jonathan likewise admitted that almost every time he walked into the Officers' Club or the ready room his mind would automatically and involuntarily begin to wonder how many of those present were there for the final times in their lives.

They had both drifted off to sleep around 9:30 last night and had slept straight through until after 7:00 this morning. Plenty of wartime news covering the past three years had been shared between brother and sister, but much more still remained to fill the rest of the journey home to Pittsburgh.

"Have you given any thought to what you're going to do once you're discharged?" Charlene now asked.

"I don't know," Jonathan quickly answered.

"What do you think?" Charlene pressed. "You know, what kind of job you're going to get? Where you and Francine are going to live?"

Jonathan blew out a deep breath. Of course he had given these questions – and others – plenty of thought. The problem was that whereas he had plenty of questions to ask, he had absolutely no answers.

❄ ❄ ❄

Pittsburgh's wintertime weather – at least this December – was both monotonous and uncomfortable. Bitter cold and snow, over and over. Today's newspaper headlines and radio news broadcasts warned that another five inches of snow was on its way, followed by temperatures diving again towards the zero mark.

Irene Coleman would spend this day making her rounds of the bakery and the butcher's shop and the market, making sure that the Coleman pantry and cupboard shelves were as well-stocked as possible. The delay in the arrival of both Jonathan and Charlene had put a wrinkle into her mealtime plans, however. With her final two arriving children originally scheduled to be in Pittsburgh long before suppertime, a glorious feast had been planned for this evening's meal. Her brother Stan Walker and his family had been invited to share in the celebration.

Now though, with both Jonathan and Charlene arriving at 7:00, Irene was forced to delay the family supper until Wednesday. She fretted that if the threatened five inches of snow did indeed arrive, her brother's family might not be able to make it to the Coleman house through the snowy and icy streets.

From early 1941 until earlier this year, Stan and Lois Walker had raised their children in their own Polish Hill home, less than a ten-minute walk from the Coleman home. Further back, beginning in 1935 with Stan out of work and their first home taken by the bank, the Walkers had actually lived in the Coleman house for more than five years. Initially Stan and Lois rented a house after being able to move out of Gerald's and Irene's, but a year later they were finally able to once again buy a home. Stan plunked down a down payment of $1,000 to purchase the house from their landlord, and they lived there for the next three years.

Years earlier in the mid-'20s Stan Walker had been captivated by the roaring stock market, and he began tucking away a few dollars here and there from his job as a railroad brakeman. By 1929 the value of Stan's stock certificates in America's industrial giants had rapidly grown to forty thousand dollars...a fortune! Alas, the stock market crash in '29 had instantly wiped out about one-third of Stan's haul, with the rest evaporating over the next few years as steadily as air being let out of a balloon.

But Stan Walker's faith in American industry and the New York Stock Exchange was unshaken by what he had endured, even as the stock markets sunk deeper and deeper during the early years of the war. Fortunately for Stan, it was mid-1942 before he was finally able to cobble together enough money for his first stock investment since the '20s...just as the stock market began its climb from its wartime bottom to nearly double by the end of the war. The same skill – or dumb luck, Stan wasn't quite certain and really didn't care – that had yielded him that temporary bounty of $40,000 so many years earlier helped Stan grow his regular stock purchases in United States Steel, Ford, Gulf Oil, and other companies to more than $20,000 this time around. This haul of stock profits wasn't quite as abundant as his earlier one, but it was enough for Stan to pull $7,500 out of the market in early '45 and use that money as a down payment on a house out in posh Fox Chapel Borough, out on the other side of the Allegheny. The new Walker home cost $25,000, nearly five times what their house in Polish Hill had cost and then had been sold for. Ten years had passed since the bank had taken Stan Walker's first family home and his family was forced to move in with the Colemans. But what a difference a decade had made!

Tomorrow, the ten miles of snowy and icy roads from her brother's plush Fox Chapel home to Polish Hill – and back again – could indeed prove to be too treacherous for Stan and Lois and their children to brave. But the weather and road conditions were out of her control; if that's what wound up happening, then so be it. If her brother still lived in Polish Hill where he belonged then there wouldn't be a problem; that was how Irene Coleman saw it.

For the rest of this Tuesday morning and afternoon, though, Irene would focus on her many chores, including thoroughly cleaning the house again later this afternoon, before Jonathan and Charlene arrived. Around 5:30 she would serve a light supper to Gerald, Joseph, Thomas, and Ruthie, and then after they all arrived back home from Penn Station Irene would serve another meal for all of them. It wouldn't be the feast that was originally intended, but she was certain that none of her children would leave tonight's late supper table less than satisfied.

Francine Donner would be in attendance at Irene's table tonight, of course, and then would be accompanying the Coleman family to Penn Station to greet Jonathan. Given her status as Jonathan's fiancé, how could she not be? Irene grudgingly accepted this fact, though she wished there were some other scenario in which Francine would yield the rich pleasure of welcoming Jonathan home to his family – to Irene – before she stepped into the picture.

Oh well, Irene thought to herself as she tidied up around the house before braving the outdoor weather, at least Jonathan will be home and close by. He would sleep in his old room for another week and a half until the wedding day, and then afterwards he and Francine would no doubt rent a small house nearby; perhaps even on the same street, but at least somewhere in the neighborhood. As long as her son was close to home, even with his new wife, things would be as they had once been – mostly – before he had gone away to war.

❄ ❄ ❄

Thomas glided the Packard down Butler Street, headed towards the Highland Park Bridge and then to the other side of the Allegheny River. Even though the bridge had been open for six years now, most people in Pittsburgh still thought of it as the "new bridge," upriver from the cluster of other ones closer to the heart of the city. A light dusting of snow was coming down again, and Gerald Coleman's warnings echoed in both Thomas' and Joseph's heads:

"You boys better both be careful; this isn't a couple of miles right around here, but ten miles each way to your cousin's. It's going to snow and neither one of you has a license. Both of you be real careful!"

Gerald would have been happy if his sons had called off this little trip, but with Jonathan's arrival at Penn Station now delayed, they both wanted to fill the time by going to see their cousin Marty Walker. Fox Chapel might be ten miles away but to Joseph's mind, if he could fly hundreds of miles through German fighters and anti-aircraft fire, then a short ten-mile trip through a little bit of snow was nothing. Besides, Tommy's driving yesterday had been uneventful; anyone would have thought that he had been behind the wheel regularly for two or three years by now.

"It's sort of strange with Marty living all the way out here," Thomas mused. He meticulously kept his eyes on the road but every so often he could catch a glimpse of the Allegheny River off to their left through the now-barren trees or in between industrial buildings. Even though he had rarely spent any time this far away from the heart of the city, there was something familiar and strangely comforting to Thomas about this late morning trek through this part of the city; that feeling of being home again; home where he belonged.

"Yeah," Joseph agreed. Yet one more thing that had changed since he had last been home, Joseph thought to himself. Being the exact same age, he and Marty had been exceptionally close growing up; especially living in the same house for all of those years. Following the attack on Pearl Harbor, both boys could talk of nothing else for months other than enlisting right after their high school graduations to fight in this new war. Indeed, both had enlisted the same day back in the spring of '42, as did Jonathan. But whereas the Coleman brothers opted for the Army Air Forces and the chance to become pilots, Marty Walker joined the Navy. He was quickly sent off to the naval training base in Chicago and then before he knew it, was on board the *USS Augusta* in time for the invasion of North Africa in late '42.

Joseph had received a couple of letters from Marty before being shot down, but hadn't heard from him at all the entire time he was held in the Luftstalag. After V-E Day, a letter from Tommy mentioned that as far as anybody knew, Marty was still in Europe and hadn't been sent out to the Pacific to take part in the eventual invasion of Japan. Joseph was looking forward to learning what his cousin had done during the war; perhaps he had even taken part in the Normandy invasion.

Ten minutes later, the final three miles of the trip had passed uneventfully and Tommy eased the Packard into the empty single-car driveway in front of the house. He double-checked the address he had written down on a slip of paper to make sure that indeed they had arrived at the right place. This house was a mansion! Well, not quite a real mansion like the stately old homes that dotted various parts of the city – Fifth Avenue on the way to Wilkinsburg, or Millionaires' Row on the north side – but compared to the Walkers' former house in Polish Hill or the Colemans' house, it sure looked like one!

"Yeah, it's the right place," Tommy said just as the front door opened and out stepped Marty Walker, accompanied by his nineteen-year old sister Lorraine. The Colemans exited the Packard and before they could take more than a couple of steps away from the car, they were swarmed by both of their cousins for hugs all around.

"Oh my God, I can't believe you're home!" Lorraine said in a broken voice, fighting back tears as she hugged Joseph. The two had never been particularly close; Lorraine and Charlene always paired off the same way that Joseph and Marty did, but the sight of her cousin after so long – and especially after those earlier months of uncertainty when everyone was all but certain that Joseph had been killed in action – brought forth a rush of emotions to Lorraine as she hugged her cousin.

"Let's go inside," Marty suggested. "I'm freezing without a coat." Both Marty and Lorraine had hurried outside without any overcoats at the sound of the approaching Packard, and even though not more than a minute had passed each of them was already freezing.

"Ma is inside," Lorraine said through chattering teeth as the Coleman brothers followed their cousins into the luxurious home. "Pop is at work, though, and Calvin is at school."

The group of cousins had barely stepped inside before Lois Walker appeared in the foyer. Yet another tear-filled hug commenced when she greeted Joseph.

"We were all so worried about you," Joseph's aunt said. "I'm so glad you're home now!"

"Come in, come in, sit down," Lois Walker said to her nephews. "Marty can show you around the house later but I'm sure you want to sit and rest after your drive."

"Sure, Aunt Lois," Tommy said as they followed her into the living room. Joseph couldn't help but notice how elegant the furniture was. He had heard from Tommy that his Uncle Stan had done well with the stocks, but until entering the Walkers' new home and drinking in the plushness and elegance, he hadn't grasped how much money his uncle must have actually made to be able to afford all of this.

"I have coffee for both of you," Lois said as she hurried out of the living room towards the kitchen. She returned quickly with two steaming cups of coffee, then made two more trips into the kitchen; the first to bring back coffee for Lorraine and Marty, and the second to retrieve a cup of tea for herself.

A good hour passed as stories were exchanged. Marty told his cousins about his role in the Normandy invasion, manning a landing craft bringing the Army troops ashore. After tiptoeing around the subject for a while, Marty finally asked his cousin about being shot down and his imprisonment. Lois asked Tommy about his upcoming long journey out to California and Camp Pendleton, and Lorraine asked for any updated news of Charlene's arrival home.

"Would you boys like lunch?" Lois asked as the clock ticked past twelve. Before either Joseph or Thomas could answer, Marty interjected:

"I was thinking that we could go over to Lou's and grab something to eat there," he told his mother.

"That would be fine," Lois answered after a few seconds. "Lorraine and I can go to the market then, before we get much more snow. But you boys be careful driving on these roads."

"We will, Ma," Marty replied, heading for the hall closet to retrieve his Navy Pea Coat. Joseph put his flying jacket and officer's cap back on, and Thomas did likewise with his civilian jacket. The boys headed outside to the Packard.

"Want me to drive?" Marty offered to his cousins. "Neither of you has a license, right? I do now, so maybe that would be better."

"When did you get a driver's license?" Tommy asked.

"About a month ago after I got home," came the answer. "Pop usually has the Buick so I don't get much of a chance to drive except on weekends. But I figured that sooner or later I'll get a car, so I might as well get the license, ya know?"

"Sure then, here ya go," Tommy tossed Marty the keys and climbed into the back seat, yielding the front to his brother.

"This place Lou's is a lounge with pretty good burgers," Marty said as he gunned the Packard to life. The car sputtered a little bit, still objecting to the intense cold. Just as Thomas had quickly figured out for himself driving the Packard, Marty let the car idle for a minute or two to settle down before backing out of the driveway.

"It's only about a mile and a half from here, but no way am I walking there in this cold," Marty said as he turned out of the residential neighborhood onto the country road leading to the main drag. "I go there for lunch a couple times a week; you know, grab a burger and a couple a beers."

"What's it like living out here?" Joseph asked. "I mean, isn't it really different than Polish Hill?"

"I'll say," Marty chuckled. "Not just the old neighborhood, but...well, you know, living in the city versus living way out here in the country. It was really strange coming home and not going back to the old house; like *everything* had changed while I was gone. You know what I mean?"

Marty's question was addressed to Joseph rather than Thomas, which both Coleman brothers knew.

"Yeah, I do," Joseph replied, and after a few more seconds offered:

"Yeah...everything..."

"You know how I just said that it was too cold to walk to Lou's?" Marty continued. "Well, until a couple weeks ago when it got this cold I would do that all the time; it's just about the same distance as from our old house to Schenley. But you're walking through...I don't know, it seems like nothing. A house every so often, all these trees, even a couple of farmers' fields...it's not like in the city where you walk a mile and a half and it's nonstop houses and stores and everything."

He paused as he made a right turn, the Packard slipping a little bit on the increasingly slick roads.

"I don't know, Pop likes it out here and Ma seems to also, but if it were up to me I'd just as soon be back in the old house and the old neighborhood."

"You mean that?" Tommy asked from the back seat.

"I don't know," came the reply, followed by: "Yeah, sometimes."

❄ ❄ ❄

The dramatic distinctions between Fox Chapel and Polish Hill notwithstanding, Lou's could just as well have been a bar in Polish Hill, or Bloomfield, or Oakland or any other city neighborhood. The outside of the aging building was red brick, with a heavy layer of black soot adhering to a good portion of the building's surface. The windows on both sides of the front door were constructed from thick opaque glass bricks, the same as many of the bars in the central working class neighborhoods. Inside, an unobtrusive wooden bar with a dozen or so unpretentious barstools was the primary gathering place, but nine or ten tables, each surrounded by plain-looking wooden chairs, were also scattered around the interior. Perhaps some early Pittsburgh-to-Fox Chapel transplant had opened up a bar specifically designed to remind himself – and his similarly-rooted patrons – of the city neighborhoods from which they had come.

A Wurlitzer 850 Peacock stood in the corner closest to the door, but when the boys walked inside no music was coming from the jukebox. They headed to the bar where only three seats remained unoccupied, but fortunately all of the open spaces were in a row at the far end away from the door. Eyes shifted as they walked by, attention drawn to Joseph's flying jacket.

"Hey Marty," one of the men sitting at the bar – a somewhat disheveled brown-haired man with bloodshot eyes and two or three days' stubble growth on his face – said when he noticed that Marty Walker was among the three newcomers.

"Hi Wayne," Marty offered back his response. "Hey Wayne; these are my cousins, Joey and Tommy Coleman, both of them just back in Pittsburgh since two days ago."

"Yeah?" the man named Wayne said, eyeing Joseph's flying jacket again. "Air Corps, huh?" he asked Joseph.

"Uh-huh," Joseph said, slowing just a touch as he passed Wayne's barstool but still walking towards the empty seats, his brother and cousin both a few steps ahead of him.

"Well, welcome back," Wayne said. "You home for good?"

This time, Joseph halted, turning back towards Wayne since he was already a couple of steps beyond where the man was sitting.

"Not yet, but probably soon," he answered. "Christmas furlough, then I'll probably have enough points for my discharge by February or March."

The man called Wayne took notice of the officer's cap that was still perched on Joseph's head.

"You a pilot?" he asked.

"Uh-huh," Joseph nodded. "B-24s," he added, knowing full well that question – "whadja fly?" – would have been forthcoming in about two seconds if he didn't preemptively offer up that information.

"Lieutenant?" Wayne pressed. Joseph's jacket was void of any rank and Joseph wasn't wearing his uniform underneath, so the man had no way of knowing exactly what rank Joseph had earned.

"Captain," Joseph answered, starting to feel uncomfortable with the game of twenty questions he had found himself in the middle of.

"Captain," Wayne repeated thoughtfully, nodding his head slowly as he spoke. Then he turned to the man behind the bar and said:

"Lou, set this captain and Marty and the other guy up with three Fort Pitts, on me." His words were increasingly slurred, and Joseph wondered just how long this guy Wayne had been sitting here at the bar drinking this day…or any day, for that matter.

"You don't have to do that," Joseph said quickly.

"Nah, I insist," Wayne retorted. "You guys were over there doing all the fighting while I was back here just trying to do my part, as little as it was."

"Well, thanks then," Joseph said, finally heading over to the empty stool Marty had left open to his right. Thomas had grabbed the stool on Marty's left, so the cousins could each sit on one side or the other from him.

Joseph had barely plopped himself onto the barstool when the guy behind the bar – Lou – appeared carrying three large beer glasses. He set one down in front of Marty, then Joseph, and was just about to lower the third one in front of Thomas when he glanced up.

"You twenty-one?" Lou asked, his eyes narrowing.

Thomas wasn't about to try and lie.

"No," he answered, adding "eighteen." If this guy Lou gave him a hard time, Thomas was ready to remind him that he hadn't even ordered the beer; that guy named Wayne had done so for all three of them.

"You in the service?" Lou inquired.

"Yeah," Thomas answered. "Marines."

To his surprise, Lou slid the Fort Pitt towards him.

"Just don't say nothin' to nobody," he said, his eyes narrowing.

Thomas was caught by surprise but quickly recovered. Lest he be accused of impersonating a combat Marine, he felt compelled to set the record straight.

"Wait…wait," he said before Lou could leave their vicinity. "I just got out of boot camp and infantry training. I wasn't in the Pacific or anything."

Lou paused and seemed to contemplate the "confession" he had just heard.

"But you woulda been sent over there to fight if the war was still going on, right?"

Thomas shrugged.

"Well, yeah," was his reply.

"Good enough for me," came the bar owner's response as he turned and headed back to the other side of the bar.

"Hey, congratulations," Marty said to Thomas when Lou was out of earshot. "Your first beer at a bar in Pittsburgh – or at least near Pittsburgh – right?"

Thomas thought about it.

"Yeah, I guess so," he answered.

"And I was here to see it," Marty grinned. He raised his glass, looked over at Joseph to his right and then back at Thomas to his left, and offered a short toast.

"To all of us making it back here safely," he said. He looked back at Thomas and added:

"You too. I've heard of guys buying it at Parris Island or Lejeune so same goes for you as well."

Three glasses clinked together and each of the cousins took a healthy swallow.

"You guys want burgers like I'm getting, right?" Marty asked and each of the Colemans nodded even as they were still drinking.

"Hey Lou," Marty raised his voice to be heard. "Three burgers and fries, okay?"

"You got it," came the answer from the other side of the bar.

"So how often you come here?" Joseph asked Marty.

"I dunno," Marty replied. "Maybe once or twice a week; some weeks a little bit more. You know, just killing time mostly."

"So what are you thinkin' about doin'?" Joseph inquired. "You know, being done with the Navy and all that. I didn't want to ask you in front of Aunt Lois; you know."

"Yeah," Marty grinned. "Could be a sensitive subject; I get it." He lowered his voice so only Joseph could hear him. "Like maybe I'm planning to sit here and drink all day, every day?"

He paused to take another swig of his Fort Pitt.

"I'm going to college," Marty pronounced, the volume of his voice raised again so Tommy could hear as well. "I'm starting at Pitt right after New Year's. You know, using my G.I. Bill money."

"College?" Joseph's eyes widened slightly. Whereas Joseph had been mostly a B student at Schenley, Marty had been a notch or two below; mostly C's, with a few B's sprinkled in here and there; even a couple of D's. To the best of Joseph's knowledge, Marty hadn't gotten a single A in his entire four years of high school. And the two of them had taken most classes together; Marty was even more of a cut-up in the classroom than Joseph had been, and had spent even more time than his cousin in the Principal's office.

"Yeah," Marty nodded. "Pop and I talked about it after I got back, and it was his idea that I take a couple months until the end of the year to…I dunno, take it easy for a little bit after the war and everything we went through, you know? And then use the G.I. Bill to go to college. Uncle Sam's gonna pay me fifty bucks a month while I'm at Pitt plus cover all of the school costs."

Joseph almost blurted out what he was thinking as Marty was talking – "Are you really smart enough to go to college?" – but since he couldn't think of a diplomatic manner in which to phrase that question, he decided to let it drop.

"Pop wants me to major in business accounting," Marty continued, "and then maybe go to work as an accountant or maybe something to do with the stock market. You know how he is…"

Marty's voice trailed off.

"Is that what you want to do?" Joseph pressed.

"Yeah, I think so," came his cousin's reply, though his voice reflected at least a touch of uncertainty. "I don't really know anything about business accounting and all that, but I figure once I get started if it's too hard I'll switch to something else."

Marty took another swig of his beer, this one finishing off what remained in the glass, as he seemed to be contemplating a particular perplexing quandary.

"I thought about goin' to get a job," Marty continued, "maybe in the steel mills or something like that. But I was thinking about in the Navy how most of the officers were college men and you could tell there was a big difference between them and us average sailors."

As if all of a sudden remembering that his cousin was an officer himself, Marty added, a bit defensively given what he had just mused about:

"Sort of like with you, right? In the Air Corps I'll bet there was a big difference between you officers and the enlisted guys, and not just in pay."

"I dunno, maybe," came Joseph's reply, "but remember I didn't go to college. Jonathan and I wound up in the flying cadet program and remember back in '42 they were so desperate for pilots and navigators and bombardiers that they didn't make you have a college degree or anything. So yeah, I get what you mean about officers and enlisted guys but I don't think it had anything to do with college."

"Well anyway," Marty said, looking over at Thomas and then back at Joseph, "I figure that if I go get my degree then I can get some fancy job downtown, maybe at Gulf Oil or Mellon Bank, and wear a suit to the office every day and all that; you know, get some job that I couldn't get unless I do go to college. That's what Pop wants me to do. He's plenty proud of working as a railroad brakeman but you know he doesn't make a lot of money; the only way we're living way out here in fancy Fox Chapel is that he got lucky again playing the stock market, and this time he didn't lose it all. We talked about it; it's the usual thing, him wanting something better for me than he had. Probably the same with Uncle Gerald and you guys and Jonathan too, right?"

Joseph shrugged. The truth was that he really didn't have much of an idea what his father's aspirations were, at least for his second son. Perhaps Jonathan had engaged in such discussion with their father at some point before leaving for the Air Corps; but not Joseph. After all, Joseph hadn't even turned eighteen when they all knew with every bit of certainty in the world the single, immutable thing that Joseph's future *did* hold: war.

"So what about you?" Marty asked. "When you finally get discharged, you know yet what you're gonna do?"

Joseph shook his head, finishing off the last of his beer as well.

"Don't know," he said, staring into the now-empty glass as if perhaps the answer to the question might be found in there.

"To be honest with you," he added, "until I actually got home Sunday night, I did my best *not* to think about anything in the future. You kinda learned that in the Luftstalag; don't think too far into the future or make any plans, because you got no idea what's really ahead. You just make it through one day at a time."

"How bad was it?" Marty asked, using the exact same words that Thomas had spoken Sunday night in making the same inquiry. Earlier in the Walker living room Joseph had told them all a little bit about being held prisoner by the Germans, but Marty sensed there was a lot more to the story than Joseph wanted to share in front of his aunt or Lorraine.

Joseph glanced across his cousin and over at Thomas – a look that said "hope you don't mind hearing it all again" – and then proceeded to give Marty mostly the same narrative he had related to his father and Thomas, then later just his brother, Sunday night in the Coleman living room. Meanwhile, the man seated to Joseph's right, on the other side of the flyer, couldn't help overhearing what Joseph was telling his cousin.

"You were in a German prisoner camp?" the man finally asked when Joseph had paused in his tale. Just then Lou the bar owner reappeared, this time balancing three plates overflowing with burgers and French fries. As Joseph's plate was placed in front of him – and after Marty ordered another round of beers for them – Joseph turned to the man to his right to answer.

"Yeah," he said. "About a hundred miles from Berlin; this town called Sagan. That was the first one; near the end of the war they moved us to a couple of others."

"Geez," the man said. "Was it like what they did to the Jews in those camps?"

Joseph quickly shook his head.

"No, nothing like that," he replied. "I mean, it wasn't a picnic or anything but it wasn't anything like what they did to all those people. The Luftwaffe was in charge of us and mostly they were flyers like we were, so there was this…I don't know, respect or courtesy or something like that. If you got called to the Commandant's or the Adjutant's office, and they outranked you, you would salute them just like you would an Air Forces officer who outranked you. Sometimes one of them would even salute a higher-ranking officer on our side; not all the time, but occasionally. Anyway, until the last couple months of the war things in the camp…well, you'd definitely rather be back at your own airfield and not a war prisoner, but on the other hand it could have been a lot worse."

By this time, most of those seated at the bar – including the man named Wayne – had picked up on Joseph's words and were listening intently to what he was saying. Another man who had walked into the bar only minutes earlier and had taken a just-vacated seat happened to catch part of Joseph's tale, and when the pilot paused for a moment the man asked:

"So how were you shot down?"

"We were jumped by a bunch of Messerschmitts and a couple of 'em shot us up bad enough we had to bail out," Joseph repeated what he had mentioned earlier before the man had arrived, then picked up where he had left off. When Joseph had finished, the man who had most recently walked in told Lou the bar owner that not only would he buy lunch for Marty Walker and his two cousins, he would also pay for their next round of Fort Pitts.

"That settles it," Marty murmured to Joseph in a voice barely above a whisper, "after you get home for good you gotta come out here pretty often, and the rest of the time I'll meet you in the city. I could probably get free beer and burgers for the next year if all it takes is you mentioning that you were a prisoner of war."

Realizing his cousin was kidding – mostly – Joseph raised his eyebrows and replied:

"Glad to know my time in the Luftstalag is turning out to be so helpful for you."

❋ ❋ ❋

Shortly after 3:00, the Coleman brothers and their cousin were on their fourth beers when a few copies of the early edition of the afternoon *Pittsburgh Press* showed up in the bar. Joseph noticed that apparently a ritual in Lou's was that when the newspapers arrived, the sections were divided up and distributed in a seemingly scattershot manner to whomever happened to be seated at the bar. One of the front sections made its way down to Marty and his cousins, and each one's eyes settled on the banner headline in all caps: 5-INCH SNOW ON WAY HERE. This of course wasn't news to Joseph and Thomas – the morning's *Post-Gazette* had offered the same warning as had the radio, and the boys' father had hammered home that point when he handed over the keys to the Packard – but it was a reminder that they needed to be back home by 4:30. Another half-hour – and maybe one more beer – they figured, and they could easily pass the remaining time skimming through the paper with their cousin.

"Hey, look at this," Marty exclaimed, his eyes settling on a short, three-paragraph story near the bottom right side of the front page that bore the small headline reading "Patton's Condition Continues Excellent." All three of them – indeed, probably everyone in the entire United States – were well aware that the famed general George S. Patton had been in a terrible automobile accident a week and a half earlier, suffering a broken neck in the collision. According to this latest report, however, General Patton had just been fitted with a new cast, and a day earlier had been allowed to sit up for the first time. It seemed that the fiery warrior would pull through after all.

"Did you guys know I met him during the war? Patton?" Marty said.

"Really?" came Thomas' incredulous reply. His cousin had been in the Navy; where in the world would he have met the famous Army general?

"During *Torch*," Marty continued, referring to the invasion of North Africa back in late 1942. "I was on the *Augusta* and General Patton came on board with Admiral Hewitt and Admiral Hall and directed the invasion from our ship. Since I was a radioman in the Captain's Bridge, I was there a lot when he was, and every so often I would hand him reports that came in, or scribble down something that he wanted me to transmit."

"Patton?" this time it was Joseph who responded to his cousin's story.

"Uh-huh," Marty nodded. "He finally went ashore after the initial invasion but he was on board for a little while."

"Wow," Thomas said. He hadn't heard that story about his cousin, even though he had been home in Pittsburgh for the entire war until six months ago. But then again, given how war news had been so tightly controlled – and how letters sent by servicemen to the folks back home were often so heavily censored – it was no wonder that this tale was news to him, even though his cousin's encounters with General Patton had happened way back in 1942. Even if Marty had carelessly included such anecdotes in a letter back home, they surely would have been excised from that letter via the censor's scissors for reasons of inadvertently conveying information about troop movements and battle formations.

When the allotted half-hour had passed – the brothers having switched to hot coffee, figuring another beer wouldn't be a good idea with the long drive ahead of them, and Marty joining along in solidarity – they made their way out of the bar. The Wurlitzer, which had been silent most of the afternoon, was now playing the Bing Crosby version of *It's Been a Long, Long Time*...which of course instantly made him think of Abby Sobol. Thus far today he had successfully kept the girl from his thoughts, but all it took was this song about reunited lovers to instantly bring her to memory.

Marty drove the Packard back to the Walker house and mostly talked with Tommy during the drive, as Joseph remained lost in his memories of Abby. When would this stop, Joseph wondered; hopefully soon. Little things like a stupid song triggering such a flood of emotions...well, that was definitely unwelcome, especially with his brother and sister due home soon. He forced himself to think about Jonathan's impending arrival, and by the time they arrived at Marty's house his mood had improved at least a little bit.

"See you tomorrow at dinner," Marty said as he jumped out of the car and Thomas came up from the back seat.

"Yeah, see you then," Thomas said as he slid behind the wheel.

"Yeah, see you then," Joseph echoed from the front seat just before Thomas shut the driver's side door.

"You good to drive?" Joseph asked his brother as the Packard backed out of the driveway.

"Uh-huh," Thomas answered.

"You sure?" Joseph pressed.

"You mean because of the beers?" Thomas asked, starting to feel a touch irritated at his brother's questioning.

"Just making sure," came Joseph's answer.

The first half of the drive passed in silence as Thomas tried to figure out why his brother's questions irritated him so much. Even back at Lou's, as Joseph's tale of being shot down and taken prisoner became somewhat of a public oratory, and as his brother and his cousin shared stories of their wartime experiences, Thomas felt relegated to some sort of second-class listener status like the regulars sitting at the bar; perhaps being the "little cousin" and "little brother" who had been slightly too young to have gone to war and didn't have his own stories to share.

The snow was starting to fall more rapidly, and Butler Street was now covered by a steadily thickening gray slush. Enough cars were still out and about this afternoon to keep the street from icing up – mostly – but by tonight, between the lesser traffic and the dropping temperatures, travel was certain to be treacherous. Gerald would be certain to be extra careful driving the family to Penn Station to meet Jonathan and Charlene, and Thomas forced himself to concentrate on driving the same as his father would. He was going no faster than twenty miles an hour right now, though every so often the slushy mix would still cause the Packard to slip and jerk to one side or the other. Leaving Fox Chapel and the Walkers' house Thomas had still been a little bit lightheaded from all of the beer consumed that afternoon, but now he was totally alert. The sheer terror of imagining what his father would do if something happened to the Packard was enough for Thomas Coleman!

"You doing okay there?" Joseph asked and this time, Thomas didn't immediately anger at the question.

"Yeah," he said, scrunching down slightly so that he could see below the accumulation of snow that had built up on the top part of the windshield, above where the windshield wipers flicked back and forth. In fact, it seemed to Thomas that the snow buildup was even underneath the path of the wipers; he would have to mention to his father that maybe the gas station should put in new wipers.

"Having trouble seeing," Thomas added, putting words to his thoughts.

"Sort of like being on a nighttime bombing mission," Joseph responded in a strange voice. "Can't really see anything outside; you just keep flying where you think you're supposed to go, and hope like hell that your navigator has you headed in the right direction."

The Packard approached the three-way intersection with Penn Avenue vectoring in from the left side and also, a few yards ahead, the left turn on 34th Street that they would make to head up into Polish Hill. Thomas slowed the car, looked back over his left shoulder – as best as he could, given the accumulated snow on the Packard's left side and back windows – at the intersecting traffic coming from Penn Avenue. Not seeing any other vehicles headed towards him, Thomas continued straight ahead.

Suddenly the blare of a car horn shattered the silence. Thomas slammed down hard on the brakes and the Packard began spinning out of control on the slickened roads. The car wound up making a complete circle, but somehow came to rest in exactly the same position from which it had started, once again facing in the right direction. Meanwhile as the car was spinning and even after it had stopped, Thomas was bracing himself for the impact of an impending collision...but there was none.

The other car must have swerved around us, Thomas realized. He quickly opened the driver's side door of the Packard – not too quickly, lest an oncoming car rip right into it – and seeing no other cars around him now, got out and quickly surveyed the Packard for any signs of damage. None! He walked another rapid circle around the car, checking each of the tires for a blowout. Again, all was well.

Silently and rapidly muttering the Hail Mary he got back into the car. Apparently the "hour of our death" mentioned in the prayer wasn't going to be this particular one, he thought to himself when he came to the conclusion of the short prayer. He began reciting the prayer again as he looked over at his brother, fully expecting to be greeted by a rage-filled face and a profanity-fueled diatribe. Instead, Joseph Coleman looked as calm as ever, as if Thomas had just pulled into some business establishment's parking lot to check the car's tires or take a peek under the hood.

"Just like flying through a flak field and coming out the other side," Joseph finally said in a detached voice.

"Guess our number wasn't up...this time," Joseph added, still in a voice that was so curiously calm, Thomas couldn't help but wonder if his brother was fully here in Pittsburgh this cold December day, or perhaps elsewhere in a different place and time of the past.

Thomas pulled the Packard over to the curb a block away from the Coleman house to give the car another looking-over. He knew that if he pulled into the parking spot in front of the house and did this, and if his father happened to look out of the window and see him doing so, there would be no hiding the close call even if indeed no damage had been done to the car. So both Thomas and Joseph exited the car where Thomas had pulled over and did a walk-around. Still, no signs of damage. Quite possibly this near-encounter could fade into history without Gerald Coleman being any the wiser.

After getting back into the car and finishing the journey home, Thomas eased into the parking spot in front of the house and both boys hurried up the stairs to get out of the cold. Inside the house, they shed their coats just as their mother came out of the kitchen into the living room.

"How is Marty?" Irene asked.

"Great," Thomas replied.

"He said he's going to college," Joseph added, apparently back in the present day and time. "Here at Pitt."

"College?" Irene responded, a disbelieving look immediately coming to her face.

"Yeah," Thomas confirmed. "He's going to use that G.I. Bill money. He said Uncle Stan wants him to go into business accounting or something like that."

Irene nodded. That made sense; even without the stock market luck bestowed on her brother, Marty had an opportunity in front of him courtesy of that government money that had been unthinkable only a few years earlier. And if Marty – a mediocre student as Irene knew all too well, having listened to her sister-in-law's complaints for years about Marty's laziness in school – could take advantage of this wonderful opportunity, her sons should be able to as well.

Irene was in the kitchen, assisted by Ruthie, and the boys were upstairs cleaning up when the front door opened a few minutes after 5:00. Not only was Gerald returning home from his shop, right on schedule, but he was accompanied by Francine, who must have been arriving at the Coleman house the same moment as Gerald.

"Irene?" I'm home, and Francine is with me," Gerald called out, loud enough to be heard in the kitchen. A few seconds later Irene came through the kitchen doorway, wiping her hands on her apron.

"Hello, Francine," she said, mustering pleasant tones into her voice. "Can you believe it? Our Jonathan is finally coming home tonight!"

Francine of course took note of her future mother-in-law's reference to "our Jonathan" but was determined not to react.

"I know," she replied sweetly as she shed her overcoat and walked to the hall closet to hang the garment. "After so long, he's finally almost home. Charlene too! I can't wait to hear all of her stories about the movies!"

Francine knew full well how Irene Coleman felt about Charlene as a Hollywood starlet, and couldn't resist throwing in that little dig.

Gerald, well aware of the subdued sparring that had already begun between his wife and Francine, was determined to diffuse the situation. Fortunately, before he could even think of anything to say to change the subject,

Joseph and Thomas came bounding down the stairs. Francine, upon seeing Joseph, burst forward to give him a huge hug.

"Joey! I can't believe it! I'm so glad you're home!" she said with genuine affection, tears coming to her eyes.

Joseph accepted the welcoming hug from his future sister-in-law, and he could feel Francine quivering as she lightly sobbed. Instantly, he began to feel a touch irritated at all of these tear-filled, quaking-voice greetings. His mother last night; Aunt Lois and Lorraine earlier today; and now Francine. Even Tommy had done that the other night, though in that case not until both boys had talked into the wee hours of the morning and were finally on their way upstairs. No doubt Charlene would reprise the greeting when she stepped off of the train just about two hours from now. He of course understood why all of them reacted this way; he had been gone for more than three years, and a good chunk of that time had been in a German Luftstalag…not to mention that for many months they didn't even know if he was alive. But he was home now, in good health and good spirits. Hopefully he wouldn't have to endure too many more of these teary-eyed greetings.

Francine released Joseph and then hugged Thomas. He had been away a far shorter time than Joseph and wasn't returning from war, but he was a returning Marine nonetheless – albeit temporarily, until he shipped out for California – and Francine was glad that the young boy she had watched grow up would not be forced to endure what both of his brothers and so many others whom Francine knew had faced.

"We were out to see Marty today," Joseph said when the greetings were finally concluded, and he proceeded to give Francine an abridged version of their afternoon.

"We went over to Schenley yesterday," he added. "Remember Sadowski?"

"Uh-huh," Francine replied.

"We told him that you and Jonathan were getting married."

For a fleeting moment Joseph thought about blurting out what Mister Sadowski had mentioned – that he remembered Francine and Donnie Yablonski going together when they had been in his class – but he held back. The truth was that for the longest time, Joseph hadn't been particularly fond of Francine Donner because of what had happened during that long-ago Christmas. He and Jonathan had wound up in a fistfight over the whole situation, and a year later during Thanksgiving Joseph had been caught by surprise – and was not very pleased – when Francine unexpectedly strolled into Jack Canter's when Joseph and Jonathan had been sitting at the lunch counter. But since that same chance encounter had led to Joseph meeting Abby Sobol, his dislike for Francine had quickly dissipated as he became enamored with Abby…not to mention Jonathan surprisingly getting back together with Francine and then becoming engaged to her.

Still, the smallest kernel of that long-ago distaste for Francine and what she had done with Donnie – Jonathan's subsequent and current engagement to her notwithstanding – was still present and would probably never die.

As planned, a light supper made its way to the kitchen table precisely at 5:30, and by 6:00 the meal had been consumed; all dishes were washed and dried and put away; and the Coleman kitchen looked as unspoiled as it had appeared earlier that afternoon. Even though Charlene had relayed word of a 7:00 arrival at Penn Station, Irene was determined that they would all be inside the station, in place on the platform, no later than 6:15 in case the train was early. After all, Joseph's train had arrived early; this one coming from out west might show up ahead of schedule as well.

The short drive to Penn Station was uneventful, despite the increasingly treacherous streets. The snow had stopped for a while as predicted – most of the snowfall was supposed to arrive sometime after midnight and pick up throughout Wednesday – but the temperature's fall below the twenty degree mark once again meant that the slush was starting to freeze. Thomas, sitting in the Packard's back seat to the right of Francine – who was perched in the middle between the two brothers – paid attention to how his father navigated the roads, and honestly didn't see much difference than how he himself had driven home from Fox Chapel…the beers earlier in the afternoon notwithstanding. The near-collision at the three-way intersection had been dumb luck, that's all: bad luck that it almost happened, and good luck that nobody got hurt and the other car was able to avoid the Packard. At least that's how Thomas saw it.

Gerald pulled the Packard into a just-vacated parking spot close to the terminal, and all were grateful that they didn't need to park on the farthest reaches away from the station. As they all got out of the car, Joseph realized that he had never come to Penn Station himself to anxiously await someone else's arrival. He had arrived home himself twice now – once with Jonathan back in '42, and then again the other night – but this was the first time he had been on the other side, awaiting a returning serviceman. It was sort of strange; but then again, so very much these days was new and different.

Once inside, all eyes looked towards the schedule board. The *Spirit of St. Louis* was still showing a 7:02 P.M. arrival, meaning that the Colemans had about 45 minutes to pass until the family was once again all together. Irene searched for a bench where they could all sit, but the sole partially open bench they could find only had room enough for herself and three others. Irene took a seat along with Ruthie, Francine and Gerald, while Thomas and Joseph decided they would wander around the station for a couple of minutes then come back with plenty of time to spare to greet their brother and sister.

The brothers were only a minute's walk away from the others when a voice called out:

"Hey, Coleman!"

Both heads instinctively turned, but it was Joseph for whom the shout had been intended. A Marine staff sergeant wearing a winter dress uniform was looking straight at them from about thirty yards away, and then at the turn of their heads he began walking in their direction. It took Joseph a few seconds to put a name with the familiar face.

"Leonard!" Joseph said. Jack Leonard had been a high school football teammate, though Leonard was the same age and grade as Jonathan. When Jack Leonard and Jonathan Coleman had been two of the better players on the Schenley High team their final two years there, Joseph had mostly been a reserve as a freshman and sophomore during those same seasons. He of course knew Jack Leonard from school and the football team and the neighborhood, but the two years' age difference was significant and other than the connection through Jonathan, the two didn't know each other all that well.

Still, Jack Leonard had recognized Joseph. He had enlisted in the Marines two days after Pearl Harbor, and by the middle of 1942 was already on his way out to the Pacific, just in time for the bloody, prolonged Guadalcanal campaign.

As Leonard reached the brothers he held out his hand to Joseph.

"Hey flyboy; you just getting home?"

"No; been home two days now. Jonathan is due in at seven, that's why we're here."

"Yeah?" Jack Leonard exclaimed. "That's fantastic! I'm just getting home myself; train just came in about fifteen minutes ago. Talk about coincidences, huh?"

"Uh-huh," Joseph agreed, then looked over at his brother.

"You remember my brother Tommy, right?"

"Yeah; little Tommy Coleman," Jack Leonard nodded, reaching out to shake hands with Thomas. "Heard you were as good as your brother in football at Schenley. Mort wrote me about you." Both Colemans knew that in this context, "your brother" referred to Jonathan, not Joseph.

Mort Leonard, Jack's younger brother, was a classmate and teammate of Tommy's. Like Tommy, Mort had enlisted shortly after high school graduation though for the younger Leonard the Army had been his choice.

"Heard you joined the Marines," Jack added.

"Yeah," Tommy replied. "Just finished up at Lejeune; headed out to Pendleton after New Year's."

"First Marines?" Jack Leonard asked, referring to the famed First Marine Division.

"Uh-huh," was Tommy's reply.

"Well," he said, releasing Tommy's hand, "I'm Second Marines; getting discharged next week, though."

"That soon?" Joseph asked.

"Got enough points," came the reply.

"Same with Jonathan," was Joseph's reply. "I'm a little bit longer; probably February or March."

As Jack and Joseph discussed their respective discharge dates, Thomas felt his eyes instinctively lower, taking in the rows of battle ribbons on Jack's uniform jacket. The Purple Heart ribbon – with two oak leaf clusters, indicating that Leonard had been wounded three times – jumped out at Thomas. Thomas' thoughts traveled back to yesterday's catching-up conversation with Mister Sadowski. The teacher had relayed that after Guadalcanal in '42, Jack Leonard had also fought on Tarawa in '43 and both Saipan and Tinian a year later. Sadowski had heard that Jack had been wounded at least a couple of times, but didn't know much more than that. But even if one or more of Jack Leonard's wounds had been serious, here he was in the flesh and seemingly okay.

"Mort's headed to Japan for the occupation, I hear," Leonard said to Tommy. "Supposedly it's going to be mostly Army over there – you know, MacArthur's running the show – but I heard that the Marines will be part of the occupation also. So you never know, maybe that's where you're headed also."

Thomas hadn't even considered the possibility of such duty. No mention of heading to Japan had circulated around Camp Lejeune, and his orders for Camp

Pendleton made no mention of any further movement. Still, Tommy realized, you never know. He might wind up in Japan after all, even with the war over.

"Hey look guys; I gotta get going," Jack continued. "I want to surprise my folks. I almost didn't get out of L.A. with all the train delays around the country, so I didn't want to get their hopes up that I was coming home for Christmas and then not make it. I got a buddy who was on the train who's gonna give me a lift home with his folks on their way out to Homestead, and they already headed out to the car while I stopped to use the john. I'll stop by your house; we'll all head out for a beer and catch up."

Jack Leonard hesitated for a moment before continuing.

"I heard about you getting shot down," he said to Joseph, reaching out with his right hand to give Joseph's left shoulder a squeeze. "Glad you're back and okay."

"Yeah, thanks; you too," was Joseph's answer as he reached out to shake Jack Leonard's hand. Thomas did likewise, and Joseph's high school buddy headed towards the station's front door, looking back over his shoulder and adding as he departed:

"Probably a lot of the other guys are already back and we can get a bunch of us together."

"Well, don't be surprised if we run into somebody else we know," Joseph said to Thomas as they both scanned the station after Jack Leonard was gone. Plenty of young men in uniform were all around, as had been the case two nights earlier when Joseph had arrived, but no other familiar faces jumped out at them as they wandered about for a while.

"I wonder whether Ma or Francine will be the first one to greet Jonathan," Thomas said after a while.

His brother chuckled.

"My money is on Francine because she's younger and faster, but that's only if Ma doesn't trip Francine when she takes off running after she spots him."

Thomas joined in the laughter then responded:

"Yeah, I'll say. Those two are gonna be interesting over the next couple days with both of them…"

"Hey, look; it's about a quarter till," Joseph interrupted, noticing the large clock face. "We better get back before Ma gets angry with us."

"Yeah," Thomas agreed as they both turned in the direction where they had left their parents, Ruthie, and Francine a little while earlier. All were still seated on the bench but Irene and Gerald both rose as the boys approached.

"Let's go wait for your brother and your sister on the platform," their father said. Ruthie and Francine got to their feet as well, and Irene led the group down towards the platform where the *Spirit of St. Louis* would soon be arriving.

Nearly twenty more minutes passed, and all of a sudden there it was: the train chugging into the station. The *Spirit of St. Louis* slowed to a stop alongside the platform, only a couple of minutes late. Francine felt her heart quicken; the glorious moment was finally here!

Each of them began scanning the many cars of the train as the passengers began departing. Irene had situated them directly in the middle of the train so like most of the families gathered on the platform this evening, an observer gazing downwards from the heavens would see a cluster of heads turning in one direction, pausing, and then rotating back the other way.

"There he is!" Francine screamed with joy, and before the words had even finished passing over her lips she was off at a gallop towards the front of the train. There was no way that Francine Donner would cede her right to race towards her fiancé and leap into his arms, just like in the movies. Her future mother-in-law would just have to wait her turn; that's how Francine Donner saw it. Meanwhile, Thomas and Joseph quickly exchanged "we called that one" looks, and Thomas actually dropped his eyes downwards a touch to see if indeed his mother had a foot stuck out, intending to trip Francine as he had sardonically mused to his brother. Nothing seemed amiss, fortunately.

Sure enough, the Air Corps pilot Francine had spotted was Jonathan himself, and he only had a couple of seconds to notice someone racing through the crowd towards him before Francine soared into him and threw her arms around him. At first her head was to one side as she fiercely hugged him, but after a couple of seconds she pulled back slightly and planted the biggest kiss she could muster directly onto Jonathan's lips.

Francine was still frantically kissing Jonathan, over and over, when the others arrived where they stood. Gerald could tell that Francine had no intentions on releasing herself from Jonathan as his eyes settled on Charlene, so he stepped forward to give his daughter a gigantic welcome-home hug.

"Hi Pop; I missed you!" Charlene murmured in return as she was enveloped by her father. Jonathan finally pulled himself away from Francine and Irene Coleman immediately filled the gap, weeping as she embraced her

oldest son. Soon everybody was hugging everybody.
Finally, Joseph – having just released his sister – turned
towards Jonathan, who had just finished greeting Ruthie.

The two brothers hugged, and this time it was
Jonathan who began sobbing as he embraced his brother
and proclaimed: "I can't believe you're home…"

❄ ❄ ❄

The Packard was significantly more crowded for the
drive back to Polish Hill than on the way to Penn Station,
but fortunately the short distance made the seating
arrangements bearable. Ruthie now sat on her mother's
lap in the front passenger seat while Charlene settled into
the middle between her father and mother; while in the
back seat Francine snuggled onto Jonathan's lap on the
left, with Thomas in the middle and Joseph on the right
side. Eight people were in the car but it seemed as if twice
that number of conversations were going on
simultaneously, as questions and answers flew
indiscriminately back and forth: the details of how
Jonathan and Charlene had stumbled upon each other in
St. Louis; their respective train rides, separately to St.
Louis and together from there; Hollywood; Hawaii;
Europe; Parris Island; Marty Walker; and seemingly a
hundred other topics. Because of the increasingly icy
roads, Gerald crawled along at no more than fifteen miles
per hour but Francine, burrowed into her fiancé in the
darkened backseat to give Thomas and Joseph enough
room, felt much the same way little Ruthie had two nights
earlier: the agonizingly slow drive could last an eternity
and she would be in heaven the entire time!

Eventually they did arrive back home and the entire group scurried into the house. The last couple of minutes of the drive had seen the snowfall begin once again – a bit heavier with every passing second, it seemed – and everyone was in a hurry to get inside. Irene immediately headed into the kitchen, with both Ruthie and Charlene tailing behind. Francine naturally would have rather nestled herself alongside Jonathan on the sofa, but she knew well enough that at least attempting to endear herself to Irene was paramount for harmony to reign after the wedding; and the best way to win Irene Coleman over was to help in the kitchen. Still, she also knew well enough that to enter the Coleman kitchen without Irene's permission was a fool's errand.

"May I help also, Mrs. Coleman?" Francine asked, sticking her head through the open doorway.

"If you would like," came the indifferent response. Francine shrugged off Irene's apparent apathy towards the offer and dutifully entered and asked what she could help with.

"You can help Charlene put the *sledzie* and the *ogorki kiszone* in bowls," Irene answered, referring to the traditional Polish herring and pickled cucumber dishes. "And then when you are finished you can fill the small glasses with *nalewka* for everyone."

Irene nodded to the cabinet where a bottle of the traditional Polish spiced fruit liqueur rested, then added:

"Rather than wait for dessert, I would like everyone to have a glass so we can all share a toast of thanksgiving that everyone is finally here. Ruthie too; just a touch for her."

Francine smiled at her future mother-in-law, all the while wondering if Irene's usage of "everyone" included her or if she was referring solely to her children. Even if it was the latter, Francine decided she shouldn't take any offense to the sentiment. She tried her best to put herself in the position of Jonathan's mother: after three long years, all five of her children – two of them returned from years of war – were about to once again be together around the supper table. Francine might be an outsider to this little reunion in Irene's mind, but it wasn't necessarily a deliberate slight; rather, Irene was feeling what Francine's own mother, and probably any other mother in Pittsburgh or around the country, would probably feel in the same situation.

Irene began handling platters of food to Charlene and Ruthie to shuttle to the table as they were ready, and as soon as Francine finished filling the glasses with *nalewka* she joined the parade of kitchen helpers. Meanwhile, Charlene began relating stories of U.S.O. Tours, particularly the one to the Philippines earlier this year. To Charlene's way of thinking, by steering the initial conversation about her new life as a movie starlet to settings related to the war, perhaps she could diffuse the inevitable radiation of disapproval that her mother would be unable to mask. Charlene told her mother about the G.I.'s from Cleveland she had met on the train who had seen her perform in the Philippines, and what they had told her. She then launched into an elongated version of how she and Jonathan had stumbled upon each other in St. Louis – a far lengthier account than had been related during the drive home – as well as how "Carla Colburn" had actually been responsible for Jonathan sitting in the living room this very moment. Perhaps if her mother also associated Charlene's little corner of Hollywood stardom with having kept tonight's supper from being short one son, then Irene's distaste for her daughter's movie career could be kept at bay, at least for a little while.

By the time Charlene had gotten to the part where she and Jonathan had boarded the train together, the remainder of the food had been ferried to the table in the small dining room area. As he had for years now, Gerald was keenly aware of the precise moment at which he should rise from wherever he might be sitting and make his way to the table, and his three sons did likewise. For a moment there was a touch of confusion as they all tried to figure out who should sit where. After a bit of shuffling here and there by the Coleman children and Francine, the old seating arrangements from years before were dusted off, with the exception of Francine being seated between Jonathan to her right and Joseph to her left; in years past the two brothers sat next to each other.

Everyone had barely sat down when Gerald rose and reached for his glass of *nalewka*. Francine wasn't sure if she should also rise but everyone else at the table remained seated so she did likewise. She did notice that just as Gerald prepared to speak, Irene reached over to the full glass that was placed in front of where Ruthie had sat and swapped it for the slightly filled one resting in front of Thomas. And, as she made the switch, Irene shot a quick glance in Francine's direction. Oh great, Francine thought to herself; not knowing where anyone was to sit, she had simply placed the slightly filled glass – the final one she had filled – at the only remaining place setting. But it seemed to Francine that Irene couldn't resist using the occasion to highlight the tiniest flaw in her future daughter-in-law's assistance in preparing the table.

"I remember standing in this very spot more than three years ago, on Thanksgiving evening," Gerald began. "That was the last time until this very moment that all five of our children sat together at the same table. I do have new words of thanksgiving to offer, but I will wait until tomorrow when Marty and Stan and Lois, and also Calvin and Lorraine, can all be with us. For now, I will just say 'welcome home' to Jonathan and Charlene – and still to Joseph and Thomas, even though they've been home for two days now – and thank the Lord that our family is all together again. *Na zdrowia!*"

"*Na zdrowia!*" was echoed by those around the table as they drank to each other's health. Gerald sat down as plates of food began making their way around the table. Even as the food was still being passed around, numerous overlapping conversations sprung up again, just as they had during the car ride home. More than an hour passed and it was close to 9:30 before everyone was finished. Even though the meal had been topped off with *kolacz* – the traditional wedding cake that had become a Christmas-time tradition among American Poles – Irene had also prepared a large tray of *makowiec* and would serve the poppy seed pastries along with coffee after everyone had adjourned to the living room. Before then, though, Irene – again assisted by her daughters and Francine – cleared the table and quickly began washing, drying, and storing the dozens of dinner plates and serving platters and pots and pans, not to mention dozens more eating and cooking utensils. The women worked efficiently and were finished within twenty minutes, though, as Gerald and his sons adjourned to the living room.

Jonathan watched his younger brother fiddle repeatedly with the Philco's dial as they all relaxed and smoked, and happened to catch Joseph's eye.

"The Marines might as well make him a radio operator," Joseph said, looking over at Tommy and then back at Jonathan.

"I was thinking the same thing," Jonathan chuckled. Thomas, meanwhile, was so intent on his handiwork that he didn't even hear his brothers discussing his obsession with the radio dial. He settled the tuner on NBC Radio where *Fibber McGee and Molly* was just beginning. Nobody really listened to the radio program, however, as the dinnertime conversations spilled over into the living room gathering. A half-hour passed and when *Fibber* gave way to Bob Hope's *Pepsodent Radio Show*. Tonight was a special program: Bob Hope's Christmas Show broadcast live from San Francisco. Thomas looked over at his sister and asked:

"You met him, right? Bob Hope?"

"Uh-huh," Charlene answered. "Last year when we were touring out in the South Pacific. We were on Tarawa, Saipan, Kwajalein…" Charlene went on to list several more Pacific islands that had become household names during the past several years despite having been unknown to almost every American before the country's entry into the war.

For a moment, Charlene's thoughts took flight to the previous summer and that Pacific tour. Beyond the shows that they had put on for thousands of troops at a time, there had been dozens of trips to field hospitals to visit the wounded Marines, soldiers, and sailors. So many of those boys were so severely wounded that it had taken every ounce of her strength to visit and sit with them, knowing how much pain they were in and having to come to grips with the fact that many of them would never leave the Pacific alive.

Charlene shook those unpleasant thoughts from her head and forced herself back to the present. Irene retreated to the kitchen halfway through Bob Hope's program and returned with a tray overflowing with donuts.

"Hey look; the U.S.O. is here!" Jonathan said, looking at Joseph as he spoke.

"I know," Joseph replied, "that's what I said the other night when Ma came out with donuts and coffee."

Sure enough, Irene made several more quick trips into the kitchen, each time returning with two cups of coffee. Ruthie had been allowed to remain downstairs for this special evening, even though tomorrow was another school day, but she had fallen asleep about halfway through *Fibber McGee and Molly* with her head resting on Charlene's lap. Now, though, she awoke and sleepily ate half of a donut before dozing off again. The family continued relaxing until the Bob Hope program had concluded, and then Jonathan said:

"I'm going to walk Francine back home."

"It's freezing out there," Irene said. "Would you like your father to drive you?"

"No, that's fine," was Jonathan's quick reply. "It's close and I want to stop in and say hi to her folks." Francine lived only about a ten minute walk away from the Coleman's house, which had been especially convenient for her and Jonathan when they began dating back in high school.

Jonathan donned his flying jacket and gloves and perched his officer's cap onto his head. The cap wouldn't provide all that much warmth, but it was better than nothing. Francine meanwhile put on her winter coat and gloves, and proceeded to say goodnight to everyone in turn before she and Jonathan went out into the frigid night air.

As soon as the front door shut behind them, Francine reached over to link her right arm through Jonathan's left one, and leaned into him as they both carefully made their way down the slick, snow-covered front porch stairs and then out onto the equally slippery sidewalk. They walked slowly; silently at first, just enjoying this first private moment together after spending the past several hours in the company of Jonathan's entire family. Finally after nearly two minutes of silence, Francine looked over at Jonathan and proclaimed through chattering teeth:

"I can't wait until tomorrow! We can start planning our life together! There is so much for us to do!"

Jonathan's response, after close to ten seconds of silence, was a surprisingly uneasy:

"I know."

4 – Wednesday, December 19, 1945

Irene Coleman's entire family, except for Ruthie, would soon gather at the breakfast table. The little girl had already been sent off to school while her brothers and sister were still asleep. Slowly, beginning at 8:15 and continuing for another hour, the others awoke and came downstairs one by one for coffee and a cigarette, waiting for everyone else to make their way to the kitchen. Gerald decided to open his shop a little bit later this morning so he could stay home to have breakfast with all of his returning children; he had already been out to the shop to put a sign on the door and then returned home. The temperature wasn't too bad this morning; by 8:30 as Gerald was walking back home the thermometer had already risen to 29 degrees.

He entered his house just as Jonathan was coming down the stairs, dressed in a pair of his old dungarees and a flannel shirt just as his two brothers had been wearing their first morning home.

"Morning, Pop," Jonathan said as he noticed his father walking in through the front door.

"Good morning," Gerald replied. "How did you sleep last night?"

"Pretty good," came the reply, but the truth was actually different. Jonathan had made it back home just after 1:00 in the morning when everyone else had gone up to bed. Francine's parents had been awake when they had reached her house, so he visited with them for about an hour until they went up to their bedroom to give Jonathan and Francine some privacy. Francine waited a respectable fifteen minutes to make sure that neither of her parents was coming back downstairs for anything, and then she looked alluringly at her fiancé and murmured:

"Now it's time to *really* welcome you back home."

Jonathan and Francine proceeded to neck for close to an hour, and several times Jonathan's hands began roving. Each time Francine clamped her hand on top of Jonathan's to wordlessly stop him. It wasn't that she didn't want him to continue; but with their wedding approaching so quickly, she figured that they could wait another week and a half to make their wedding night everything she had dreamed of since she had been a little girl.

Jonathan eventually accepted the blockade Francine imposed on him for what she would and wouldn't allow as they continued kissing on her parents' living room couch. At least while he and Francine were necking he didn't have to talk or think about anything beyond tonight. Still, when he made it home it was a good three hours before the long parade of jumbled thoughts finally faded away and Jonathan fell asleep.

Jonathan followed his father into the kitchen. He sat down next to Joseph, who was already holding out a pack of Chesterfields to his older brother just as his mother placed a cup of steaming hot coffee in front of him. He took the pack, removed a single cigarette, and then passed the pack to his father who did likewise.

No more than a minute had passed before heaping plates of scrambled eggs, sausage, and potatoes made their way to the kitchen table, courtesy of Irene and Charlene. As soon as Gerald and his sons were all served Charlene took a plate of food for herself and sat down, as did Irene a few seconds later. The brothers talked about what they could do today before deciding that Joseph and Thomas would catch the late morning showing of *House of Dracula* that was just opening today down at the Senator. Jonathan had already promised Francine that he would go back to her house so they could put the finishing touches on the plans for their wedding day, so despite his brothers' pleadings ("Come on Jonathan; Frankenstein, Dracula, *and* the Wolfman all together!") Jonathan had to decline going to the movies with them.

Gerald and his sons all headed upstairs to wash up after finishing their meals, while Charlene helped her mother clean the breakfast plates and cooking pots.

"What are you going to do today?" Irene asked her daughter, who replied:

"I'm not sure; I think I'll just stay around the house and relax after such a long train ride. Even as tired as I was last night, it took me a long while to fall asleep."

Irene seemed to hesitate, as if deciding whether or not she really wanted to blurt out what was on her mind, but then she responded with:

"Why don't you go down to the movies with your brothers? Maybe you can sign autographs in the lobby."

Charlene looked sharply at her mother.

"Come on, Ma!" Charlene immediately retorted, struggling to keep the flash of anger she immediately felt from turning her response into a wrath-filled one. "Enough with all of this 'my daughter the snooty movie star' business already!"

"I'm just saying…"

Charlene cut off her mother's response.

"You're just saying that you don't approve of what I've been doing ever since I graduated from high school and went out to Hollywood. Fine; I understand how you feel and I guess I have to accept that. Maybe someday you'll understand better and be proud of me instead of..."

This time it was Irene's turn to interrupt.

"I *am* proud of you!" she replied defensively. "I'm just worried about that kind of life for someone like you who is still so young, with all of those actors and directors and producers."

Irene's eyes narrowed as she peered at Charlene, then added:

"You know exactly what I'm talking about, so don't pretend."

Charlene sighed. This conversation was turning into a repeat of the one she had had with her mother a little more than a year and a half earlier, when Charlene had passed through Pittsburgh on a War Bond Tour shortly before her summer of '44 travels to the Pacific with the U.S.O. That visit had been her first return to Pittsburgh since leaving for Hollywood a year earlier. Charlene's first film was playing at the Strand over in Oakland those very same days, with another queued up for a mid-summer release. After supper, her father "conveniently" had to pay a visit to his cobbler shop and took Ruthie with him, leaving Irene and her eldest daughter alone. Her mother all but directly asked Charlene if she was sleeping her way around Hollywood, and Charlene had erupted at her mother's insinuations. The truth was that while she had dated an RKO actor a couple of times and then went out for a little while with another actor from Paramount, she had still been a "nice girl" – in her mother's terms – and as such had even acquired a reputation among the movie crowd as a bit of a prude.

"Maybe you'd still like to think that I jumped into one bed after another all over the Pacific and then did the same back in Hollywood, just like you insinuated last time I was home," Charlene responded through clenched teeth. "I'm sorry to disappoint you but that's still not the case!"

Charlene laid her drying cloth onto the side of the kitchen sink (even as furious as she was, she knew better than to angrily throw or slam anything – even a cloth! – in her mother's kitchen) and turned to leave. Her mother reached out to take hold of her daughter's right arm, causing Charlene to pause and look back.

"I'm sorry," Irene said. "I didn't mean to imply that…"

"Yes you did, Ma," Charlene interrupted. "I understand why you feel the way you do, but just because you automatically assume that everyone out in Hollywood is doing…you know, doesn't mean that I am. Maybe you've started reading the gossip magazines that talk about other actresses and all the things they do and the men they're with, but that doesn't mean that I'm doing the same thing."

"I'm sorry," Irene Coleman said again before picking up the drying cloth and handing it back to Charlene…a peace offering of sorts. Charlene accepted the cloth and continued helping her mother finish the breakfast dishes.

The truth was, Charlene was forced to admit to herself, that her mother wasn't entirely wrong. Charlene might not be brazenly slipping from one actor's or director's bed to another the way so many other actresses did, but she had finally given in this past New Year's Eve to the advances of that same RKO actor. She hadn't seen him since before her U.S.O. Tour but ran into him at a big New Year's Eve bash. The party had been a slightly subdued one because of the massive German counterattack that was then underway; the one that would become known as the Battle of the Bulge. Still, Hollywood loves a good party and much of the Nazi offensive had already been blunted, and most of those in attendance were confident that 1945 would be the final year of this terrible war despite the setback over in Europe.

The RKO actor had spotted Charlene before she noticed that he was present, and the two of them quickly fell into that type of intimate, alcohol-fueled party conversation that Charlene was all but certain would end up with her in his bed that night; her inexperience notwithstanding. And that was exactly what had happened. They saw each other for only another week – not long enough for the movie magazines or the gossip columnists to catch on – before they each headed their separate ways for different movie projects. Charlene was filming in Burbank, while the RKO actor headed to the Pacific Northwest to film a war picture, with the dense forests up there standing in for those of Central Europe. Detached promises had been made that they would get together again sometime after their respective films had been completed, but the entire year of 1945 had passed with those promises remaining unfulfilled.

Compared to most of the actresses she knew, Charlene might be a prude; but she was well aware that her old-fashioned mother had a black-and-white view of such matters, and to Irene Coleman even that single brief fling almost one year ago now would be enough to categorize her daughter for all time as a "Hollywood Hussy."

❄ ❄ ❄

Attempting to instill a truce of sorts with her mother, Charlene offered to accompany Irene to the market, the butcher shop, and the bakery in preparation for tonight's family feast. They would leave the house shortly after Gerald came home at noon for his midday meal.

Around 11:30 Irene was upstairs making up more beds than she had made up in years and Gerald hadn't yet returned home. Charlene was downstairs in the living room by herself, listening to the radio, when the doorbell rang. She walked over, opened the door, and on the other side stood a Marine staff sergeant who seemed to do a double-take before his mouth fell slightly open.

For his part, Jack Leonard – the Marine standing just outside the Coleman's front doorway – immediately felt as if he had slipped into yet another one of those disorienting yet vividly realistic dreams he had experienced during so many nights on one of those far-away Pacific Islands. He had walked up the stairs and knocked on the door of his high school buddy Jonathan Coleman's house...yet when the door opened, the girl on the other side looked just like that actress Carla Colburn!

At first Charlene was as perplexed as this Marine was. He was acting just like one of the battle-fatigued Marines or soldiers she had seen walking around the hallways of one or another of those island field hospitals.

"Can I help you?" Charlene finally asked. "Are you looking for somebody?"

"Um...yeah," Jack Leonard finally stammered out. "I was looking for Jonathan Coleman...or maybe Joey Coleman..."

"They're not home right now," Charlene replied. "Jonathan is over at Francine's – his fiancé's – house, and Joey and Tommy are at the movies downtown at the Senator."

Charlene's response only served to confuse Jack even more.

"You look like..." he began to blurt out, then halted.

Charlene suddenly understood the Marine's confusion but before she could respond he spoke again.

"Aren't you Carla Colburn? You look just like her!"

Charlene couldn't help the fit of giggles that came over her.

"Well, yes, but I'm Jonathan's and Joey's and Tommy's sister."

Her explanation was of no help whatsoever to poor Jack Leonard.

"I'm Charlene Coleman," she tried again. "Carla Colburn is my stage name."

Suddenly Charlene looked past the Marine's confusion – and his uniform – and realized that his faced looked familiar.

"I'm sorry, but who are you?" she asked.

"Um...Jack Leonard," came the reply.

"I know you!" Charlene blurted out. "You went to school with Jonathan! You played football together, right?"

"Uh, yeah; we did."

"Oh my God, come on in! It's freezing out here! Jonathan will be so glad to see you! He's not home, like I said, but I can give you directions to Francine's house after you warm up."

The still-confused Marine could only follow Charlene into the Coleman house.

"I saw Joey and Tommy at Penn Station last night, and they said Jonathan was coming in a little bit after me; I just got home last night."

"I was on the same train with him," Charlene nodded. "We got in a little bit after 7:00."

"I'm really sorry," Jack said, "but did you say that you *were* Carla Colburn?"

Charlene giggled again, but the giggles gave way to a warm smile.

"I am, but that's not my real name, of course. I'm Charlene Coleman; Jonathan's sister," she repeated.

"Jonathan's sister?" Jack Leonard searched his memory and honestly couldn't recall even knowing that Jonathan had a sister, let alone one who was a Hollywood actress!

"I'm two years behind Joey so I was still in eighth grade when you and Jonathan graduated from Schenley," Charlene replied. "I remember going to Jonathan's football games and you being a very good player, just like Jonathan."

Jack Leonard blushed slightly at the complement.

"I didn't know that you were…I mean that Carla Colburn was…"

Charlene smiled again, slightly amused at how tongue-tied this Marine – this older boy from the neighborhood – was becoming in her presence.

"I went out to Hollywood after I graduated from Schenley; back in '43," Charlene said, then related an abbreviated version of having caught Gene Kelly's eye while performing for the high school show and that happenstance "audition" eventually becoming her gateway to the movies.

"I saw you with the U.S.O. on Saipan," Jack blurted out. "You came to the field hospital with Bob Hope and did a show for all of us guys who had been wounded."

"Really?"

Charlene noticed that the Marine was already blushing again.

"Bob Hope came around to shake hands with me, and I said to him, 'Nice to meet ya, Mister Hope, but can you send some of those good-looking starlets over instead?'"

"You did not!" Charlene challenged, good-naturedly.

"Yeah I did; I swear!" Jack insisted.

"Did I come over to visit you?"

Jack shook his head.

"No, you were already over in another wing," he replied, "but I did meet Frances Langford."

Charlene smiled.

"Well, I'm sorry I didn't come over to see you," she said, her eyes traveling to the rows of battle ribbons much as Tommy's eyes had done the previous night.

"You were wounded more than once?" Charlene asked, taking note of the oak leaf clusters on Jack's Purple Heart ribbon.

"Uh-huh," he said quietly, then quickly changed the subject.

"I'm still trying to remember you from the neighborhood, but I can't. I knew Joey from when he was on the team, and I knew about Tommy from my brother Mort being the same age as him. But I just don't remember ever meeting you…"

"That's alright," Charlene replied. "We met now, didn't we?"

❄ ❄ ❄

"Ma, do you remember Jack Leonard? One of Jonathan's friends?"

Irene Coleman had just come downstairs and halted in place when she saw Charlene sitting on the sofa next to a handsome Marine who looked to be about 22, maybe 23 years old.

"Of course! Jack Leonard! I'm so glad you're home safe!" Irene crossed over to where Jack Leonard had risen from the sofa and she gave him a warm hug.

"Hello, Mrs. Coleman," Jack replied. "Gosh, I haven't seen you in a long time!"

"I know," Irene offered a sad smile. "It's been so long since all of you boys went away to the war. And you went away early, right?"

"Uh-huh," Jack nodded. "Enlisted right after Pearl Harbor…"

"That's right," Irene interrupted. "I remember. I haven't seen your mother for…I don't know, it seems like many months now. How is she?"

"She's fine; my Pa too, thanks for asking," Jack replied. The small talk continued for another couple of minutes until the front door opened.

"Gerald! Look who's here; Jack Leonard!" Irene called out to her husband.

A warm smile came to Gerald Coleman's face as he took four or five steps to where Jack was still standing in front of the sofa.

"Welcome home," Gerald said, offering his right hand and at the same time, giving Jack a friendly squeeze on the Marine's right shoulder with his own left hand.

"Thank you sir," Jack responded, "I'm glad to be home."

"Jack came by looking for Jonathan," Charlene interjected. "He said that he saw Joey and Tommy at Penn Station last night just before Jonathan and I arrived."

"That's right," Jack confirmed, then looked over at Charlene and then back at Irene. "I never knew that Carla Colburn was actually Jonathan's sister, though, until just now."

Charlene's eyes traveled to her mother's face, expecting to see some sort of distaste appear at the mention of her stage name. To her surprise, her mother's face seemed to light up.

"Isn't that something?" Irene Coleman said. "Have you ever seen any of her pictures?"

Jack Leonard shook his head.

"We didn't get many movies over in the Pacific, but I was telling Carla...I mean Charlene, that when I was in the field hospital in Saipan I actually saw her with Bob

Hope and Jerry Colonna and Frances Langford and all of them."

"Jack said that he told Bob Hope to send over" – Charlene paused, and then turned to the Marine – "what was it you said?"

Jack repeated to Charlene's parents what he had told her a few moments earlier, and both Gerald and Irene chuckled.

"I was just going to fix Jonathan's father his lunch before Charlene and I go to the market," Irene said to Jack Leonard. "Would you like to join us?"

Even as Jack was gratefully accepting Mrs. Coleman's invitation, Charlene realized what her mother was up to. But for one of the few times in her life when it came to boys, Charlene had no objection whatsoever to Irene Coleman's meddling.

❄ ❄ ❄

After the noonday meal was finished, Jack Leonard accepted the scrap of notebook paper upon which Charlene had drawn a crude map from the Coleman's house to Francine's. Charlene half-expected Jack to ask her out to dinner or a movie right on the spot, and was surprisingly disappointed when he departed without doing so. Maybe, despite the ease with which the two of them had conversed all the way through lunch, he was intimidated by the whole "Carla Colburn, Hollywood Starlet" aura. Or maybe he felt the need to wait an appropriate duration from the time he first met Charlene until he actually asked her out. Time would tell, Charlene figured.

In the meantime she spent the next two and a half hours with her mother making all the necessary stops for tonight's supper. The weather had turned mild – almost – with the thermometer hovering stubbornly right around the freezing mark all afternoon. Not quite Hollywood weather, Charlene thought to herself; but all in all, not too bad for her first afternoon home given that the calendar had slid past mid-December.

By 3:30 Charlene and her mother had returned home, and Ruthie had likewise returned home with school finished for the day. Irene and her daughters went to work with an eye towards 6:00 as the dinner hour. Over the next two hours the Coleman men trickled back to the house: Thomas and Joseph first, then Gerald, and finally Jonathan, accompanied of course by Francine. Finally, with less than ten minutes to spare before the dinner hour, Stan Walker's royal maroon '42 Buick Super eased in behind Gerald Coleman's battleship gray Packard Six, and the Walker clan disembarked and then headed into the house.

A lengthy round of everybody-welcoming-everybody-else embraces ensued; even the greetings that had been made a day earlier at the Walker home in Fox Chapel were reprised. Nearly two full minutes passed until all of the hugs and teary-eyed "welcome home!" proclamations were concluded. Given the closeness of the appointed dinner hour, tonight Irene Coleman summoned the clan to the dining room table even while Lois Walker and Lorraine – and Francine – joined Irene, Charlene, and Ruthie in the ritual ferrying of serving platters to the table.

When all of the food had been placed on the table, Gerald Coleman rose as he had done the previous night.

"Last night," he began, raising his glass of *nalewka*, "when most of us except for Stan's family were here, I offered my thanks for our boys' homecoming, but I said that I would wait until tonight when everyone was gathered together to say more."

Gerald paused, and spent the next ten seconds gazing around the table at each and every face present. Unlike most lengthy silent pauses, this one was not an uncomfortable one for anyone sitting at the Coleman table this evening. Finally, he continued.

"Everyone here tonight was also here more than three years ago for Thanksgiving, except for Marty" – Gerald looked directly at his nephew – "who was already off at war. I remember saying that the first Thanksgiving of the war was a special day for us because not only were things with the war getting a little bit better, but also that we were all fortunate enough to gather together for one final time before my own boys headed off to the war themselves. I made note that Marty wasn't there, and we all missed him."

Everyone present looked over at Marty, who in response lowered his eyes to the table. His own thoughts time-traveled to that same Thanksgiving when he was aboard the *U.S.S. Augusta* as the heavy cruiser was making its way back to the United States following its role in the North Africa invasion. He was so incredibly homesick then. He knew that his parents and brother and sister would be missing him that Thanksgiving Day; but his Uncle Gerald's words were the first inkling that his absence had been noted beyond Marty's immediate family.

"Tonight," Gerald Coleman continued, "*everyone* is here. Our three boys – Jonathan, Joseph, and Marty – have all come back safely from the war, and we have the

Lord above to thank. Charlene is home as well, and she was just telling us last night about her travels with Bob Hope to all of those Pacific islands to entertain our boys who were fighting over there, and some who had been wounded."

Gerald looked directly across the table at his youngest son.

"And Tommy is here tonight. He is a good, strong Marine and I'm very proud of him, but I can only thank the Lord that the war ended before he had to go fight like his brothers and his cousin did."

Gerald lowered his eyes briefly towards the table and continued speaking even before looking up a few seconds later.

"All across Pittsburgh and all around this country, families are gathered together who aren't as fortunate as ours. A son or nephew went off to war and didn't come back, or maybe did return but was terribly wounded. Even those families who were fortunate enough not to lose anyone might still have someone over in Europe or the Pacific, or maybe stranded out west or down south because of all the bad weather and the railroad delays all over the country. Hopefully those boys will make it home in time for Christmas, but you never know."

Gerald took another short pause before continuing.

"But here we are; all of us, together again. Tonight isn't Thanksgiving or Christmas; it's just another night. But tonight might as well be both of those holidays combined as one."

He raised his glass and everyone at the table quickly did likewise.

"Here's to Jonathan and Joseph and Marty, for helping us win the war. Here's to Thomas, for being ready to do the same thing, even though he fortunately didn't have to. Here's to Charlene for entertaining the boys who won the war. And here's to all of us, for enduring those long years of war and now being able to gather here together tonight to welcome all of them home. *Na zdrowia!*"

"*Na zdrowia!*" came the response from everyone gathered around the table, even Ruthie who – like last night – had been given a glass containing a few sips of the spiced fruit liqueur.

Gerald sat down. He knew that his words had been awkward ones; toasting and formal speaking had never been his strong suits, nor would they ever be. But his words had come from the heart, and he was certain that everyone present at his table tonight knew that. Nobody would ever etch words uttered by Gerald Coleman's into a monument nor recite them in school classrooms for decades to come, but for the purposes of welcoming home four of his children and also his nephew, he was confident that what he had just spoken had been satisfactory.

Conversations began flying, just as had happened the previous night, as the platters of food were passed around the table. Last night it had seemed that a dozen conversations were occurring in parallel; tonight it might well have been two or three dozen! Colemans and Walkers talked to whomever might be to the left or the right, and also conversed with whomever was across the table. Subjects ranged from the war to the day's news to...well, most anything was fair game for discourse tonight.

"Did everyone hear that Marty is going to college?" Stan Walker eventually asked, loudly enough to halt most other conversations in their tracks.

"At Pitt? Starting in January?" Stan added.

"We did," Stan's sister Irene Coleman nodded. "I think that's wonderful news!"

Irene looked pointedly at Jonathan first, and then Joseph.

"Jonathan should do that, and then as soon as Joseph gets his discharge he should do that also."

Irene then swiveled her gaze around the table; that consensus-seeking maneuver.

"Doesn't everyone think so?"

Amidst the chorus of "uh-huh" and "of course" responses, Francine Donner's eyes narrowed as she slowly turned to her right to peer at her fiancé, who in turn looked away from Francine.

❄ ❄ ❄

"Tell me everything!"

Lorraine Walker's excited voice might well have carried downstairs where everyone else was gathered in the living room, no doubt continuing to discuss anything and everything. For her part, Lorraine cared only about one thing: hearing all of the delicious gossip about Hollywood and movie stars, first-hand from her own cousin!

The scene was a familiar one: Lorraine and Charlene quietly sequestered in the Coleman girl's bedroom, sharing secrets about boys and aspirations and most anything else that neither wanted anyone else to know. Only four years had passed but it seemed like an eternity since these same two girls had sat in this very same room, in the very same positions on Charlene's bed, when Charlene blurted out that she had just become secretly engaged to Larry Moncheck. That "engagement" had been short-lived – actually, more of a false alarm – but that particular secret was emblematic of the confidences the girls shared between them.

"There's not really much to tell," Charlene answered lamely, knowing her cousin would never go for that assertion. "Making a movie is hard work; it's not all glamorous like we thought…"

"But what about all the Hollywood parties?" Lorraine interrupted. "You get to go to parties with Clark Gable and Gene Kelly and Jimmy Stewart and…"

"First of all," Charlene interrupted right back, "Clark Gable was off at war, and Jimmy Stewart was also. Gene Kelly is nice enough but he doesn't go to a lot of Hollywood parties. *I* don't even go to a lot of Hollywood parties. Remember that I made two trips to the Pacific with the U.S.O. so I was gone for months at a time…"

The interruptions continued; again it was Lorraine's turn.

"But you got to travel all over the Pacific with Bob Hope and all of those other stars," she protested. "Wasn't that a dream?"

Charlene sighed.

"Sort of," she said, "but we were going to all these islands where either the fighting had just stopped or maybe even was still going on, on the other side from where we were. It's hard to describe, but even though the shows were fun to do it all was really nerve-wracking. You know, being in the middle of a war and all that, with Japanese planes probably not too far away. Every time you got in a plane you wondered if you were going to get shot down or crash; look what happened to Glenn Miller last year, and Leslie Howard a couple of years ago. Plus all of those poor boys in the field hospitals on those islands who had been wounded…"

Mentioning wounded fighting men in the field hospitals triggered a thought in Charlene's head.

"You remember Jack Leonard, right? He played football? Graduated the same year as Jonathan?"

"Uh-huh," Lorraine replied. "He went into the Marines, right?"

"Uh-huh," Charlene replied, and then gave an abbreviated description of Jack Leonard's visit to the Coleman house earlier that afternoon.

"So what do you care about Jack Leonard?" Lorraine finally interrupted as she impatiently listened to her cousin's story. "You were in a movie with Gene Kelly and Frank Sinatra! Think of all the Hollywood stars you've met so far, and all the ones you will meet!"

Charlene sighed again.

"I know, but…"

Lorraine interrupted again.

"Remember when you were home last summer for the War Bond Tour? I mean the summer of '44, not this past summer?"

"Uh-huh," Charlene nodded, realizing where this conversation was going even as her cousin continued speaking.

"You were telling me about…" she mentioned the RKO actor whom Charlene had dated for a little bit in early '44.

Charlene was helpless to prevent the fierce blush that instantly reddened her face.

"Ah-hah!" Lorraine exclaimed at her cousin's physical response. "I knew it!"

Charlene looked away from her cousin. At one point in her life, she would have preemptively and gleefully volunteered to her cousin the most minute details of what had happened this past New Year's Eve, and would have expected Lorraine to do likewise with the tale of any salacious encounter of her own. Now, though…well, doing so when the man involved was sort of a household name seemed not just gossipy, but somewhat unsavory.

Still, it was her cousin Lorraine Walker sitting in Charlene's old bedroom on Charlene's old bed, just like old times. And so, Charlene lowered her voice and after swearing her cousin to secrecy, shared the details of how she had lost her virginity to a man Lorraine had seen on the movie screen only last week.

❄ ❄ ❄

Goodbyes were said in the Coleman living room around 8:45, and the Walker clan trudged out to the Buick for the ride home to Fox Chapel. Irene shuffled Ruthie off to bed; no evening snack or staying up late tonight for the little girl. Jonathan walked Francine home and dawdled a little bit at her house before finally being able to excuse himself to return home. He made it back for the final few minutes of Eddie Cantor's radio program, but just as *Mr. District Attorney* – the crime drama inspired by the anti-racketeering days of New York Governor and presidential candidate Thomas Dewey – began, Jonathan looked over at Joseph and said:

"Whaddya say we go get a drink somewhere?"

At first, Joseph seemed caught off guard at his older brother's suggestion. But after mulling over the idea for a few seconds, he replied:

"Yeah, okay; someplace close, right?" Ten degrees had been shaved off of the thermometer since late afternoon, and Joseph could almost feel the bitter cold again of his frosty walk around the neighborhood two nights earlier.

"Uh-huh; is Leo's still around?" Jonathan suggested, referring to a popular Polish Hill corner bar a couple doors down from their father's cobbler shop.

Joseph shrugged, then looked over at his father who was listening to the brothers' conversation.

"Pop? Is Leo's still there?"

Gerald Coleman nodded.

"It is," came the reply. "You boys sure you want to go out there on a cold night though?"

Jonathan hesitated before replying.

"I want to catch up with Joey just this once; you know, one on one. We haven't had a chance to do that yet with everyone here." He almost added "and me at Francine's all day" but decided expressing that sentiment wasn't the wisest thing to do at the moment.

Gerald nodded.

"Okay but you boys be careful," he said, thinking even as he spoke how foolhardy those words sounded. Be careful walking a couple blocks? Be careful out in twenty degree weather? Be careful in the neighborhood bar? These two boys – these two *men* – had just fought and won a war against the Nazis, flying so many dangerous missions over occupied Europe. Joseph had also survived being shot down and being a prisoner for such a long time until his eventual liberation. The last piece of advice they really needed was their father telling them to be careful now that they were back at home.

Neither Jonathan nor Joseph took offense at what their father had said, though. Joseph went to the coat closet and retrieved his B-3 flying jacket as well as Jonathan's. They each were donning their coats when Thomas asked:

"Can I come with you guys?"

Jonathan hesitated before answering. He hated to say no to his youngest brother's request but he desperately felt the need to talk one-on-one with Joseph.

"They probably won't serve you," Joseph interjected. "You know, being eighteen and all that. This isn't like the bar in Fox Chapel."

Thomas began to object, but even as he started speaking he caught on to the fact that his two brothers wanted time alone; just the two of them. Thomas did his best to tamp down the hurt feelings that were bubbling up. He tried to tell himself that it wasn't so much that they wanted to exclude him, but rather that the two of them – the two war veteran Air Corps flyers; two brothers seeing each other for the first time in years – probably had things that they wanted to discuss just between them.

Still, the rejection stung.

❄ ❄ ❄

"I felt bad telling Tommy he couldn't come along," Joseph said as they both reached the sidewalk in front of their house and began their trek to Leo's.

"I know," Jonathan said, shoving his hands in his jacket pocket to ward off the cold. "Just for now, though. And besides, like you said, he probably wouldn't even get served. But what's this about some bar in Fox Chapel?"

Joseph related the tale of yesterday afternoon's visit to Marty to his brother, which filled the time until they arrived at Leo's. Both Jonathan and Joseph had been in the place a couple of times, but neither had ever ordered a beer or a shot there because both had been under 21 at the time. Mostly they would go there to shoot a couple of games of pool and feel older than they actually had been.

They walked inside and scanned the half dozen or so faces at the bar and over at the pool table. Nobody looked familiar at first glance, which was fine with both of them. Tonight was earmarked for conversation between the two of them, not for finding old friends and catching up. They headed to the bar and grabbed two seats at the far end, away from the three men seated together at the other end. Both brothers were aware of the eyes of everyone in the place following them, courtesy of their Air Corps jackets and officers' caps.

"Aren't you Gerald Coleman's boys?"

The words came from one of the men who had been among the three they had walked by on their way to their barstools. Jonathan looked back across the bar at the man who had spoken. He looked to be about sixty years old at least; maybe even older. As Jonathan peered at him, the man still didn't look familiar.

"Uh-huh," Jonathan said as he removed his officer's cap. "Just got home," he added.

"I heard about you boys," the man replied. "Heard you really gave it to the Krauts over there. One of you was shot down, right? Taken prisoner?"

Joseph sighed.

"Yeah, I was," he replied.

"But you made it back," the man replied. "Good for you."

Joseph's only reply was one of those half-nods, half-shrugs; that wordless acknowledgement that hopefully conveys to someone else that further conversation isn't necessarily welcomed.

"Hey Stosh," the man called out, apparently addressing the bartender. "I'm buying these guys an Iron City."

"You don't have to do that," Jonathan quickly replied.

"Nah, I wanna," came the slurred reply. "Heard you really gave it to the Krauts over there," the man repeated what he had said a few moments earlier.

Joseph was sitting to Jonathan's right, closest to the other side of the bar, and he shifted his body away from that side so hopefully the other men couldn't notice him speaking.

"Geez, almost a replay of yesterday in Fox Chapel," he muttered in lowered tones. Realizing that on the way over here he had neglected to tell Jonathan that the one guy at

Lou's had bought lunch for Marty, Thomas, and himself, he quickly mentioned that fact to Jonathan, who mused:

"Too bad we're both full from Ma's cooking; we could probably get one of these guys to buy us free pierogi or something."

"Yeah, let's come back tomorrow around dinner-time," Joseph answered, only half-jokingly.

The two Iron Cities appeared in front of the brothers. Jonathan picked his up and faced his brother.

"To you making it out of your plane and out of the Luftstalag," he said.

Joseph let out a deep sigh, pausing for a few seconds before he clinked glasses with his brother.

Both brothers sat silently for nearly two minutes.

"My train went through Phoenix," Jonathan finally said. "I actually thought about getting off and heading up to Thunderbird to look around, but I knew both Ma and Francine would kill me if I wound up not making it home. You know, if I had to wait a couple days for the next open train but instead that train got caught by the snow and was stuck. As it was, both Charlene and I almost got stuck in St. Louis."

"Man, that seems like so long ago," Joseph replied, thinking about Thunderbird Field out in Arizona. "It's only three years ago we were there but it seems like...you know..."

Jonathan nodded.

"Yeah, I know what you mean," came the detached response as Jonathan's thoughts did a touch of time-traveling. "We thought the toughest thing we would ever face was learning to fly, remember?"

Joseph let out one of those wistful snorts.

"Yeah. Who could have known what was ahead of us?"

"You especially," Jonathan responded. "You know, getting shot down and being a prisoner and all that."

"Yeah, but you wound up flying more missions than I did because of that," Joseph countered. "So you probably had more close calls up in the air."

Seeing his brother look away, Joseph added.

"Am I right?"

"Yeah," Jonathan replied after a few seconds. He didn't add anything, so his brother didn't press the issue. Just like with himself, Joseph knew that his brother had things that he didn't particularly want to talk about. Maybe for now; maybe for all time.

"Is something up with you and Francine?" Joseph abruptly inquired. "I mean, you seem all...I don't know..."

Another shrug from Jonathan; another healthy swig of Iron City.

"I dunno," was Jonathan's hesitant answer. "I mean I'm really glad to see her and I'm glad she waited for me, and I'm glad we're getting married. But...I mean..."

Joseph wasn't sure if his brother was having difficulty putting his feelings into words, or if he knew exactly what he wanted to say but was just hesitant to do so.

So he just drank and waited.

"She has all these ideas about us buying a house," Jonathan finally blurted out. "Right after New Years, too. We spent the first part of this afternoon talking about the wedding. You know, she was telling me all these plans she and her mother have for the whole thing. That's all fine. Though I think Ma is getting steamed that Francine and her mother are sort of doing this all by themselves without involving Ma."

"That's for sure," Joseph quickly agreed. "Me and Tommy were talking about that, and we were talking to Pa about it."

"Well anyway, that's what girls do," Jonathan shrugged. "You know, get all caught up in all of that wedding stuff. I figure all I have to do is go along with it and she's happy, which means everybody is happy."

"Except for Ma," Joseph grunted.

"Well yeah," Jonathan agreed. "Anyway, then she starts telling me about how we should start looking right after New Year's for a house to buy, and I tried to tell her that right now there's really no way for that to happen. You know, Uncle Sam is gonna give me twenty bucks a week while I'm looking for a job, and you can't buy a house on that. I tell her that but Francine starts talking about the new veterans' house loans that you don't need any money for a down payment, and I'm still trying to tell her that we should at least hold off on all of that until I find a job…"

"Oh yeah," Jonathan interrupted himself. "And then tonight at dinner Ma says that you and I should go to college just like Marty, and when I was walking Francine home she starts giving me an earful about what Ma said. You know, how if I go find a job real soon then we can get a house, but if I listen to Ma and go to school I only get fifty bucks a month like the other G.I.'s going to college…"

"Seventy-five," Joseph interrupted.

"Huh?"

"Seventy-five bucks," Joseph repeated. "Because you'll be married. Single guys like Marty get fifty bucks, but he was telling us that married guys going to college get seventy-five."

"Didn't know that," Jonathan said, shrugging.

"Two more?" Stosh the bartender appeared and Jonathan silently nodded in response.

"Anyway," he continued, "You know what we're doing for a honeymoon; taking the train to Washington to freeze while we sightsee in the middle of winter, because that's all I can afford. Francine wants to go all the way down to Florida where it's warm, but I don't have the money for that."

Jonathan took a healthy pull from his Iron City a few seconds after the bartender plopped down a new round for the brothers.

"I've been home what; a little over 24 hours?" Jonathan continued. "I know I shouldn't feel this way but between Ma and Francine, I'm feeling...I don't even know how to describe it."

"I know what you mean," Joseph replied after a long pause. The two new Iron Cities were plopped down in front of them, and the younger brother gave the bartender time to get out of earshot.

"I've been home for three days now, and every day feels strange. I told you about when Tommy and I went to Schenley, how Sadowski looked at me like I was a ghost?"

Jonathan nodded.

"Then thinking about Tommy Bonnaverte and how he didn't make it back. And knowing Abby is engaged to some other guy. I mean I knew about all of that after Tommy wrote me, but now that I'm back home it really sunk in."

Joseph took a swig of his beer before continuing.

"Also…well, I know this sounds bad but if one more person starts crying when they hug me and telling me how glad they are that I'm home like I just came back from the dead, I think I'm gonna explode."

Too late, Joseph realized that his older brother had done just that at Penn Station the previous night.

"Sorry, I didn't mean…"

"Nah, forget about it," Jonathan waved off his brother's start of an apology. "I get how you feel. Just remember for a long while we all thought you really might *be* dead, and besides nobody's seen you anyway since '42. Hell, *I* haven't seen you since early '43 when we both headed over to England. So just bear with it, ya know?"

"Yeah, I know," Joseph replied, his eyes downcast.

"You know what I think it is?" Jonathan said.

"Huh?"

"Why we both feel…I dunno, whatever you want to call it? Strange? Out of place?"

Joseph responded with a no-I-don't-know shrug.

"I must have dreamed a couple hundred times since we left that I was finally home," Jonathan mused. "Actual dreams. The war was over, or at least I was done fighting. I was back home, and everything was…I dunno, just sort of peaceful, you know? I honestly don't remember too many details from all of these dreams, I only remember that…peaceful feeling, or whatever it was."

Jonathan sighed, started to take a swig of his beer but halted.

"Well, I know it's only one day," he continued, "but all of a sudden there's all this pressure from Francine about a house and getting a job soon, and then Ma brings up me going to college right away; you know, just a couple weeks from now. I mean, I'm glad to be home and all that, but at least for right now everything doesn't feel all that peaceful like it did in those dreams."

Jonathan paused for a second or two before continuing.

"It doesn't feel like I'm really home yet, you know?"

Part II:
As We Face Our Destiny

"It is well in this solemn hour that we bow to Washington, Jefferson, Jackson, and Lincoln as we face our destiny with its hopes and fears; its burdens and its responsibilities. Out of the past we shall gather wisdom and inspiration to chart our future course."

President Harry S. Truman's Christmas Address, December 24, 1945

5 – Monday, December 24, 1945

Gerald Coleman was a cigarette man. For years he had mostly smoked Pall Malls and Old Golds, though when the war came he found himself smoking Chesterfields more and more.

On occasion, though, Gerald would spurn his cigarettes, whatever the brand, for a Kaufman Brothers Army & Navy brand pipe. Ruthie and Thomas had gotten together to buy that pipe for their father's Christmas of '43 present. During the past two years, Gerald had found that the pipe was preferable to his usual cigarettes on occasions when deep thought was required.

Occasions such as this Christmas Eve morning.

There was no doubt about it: storm clouds were stirring at the Coleman home, despite tomorrow's Christmas holiday and this coming Saturday's wedding. Or maybe the storm clouds were actually because of those occasions, at least in part.

Jonathan had been home for five days now. He frequently was over at Francine's house and inevitably when he would return home, he would be especially quiet and moody. Gerald wasn't sure exactly what the problem was, but most likely it had something to do with everything moving so fast for his oldest son, so soon after his return from the war.

Gerald wasn't particularly fond of his brother-in-law Stan Walker, but he could admit that Stan's advice to Marty upon the sailor's return – "just take it easy for a couple months; take things slow, and get used to everything again" – was exactly what Marty needed to readjust to peacetime life in Pittsburgh.

Jonathan, unfortunately, wasn't afforded that luxury with his wedding approaching so quickly. It wasn't the wedding so much, either, but more a matter of suddenly needing to support a wife; a matter of being mercilessly plopped into yet another entirely different life after his years in the Army Air Forces. Where would Jonathan and Francine live? Could Jonathan find a job as quickly as he needed to...and if so, doing what? But then, what about Irene's now-daily suggestions that Jonathan take advantage of that government G.I. money and go to college? Gerald had a pretty good idea that Francine wasn't particularly enamored with that idea, which of course meant that Jonathan was caught in the middle between his mother and his future wife.

Gerald inhaled deeply, his thoughts switching to Joseph. Two mornings in a row Gerald had walked by Joseph's room and heard muffled shouting. No doubt the boy was suffering nightmares, and Gerald had a hunch these weren't ordinary and occasional nightmares but regular and deeply disturbing ones drawn from Joseph's wartime ordeal.

Even Ruthie was starting to act up. She began crying Friday morning that she didn't want to go to school, and offered a repeat performance yesterday morning before Irene shuffled the family off to Sunday Mass at Saint Michael's. Gerald was certain that her sudden rebellious nature was because of all the attention being offered to her returning sister and brothers. Hopefully with the arrival of Christmas tomorrow – and of course Christmas presents – her disposition would improve.

Most worrisome of all to Gerald, however, was how his wife had been acting for the past four or five days, ever since Jonathan and Charlene had joined Joseph and Thomas at home. Well, maybe not how she was "acting"; there was nothing particularly blatant in what Irene Coleman had done or even said on any given day since the middle of last week. But Gerald had been married to this woman for nearly 25 years, and by now he knew her thoughts almost as well as his own.

Irene Coleman wished to turn back the calendar to before the war and then move forward from that point. An impossibility, of course; but Irene seemed to want the laws of time and nature revoked. Her five children were all together under her roof once again, but she desperately wanted more. So what if two of her sons had been away fighting a war, suffering through hardships and tragedies that neither Gerald nor Irene could imagine? So what if her older daughter had not only grown past the precocious, starry-eyed teenager she had once been, but also on most days could be seen acting on a movie screen in at least one theater somewhere in Pittsburgh? Or that Irene might walk into the Sun Drugs or past a newsstand and possibly see Charlene's photograph actually on the cover of a movie fan magazine? Gerald could almost envision Irene's own thoughts of Jonathan and Joseph once again having little more to do than tossing around a football out in the street; of her exasperations to come because of yet another new and suspect boyfriend who suddenly was Charlene's latest love of her life.

Gerald was thankful that his two older boys had come back from the war safe and – mostly – sound. He was thankful that his daughter was able to take time away from her busy Hollywood schedule to travel across the country to be with her family for this all-important first Christmas following years of war. He was also thankful that his youngest son, despite surviving the rigors of Marine Corps training, wasn't training on some Pacific island right now for the brutal invasion of Japan that would no doubt have cost hundreds of thousands more American lives. Tomorrow might be Christmas, not Thanksgiving, but for Gerald Coleman the two holidays might as well be rolled into one, similar to what he had expressed in his toast last week at dinner.

Gerald inhaled deeply again, sighed, and thought to himself that hopefully before too long, his wife would come around to his way of thinking rather than yearning for days of old that were gone forever, despite her desire to repeal the immutable march of time.

❄ ❄ ❄

Irene Coleman hurried to the front door. Whoever was on the other side was certainly impatient; whereas front door etiquette called for a few rapid knocks followed by a suitable pause to give someone inside time to answer the door, this person was all but pounding nonstop on the Coleman's front door. Irene had still been cleaning the breakfast dishes and pans, and whatever this interruption might be was only serving to disrupt her household rhythm.

Irene's heart nearly halted when she saw the Western Union man on the other side of the screen door. If she could have given herself a few seconds to gather her thoughts Irene would have realized that at the end of 1945, with the war over and – more importantly – all five of her children safely under her roof, the chances of this telegram bearing terrible news were very small indeed.

Still, four years of war with nearly everyone in America eventually being conditioned that telegrams could only bring tragic news…well, that automatic, panicky reaction would take time to get past. Besides, the sight of a Western Union man on her front porch bearing flimsy yellow paper instantly took Irene back in time two years when a similar delivery had coldheartedly informed her that Joseph was missing in action.

For his part, the Western Union man was invariably irritated at reactions such as those exhibited by Irene Coleman. The woman's hand flew to her mouth and her eyes opened as wide as they possibly could as soon as she saw who was at her door. Didn't these people realize the war was over? True, there was still the occasional telegram bearing word that a serviceman had died over in Europe or Japan. But still…

"I have a telegram for Captain Joseph Coleman," the Western Union man said, ignoring the shocked reaction of this woman…probably this Captain Coleman's mother, he figured.

Geez, he thought to himself; the woman is still standing there like a statue with her hand over her mouth.

"Telegram for Captain Coleman?" the Western Union man repeated. Today being Christmas Eve and all, the Western Union man wanted to finish his rounds and get home. People like this lady were sure slowing him down, he grumbled to himself.

Finally, the rational portion of Irene's mind fought through the terror and panic. She turned back towards the doorway to the kitchen, where Joseph was sitting at the breakfast table with Charlene and Thomas (Jonathan was, of course, again over at Francine's house), and in a raised voice called out anxiously:

"Joseph? You have a Western Union telegram!"

A few seconds later Joseph appeared in the kitchen doorway and continued over to the front door, a puzzled look on his face.

"You Captain Coleman?" the Western Union man asked.

"Uh-huh," was Joseph's response.

"Well here you go, Captain," the man said as he handed the paper to Joseph.

For his part, Joseph immediately felt much the same reaction that his mother had…which was strange because he had been far away from the American Home Front during most of the war years. And before he and Jonathan had left for Air Corps training in mid-'42, American fighting men hadn't been nearly as engaged in combat as they would soon be; thus the specter of Western Union men regularly delivering teletyped messages of death hadn't yet taken hold of the American psyche.

However, just as with his mother, within a few seconds rational thought won out over instinctive emotional reaction and Joseph accepted the telegram from the delivery man.

"Thanks," he said.

"Yeah, no problem," was the indifferent reply as the Western Union man continued his rounds amidst the icy ten degree temperature that had settled over Pittsburgh at nine o'clock on Christmas Eve morning.

"What is it?" Irene Coleman anxiously asked her son as she shut the door.

"Don't know, Ma," was the detached reply as he was opening the telegram.

A few seconds later:

"Well, I'll be a son of a…" Joseph's voice trailed off.

"What? What is it?" Irene frantically demanded.

"I got my discharge," Joseph said, looking up at his mother. "They moved my date up to the thirty-first. Gave me extra points, and moved me up a couple months."

He paused for a minute, then continued.

"The thirty-first," he repeated. "Of December. Next Monday. Same day as Jonathan."

His right hand that held the telegram dropped to his side, still clutching the yellow paper.

"I got my discharge," he said once again as a curiously melancholy smile came to his face.

❄ ❄ ❄

Four and a half hours later, about an hour after lunch had been served and then quickly cleaned up, a peculiar scene occurred at the Coleman home. Another round of persistent knocking on the front door occurred, and when Joseph Coleman opened the door, a Western Union man stood on the other side. This was a different Western Union man than the one who had appeared earlier that morning, but Joseph of course felt a sense of déjà vu.

"I got a telegram," was what this Western Union man said. "For Coleman."

"I'll take it," Joseph said. Even as the Western Union man was handing over the envelope, Joseph was certain that the War Department had mistakenly issued a duplicate telegram informing him of his sudden upcoming discharge from the Air Corps. His certainty was unshaken when, upon opening the telegram, his eyes immediately settled on the word "discharge" in the middle of the message.

Joseph almost closed the telegram without reading it further – after all, he had already read its earlier incarnation, had he not? – but when his eyes detected a different date of "27 DECEMBER 1945" he stopped and began reading from the beginning.

He couldn't believe what he was reading, and scanned the telegram a second and then a third time.

He took a deep breath and walked slowly into the kitchen. By now Irene Coleman was out shopping at the market and Joseph had been sitting around the table, smoking cigarettes and talking with Charlene and Thomas long after they had finished their lunch.

"Who was it?" Charlene asked.

"Western Union again," Joseph said after hesitating for a second or two.

"Again?" Charlene asked.

"Uh-huh," Joseph replied, then looked over at his brother.

"Hey Tommy?"

Thomas looked up at his older brother.

"Yeah?"

"You're getting discharged, too."

❄ ❄ ❄

"Apparently the Marines are discharging a whole bunch of guys now that the war is over," Joseph Coleman was explaining to his father. Joseph had walked down to his father's shop, arriving just after 2:00. With today being Christmas Eve Gerald had brought a sandwich with him and worked straight through lunch, taking a bite of the sandwich here and there as he stitched and cut, so he could get home a little bit early.

"They gave Tommy a discharge date of the 27th – this Thursday. Just like that."

"Are you sure?" Gerald Coleman asked. "Wouldn't they let Marines who had been in the war get out first?"

Joseph shrugged.

"I dunno," he said. "Maybe they already did let all the combat Marines out who aren't on their way to the occupation, and now they're going through the new guys like Tommy. All I know is what I read. The telegram told him to report Thursday morning to the Marine station down on Forbes Street in Oakland for a physical and then get processed out."

"Is he happy about it?" Gerald inquired, fairly certain of the answer to his question but still asking it anyway.

Joseph shook his head.

"I don't think so," was the answer. "Probably because Jonathan and me went away, and he wants to do the same thing we did; something like that."

"I suppose so," was his father's reply. "I think I'll go home now to talk to him."

"Yeah," Joseph nodded, "good idea. It's probably a big shock right now but after it all sinks in, he'll be fine. He gets to stay home and doesn't have to go all the way out to California after New Year's. And then who knows where the Marines would have sent him."

"I'll finish this fast," Gerald said, meaning his the other half of his lunchtime sandwich, still uneaten. Gerald wanted to get home as quickly as possible but his Great Depression instincts were still intact: no way would he waste precious food. While his father quickly ate Joseph lit a Chesterfield and looked around the shop.

"You got our Christmas presents hidden around here like you used to?" Joseph asked.

Gerald lightly laughed even with his mouth full. After he had swallowed, he answered:

"I don't know what you're talking about. Santa Claus brings the presents, I've got nothing to do with it."

"Yeah, right," Joseph laughed, then said:

"You remember when Ruthie used to call it 'Crispmas'?"

"I do," Gerald nodded. "You used to say something like that when you were little too; all of you kids did."

"Yeah, you and Ma had said that," Joseph replied. "I just remember Ruthie doing it since she's the youngest."

"Well," Gerald responded, almost finished with his sandwich, "that next Christmas after you boys left was when she stopped saying it that way. I don't think it had anything to do with you not being there, but she just did."

"Yeah, I guess we're all going to get older; even Ruthie," Joseph said thoughtfully. "I hope Ma is okay with that...you know, things changing so much?"

Gerald – half-surprised at his son's prescience – could only shrug in response and say:

Alan Simon

"I hope so also."

Once Gerald finished the remainder of his sandwich, father and son headed back home from the shop. While Gerald certainly could have continued working through the remaining couple of hours of this Christmas Eve afternoon, none of his queued-up work was so time-sensitive that it had to be finished today. He wanted to make sure that Thomas was okay, and figured that afterwards he would just call it a day and relax at home until it was time for Christmas Eve supper and the family's traditional Christmas Eve gathering, rather than return to his shop.

The first thing both Gerald and Joseph noticed as they turned the corner shortly before 2:30 and had line of sight for the Coleman home was that the parking space in front of the house was empty: sans Packard.

"Where's the car?" Joseph asked, half-knowing the answer even as he asked his father that question.

No response.

Joseph looked up at his father who was also peering at the empty parking space. Gerald then looked over at his son, as they both quickened their pace.

❄ ❄ ❄

"I'm gonna make a call," Joseph said.

Joseph was on the phone when Jonathan walked in the front door, seemingly lost in thought. A pained look was splattered across his face, but the moment he gazed at his father's own worried face he asked:

"Is something wrong, Pop?"

"Tommy's not here and it looks like he took the car somewhere," was the answer. Gerald gave Jonathan an abbreviated version of the two discharge-bearing telegrams that had arrived at the Coleman house earlier this day. Gerald had just finished his condensed narrative when Joseph hung up the phone and turned to his father and his brother.

"Marty is gonna check that bar in Fox Chapel," he said. "I'm pretty sure that's where he went."

"Yeah, you're probably right," the light bulb going off in Jonathan's head as well. "If that bartender let him drink there like you said then that's exactly where he went, and why he needed to take the car."

"We gotta go get him," Jonathan added.

"Yeah, if he's there," was Joseph's reply. "Marty's gonna call us if Tommy is there. He said he'll wait with him. You know, keep an eye on him; not let him drive."

A thought occurred to Joseph all of a sudden.

"But how we gonna get there? Tommy has the car."

"Oh yeah," Jonathan said, then looked over at their father.

"Pop, you know anybody else who's got a car who can drive us to get him?"

Gerald was starting to think of a solution when someone knocked on the front door.

"Geez, it's like Penn Station here today," Joseph muttered. "Better not be another telegram or anything."

Joseph was just about to open the door when he paused and looked back at his older brother.

"You haven't gotten one today. Maybe it's for you, telling you that you *aren't* getting discharged, you know?"

Jonathan's eyes widened.

"Don't even joke about that," Jonathan tersely responded. He honestly didn't think that was a possibility but just the thought of such a telegram only seconds away from being delivered…

No Western Union man this time; on the other side of the now-opened front door stood Jack Leonard. Ever since Friday night, when Charlene had met Jack for pie and coffee after the entire Coleman clan had finished their first family downtown Christmas shopping sojourn in four years, the two of them – Charlene and Jack – had spent plenty of time together. They had gone to the movies on Saturday night and then again yesterday afternoon. (At Jack's insistence, Charlene shared a few juicy gossip tidbits about the stars of each of the pictures they saw.) Earlier on Sunday, they sat next to each other at Saint Michael's. Then, last night, Jack returned after supper to take Charlene to the Crawford Grill jazz club and hadn't returned her to the Coleman house until well after midnight.

"Hi Jack," Joseph said. "Come on in. We got some excitement going on here."

"Yeah? What?"

Joseph gave Jack Leonard roughly the same abbreviated version of the day's events that Gerald had related to Jonathan a few moments earlier. Meanwhile, Charlene came bounding down the stairs, eager to give Jack Leonard a big kiss hello. Upon seeing her father home early, though, she halted and instead just smiled warmly at Jack.

"We're trying to figure out how to get out to Fox Chapel if that's where Tommy is," Jonathan said to his high school buddy.

"I could drive you if you want," was Jack's reply. "Charlene and I were only going to go over to Jack Canter's for pie and coffee."

Even though Jack had just returned to Pittsburgh a few days ago, he was one of the few Schenley guys in Jonathan's class to obtain a driver's license while still in high school. Plus during the war he logged many miles in Marine Corps Jeeps; so of everybody present in the living room this afternoon – even including Gerald Coleman – he was the most experienced (or, more accurately, the "least inexperienced") driver.

Seeing the hurt look suddenly come to Charlene's face, Jack quickly said:

"I didn't mean it like it sounded. I just meant that if Tommy is all the way out in Fox Chapel and the guys need me to drive them...I mean, you understand, right?"

Charlene sighed.

"I guess so," she said.

"I'll be back soon," Jack said, trying to soothe Charlene's hurt feelings. "I'm sorry, but it's your brother..."

"That's okay," Charlene interrupted. She wasn't upset – not really – but she liked the feeling of having Jack Leonard, the combat-hardened Marine with his three Purple Hearts, all but wrapped around her little finger after dating for only a couple of days. Even better, it had nothing to do with her being Carla Colburn, Movie Star, either!

The phone rang and Joseph hurried over to answer it.

"Hello?" Pause. "Yeah?" Pause. "He is?" Pause. "Okay, can you stay there with him?" Pause. "Yeah, we'll be there as soon as we can." Pause. "No, you remember Jack Leonard?" Pause. "Yeah. He said he'll drive us."

"He's there," Joseph confirmed to everyone else as he hung up the phone. "Marty said he's sitting at the bar like we did last week and gulping down Fort Pitts."

"He's not going to get in the car and drive, is he?" Charlene asked, worried.

"Marty said he would stay with him," Joseph answered. "I don't think Tommy will try to go anywhere but if he does, Marty'll stop him. He said he would get help from the other guys at the bar to tackle Tommy if he has to."

"Just hurry," Charlene urged.

"We will," Joseph answered his sister. He had never taken off his flying jacket after walking into the house, and both Jonathan and Jack were still wearing their own military jackets.

"You boys all be careful," Gerald Coleman said. "You too," he added, looking straight at Jack Leonard.

"I will, sir," was the Marine's reply. "We'll be back before too long."

"Tommy's mother will be home soon," Gerald said. "I'll tell her you boys went to get Tommy. No sense in trying to hide it from her, she'll figure it out sooner or later."

"That's Ma," Charlene said, raising her eyebrows. "If there's a secret to be found, she's the one to find it."

"Just be careful," Gerald said again as the three servicemen headed out the front door towards the Hudson Super Six Jack Leonard had borrowed from his father.

❄ ❄ ❄

The drive to Fox Chapel was mostly a quiet one, with a few topics of conversation here and there. As soon as Jack pulled away from the Coleman house, Jonathan turned around to look at Joseph, sitting on the left side of the back seat, and said:

"So you're getting discharged early, huh?"

"Yeah, can you believe it? Same day as you; next Monday. We can go down there together."

"That's great that you don't have to go anywhere now just for a couple months," Jonathan said. "You got all your gear with you?"

"Yeah," Joseph replied, "but even if I didn't who cares, you know?"

Joseph looked out the passenger window for a few seconds and then turned back towards his brother.

"When I first got that telegram I was in shock, you know? I mean, I wasn't quite sure how to take it. But the more I thought about it, the happier I was. I just want to get back to normal; like before the war."

"You and me both," was Jonathan's reply, which was followed by Jack Leonard interjecting:

"Same with me, that's for sure. I figure we all did our duty; time to move on."

Another topic of conversation during the drive was General Patton's funeral earlier today, over in Luxembourg. Despite the reports last week that Patton's condition had improved dramatically following his terrible automobile accident, his health had soon taken a terrible turn for the worse and the fierce warrior died this past Friday. All across the country and the world, Americans were in shock. Vaunted generals who gained fame by magnificently winning wars eventually die; everyone knew that. Washington, Scott, Grant, Sherman…none of them had been immortal, of course, but each one had lived for a number of years following his wartime leadership. For that matter, General Pershing was still alive, nearly thirty years after the Great War had concluded. Thus for "Old Blood and Guts" Patton to be suddenly gone before this victorious year of 1945 had even concluded was a severe shock to one and all.

It turned out that the directions Joseph gave Jack Leonard for how to get to Lou's were somewhat off base. He hadn't really been paying attention when Marty had driven them there and back, so he was uncertain which turns to make once they got to the other side of the river. Finally, after about fifteen minutes of one wrong turn after another and with all those in the car unanimous in agreement that while Captain Joseph Coleman might have been aces as a B-24 pilot he wasn't much of a navigator on the ground, they pulled into a service station and got directions from one of the attendants.

Shortly after 3:15 they spotted the tired-look bar and pulled into the mostly empty parking lot. No doubt a few of the hardened regulars were drinking away this Christmas Eve afternoon, but many others were already home with their families preparing for the evening's celebrations.

The brothers and Jack Leonard walked inside and Joseph's eyes immediately went to the far side of the bar, where he and Tommy had sat with Marty last week. Sure enough, there they were: Tommy with Marty to his right, sitting there drinking but not talking…at least at the moment.

Marty's head swiveled towards the newcomers as they walked over towards that side of the bar, and Tommy's did likewise a couple of seconds later. Tommy took in the sight of his brothers and…was that Jack Leonard with them? But he wordlessly turned back towards his Fort Pitt and finished off the remainder in that glass.

Jonathan took a seat to the left of Thomas, and Jack Leonard continued on to plop down to Jonathan's left. Meanwhile Joseph settled in to Marty's right. The owner – Lou – came over and Marty waved for a round of Fort Pitts for everyone.

"We were all worried about you," Jonathan began, "taking the car without asking Pop."

"And you don't even have a driver's license," Jonathan added.

"Well I drove just fine last week before you got home, license or not," Tommy retorted.

"Yeah, but you almost got us killed on the way home," Joseph interjected.

Jonathan's eyes widened.

"What's this?" Jonathan asked.

"Yeah, what?" Marty chimed in.

Thomas glared at Joseph.

"Thanks a lot, Joey," he snarled. "I thought you weren't gonna say nothin' about that."

"I'm serious," Jonathan demanded. "What's this about almost getting killed?"

"Ah, it wasn't that bad," Joseph tried to smooth over his own breach of brotherly trust. "Some guy at Penn and Butler came flying at us from the left side and we went into a skid, but Tommy handled it like a champ. Not a scratch on Pop's car."

"Uh-huh," Jonathan said slowly, certain that he hadn't heard the whole story but willing to let the matter lie for now. After all, the rescue cavalry hadn't made its way to Fox Chapel to lecture Thomas about driving safety.

"So what's eating you?" Jonathan tried again.

"Nothing," Thomas muttered, his gaze following Lou carrying a tight cluster of five beer glasses. The conversation halted while the Fort Pitts were dispersed.

"Come on," Jonathan pressed when Lou was out of earshot.

"Look," Thomas swiveled his head to his left, his eyes narrowing. "I said I don't want to talk about it, okay?"

For the next minute the five of them sat silently, sipping their beers. Then, all of a sudden, Thomas blurted out:

"What am I supposed to do now, huh?"

Sensing an opening, Jonathan asked:

"What do you mean, what are you supposed to do? You mean after getting your discharge notice? Hell, now you can do anything you want!"

Thomas Coleman's voice quivered and he seemed on the verge of tears as he responded.

"I was all set to go out to Camp Pendleton and then maybe overseas, and be a real Marine, ya know?"

Jack Leonard leaned almost totally across where Jonathan sat as he joined the conversation.

"You *are* a real Marine. Once a Marine, always a Marine. Semper Fi, right?"

"Not like you guys." His response was specifically directed at Jack Leonard but he was again staring somberly at the beer glass in front of him.

Jack snorted, leaned back to take a swig of his beer, and then leaned forward again. His eyes were hard and his words edgy as he replied to what Tommy had just said.

"Let me tell you, Tommy, you're one lucky son of a bitch, you know that? Nah, I guess you don't, huh? You did your duty. You enlisted as soon as you could right after finishing high school. You made it through Parris Island and Lejeune like any other Marine. You were ready to go off to fight, but you didn't have to because the war was over by then. So now you're able to stay here in Pittsburgh and you got everything ahead of you, just like your brother said; you can do anything you wanna do. You're as much of a Marine as any of us, whether or not you were on any of those islands."

Almost as if he had only half-heard what Jack had said, Thomas retorted with:

"But the war ended before I had a chance to..."

"Are you kidding me?" Jack interrupted. "Like I said, you're one lucky son of a bitch. You didn't have to go through the hell that we did."

Now Jack's voice was the one that quivered when he spoke, as he repeated:

"One lucky son of a bitch, I'll tell you…"

His voice trailed off.

Thomas looked over at Jonathan, then at Joseph, and then back at Jonathan.

"What about that night last week? Wednesday after dinner? You and Joey went to Leo's by yourself and you didn't let me come with you. I know you guys said it was because I was underage and couldn't get served, but you really didn't want me along, right?"

Jonathan sighed.

"Yeah, I know," he said. "We both felt real bad about it. But it wasn't so much that we didn't want you along, it's just…"

He struggled for the right words.

"I dunno, Joey and I had been through so much together back at Thunderbird and we both were flying out of different parts of England until he got shot down…we had things that we had to talk about, just him and me and just that one time, because we had been through them together, you know?"

"See? That's just it!" Thomas challenged. "I know the war was tough and all that, but you guys shared all of those things and people will always look up to you. I got cheated out of…well maybe not cheated, I don't even know how to say it. But I didn't do the same things and fight the same as you guys did, and you guys will always be able to talk about what you went through, right?"

"Yeah?" Jack Leonard interjected again, half-sighing and looking down at the bar as he spoke. "Here's what we went through that you're missing out on. Four times I watched a guy right next to me take a bullet in the throat.

Twice on Tarawa, once on Saipan right before I got hit myself, and again on Tinian. Every single time, the guy grabbed his throat and the blood was spurting out between his fingers, and you know the guy ain't gonna make it. I swear I just want to forget seeing that, but I never will."

Jack's penetrating gaze was now aimed directly at Tommy.

"I guarantee you that if I ever go to some reunion with the guys who were on those islands, or if maybe I wind up getting together with some of my buddies from my unit one day just like we're all sitting here now, nobody is going to come right out and say 'Hey, remember when Mickey Gabrowski took a bullet right in the throat on Tarawa?'"

Jack shook his head, rapidly, as if trying to shake away those unwelcome images that no doubt were starring in the theater of his mind at that very moment.

"It's the same with us," Jonathan jumped in. "Joey and me, and every other guy who flew during the war. The other night when we were at Leo's? I'll tell you there's things that I didn't even want to talk about with Joey, and there's things that he doesn't want to talk about with me. Not just him being a prisoner, but from also from his missions before he was shot down. And we went through training together and did pretty much everything the same even though we were flying in different units, until he was shot down. I'll probably go to some Eighth Air Force reunion someday, just like Jack was talking about, and I can guarantee you that even though I'll be glad to see those guys nobody's gonna bring up the time that…"

Jonathan's voice quivered and then trailed off, his mind replaying one particularly horrific image of that B-17 off his left wing suddenly sliced into three sections, each one spiraling downwards…and the parachutes that never appeared…

Tommy looked to his right at his cousin, and now it was Marty Walker's turn.

"Same here," Marty said. "When we were coming into Omaha Beach on the first wave…"

He could get no further. His voice didn't just quiver like his cousin's and Jack Leonard's had when each had spoken up. Marty began sobbing, loudly enough for those at the other end of the bar to quickly look in his direction. Knowing that Marty had been in the war, and most likely the other guys with him had also been, the other patrons at Lou's glanced away to give these boys some privacy…or as much privacy as a group of just-returned war veterans might have in a bar on Christmas Eve afternoon.

Joseph draped his left arm over his cousin's shoulder; that "it'll be all right" gesture.

Wanting to draw attention away from Marty, Jack Leonard looked over at Thomas.

"Look, I get how you feel," Jack said sympathetically. "Probably for the next forty or fifty years us guys who were in the war will always have that bond or whatever you want to call it among us. But I swear on a stack of Bibles that if I could be like you and be sitting here right this very minute with my discharge but never have had to go through all of that, I'd do it in a heartbeat."

Silence took hold of the group once again as each of them nursed his beer…and thought. Finally after a couple of minutes had passed, Thomas blurted out much the same thing he had said soon after the others had arrived:

"So what am I supposed to do now?"

"If I was you, Tommy," Marty quickly answered, "I would go down to Pitt the day after Christmas and sign up for college. You get the same exact government money that any of us get, even though you weren't in the war."

Marty looked across Thomas at Jonathan, and then at everyone else in the group.

"In fact all of you guys should sign up," he proclaimed, then looked back at Jonathan and added:

"Even you."

Jonathan gritted his teeth.

"Look, don't you start too, okay? I'm getting it from both sides between Ma and Francine. Uncle Stan said that about you going to college last week at dinner and now Ma brings it up fifteen times a day; and then fifteen times a day Francine tells me that she wants me to find a job soon so we can buy a house soon. Ask Joey; he's heard that enough from me."

"I'm telling you," Marty pressed, "you should just tell Francine that you're going to Pitt and that's that...'

"Hey guys," Joseph interrupted. "I just realized we got a problem. How we gonna all get home? We got three cars here."

"Whaddya mean?" Marty turned around to face Joseph. "You guys go back to Polish Hill and I'll take my Pop's Buick back home."

"Nah, ain't gonna work," Joseph shook his head. "Only Jack has a driver's license and he has to drive his Hudson. Who's gonna drive Pop's Packard back home?"

"I will," Thomas immediately responded. Even without his slurred speech, the other four still would have raised their objections in unison:

"No!"

"No way!"

"You're not driving!"

"Forget about it!"

"Your driving days are over for a while," Jonathan chided his youngest brother. "You think Pop's gonna let you take the car after you ran off with it? Especially without a driver's license?"

Suddenly Jonathan's eyes widened.

"Hey, that's something! You can go get a driver's license now," he said to Tommy. "I need to get one, and now Joey can too. We should all go down to the motor bureau at the same time; maybe right after I get back from the honeymoon."

"Fine, but what are we gonna do about Pop's Packard?" Joseph asked again.

"Jack can drive it; he has a license," Thomas chimed in.

"Um…hey Tommy?" Joseph asked.

"Yeah?"

"If Jack drives the Packard, then who's gonna drive his Hudson?"

Realizing how foolish his foggy-brained suggestion had been, Thomas just shrugged.

"Yeah; he definitely ain't driving us home," Joseph rolled his eyes as he looked over at Jonathan.

It took about two minutes before they all arrived at a workable Rube Goldberg solution. Marty would quickly drive home and then come back to Lou's with his father. Jack would drive his Hudson back to Polish Hill, while Marty would drive Gerald Coleman's Packard and Stan Walker would drive his own Buick. The other three would fan out among the cars. Once safely arrived back in Polish Hill, Stan and Marty would drive back to Fox Chapel with enough time to spare before Christmas Eve supper.

The procession of vehicles pulled out of Lou's parking lot a few minutes before five o'clock. Jonathan was in his Uncle Stan's car while Joseph rode with Marty, and Thomas was poured into the front seat of Jack Leonard's Hudson. Thomas was feeling increasingly woozy, but one look at the tough Marine staff sergeant told him that if he wound up getting sick in the Hudson he would be really sorry for having done so.

"You feeling any better?" Jack Leonard looked over at Tommy as the Hudson crossed the Highland Park Bridge. "I don't mean being drunk and all; you ain't gonna feel too good from that for a while. I mean about your discharge."

"I dunno," Thomas replied. "Maybe."

Jack looked back at the road as the Hudson swung onto Butler Street, and then back at Tommy.

"So you want to hear how I got wounded? The first time on Guadalcanal back in '42?"

Thomas hesitated, not sure if he really wanted to hear the story. But he was powerless to do anything other than nod.

"A couple days after the landing, the brass sent a group of intelligence guys in to do a recon mission up the

Matanikau River, and a couple of us regular Marines got pulled to go along with them.”

Jack braked the Hudson when traffic on Butler Street began slowing.

“What we didn’t know,” he continued, “was that the Jap Navy was sitting there waiting for us, and their Marines attacked us and wiped out almost the entire patrol. A couple of us got hit but were able to make it back. The rest of the guys…”

“Anyway,” Jack interrupted himself, “I wound up in the field hospital for about a week. I was lucky; took a bullet through my left thigh but it didn’t hit nothin’ serious, it was sorta on the outer side of my leg. They patched me up and after I got out of the field hospital, I was right back on the line.”

“Geez,” Thomas said.

“I figured that I was the lucky son of a bitch that time, even getting hit and all. Like I said, most of those intelligence guys bought it on that mission.”

Jack sighed.

“From then on, I figured I was on borrowed time, ya know? So when I got it again on Tarawa, and then again on Saipan, and then each time I was out of the hospital in a week or two, I figured I got an angel looking out for me, or something like that; ya know?”

“Yeah, I guess so,” Thomas agreed.

“I’m telling you,” Jack said, “just like I said – like we all said – back there at the bar. I get how you feel but you gotta try to realize how lucky you really are. And you know what else?”

“Huh?” Thomas answered.

"We're gonna be in another war before too much longer; I just feel it. Maybe two or three years, or maybe five or six years; but there's gonna be one. Probably the Russians, but maybe the Chinese; hell, maybe even the Germans or the Japs again. And whatever G.I.'s and Marines happen to be sitting wherever the next war starts when the shooting breaks out, and also the other poor bastards who have to go in on the first wave while the others are trying to hold out...they're all gonna get clobbered. It'll be just like Pearl Harbor or Wake Island all over again, because we won't be able to hold with the number of soldiers being so low with all of the discharges and everything."

Jack looked over at Thomas again.

"And you're gonna be real glad then that you got your discharge and aren't one of those guys getting slaughtered."

They drove along in silence for a couple of minutes. Thomas, by now exhausted from all of the talk about his discharge and its implications, changed the subject and asked:

"So what's with you and Charlene?"

Jack let out a sigh and even in the now-darkened car Thomas could see a sad smile come to the older Marine's face.

"I dunno, we seem to have really hit it off. It's really strange because she's a movie star and everything..."

"It's funny that you think of her that way," Thomas interrupted. "To us she's just our plain old sister, like she's always been. But it's strange seeing her in movies just like Betty Grable and Judy Garland, that's for sure."

"Well yeah, that's the problem," Jack continued, his voice resigned. "She's going back to Hollywood a couple days after New Year's, and I guess that'll be that."

Thomas was just about to offer the standard reply to such a proclamation – "you never know, it might work out" – but then he remembered his brother Joseph and Abby Sobol back in late '42 in much the same circumstances. And look how that had turned out for Joseph. Instead, Thomas just offered a silent sympathetic shrug of his shoulders that he wasn't sure if Jack Leonard would even notice or not.

❄ ❄ ❄

Stan Walker fiddled with the Buick's radio dial until the static gave way to the local Mutual Broadcasting Network station.

"Truman's coming on in a couple of minutes," he said, referring to the President's scheduled Christmas Eve address. "He's lighting the Christmas tree at the White House and giving a speech."

"It still seems so strange hearing 'President Truman'," Jonathan mused. "Roosevelt was President for...almost forever, it seemed."

"I know what you mean," Stan agreed. "After all those years it was like Roosevelt was the only person who could actually be President. Plus Truman had only been Vice President for a couple months, and all of a sudden he's in the White House for both V-E Day and V-J Day."

After a commercial for Lux and another for Pepsodent, Mutual cut to the White House where the President began:

> "This is the Christmas that a war-weary world has prayed for through long and awful years. With peace comes joy and gladness. The gloom of the war years fades as once more we light the National Community Christmas Tree."

Jonathan and his uncle listened in silence as the President continued speaking, each lost in his own thoughts as Truman's words oscillated between Biblical references and tributes to America's glorious past. Both Stan Walker and Jonathan Coleman took particular notice when the President proclaimed:

> "It is well in this solemn hour that we bow to Washington, Jefferson, Jackson, and Lincoln as we face our destiny with its hopes and fears; its burdens and its responsibilities. Out of the past we shall gather wisdom and inspiration to chart our future course."

The President's speech continued for another minute or so, and then Mutual cut back to the delayed 5:00 P.M. national news. Stan Walker twirled the car radio's volume dial half a turn to lower the sound volume, and then looked over to Jonathan for a split second before turning his eyes back to the road.

"You know that one part President Truman said? That thing about facing our destiny with all of the hopes and fears and wisdom? Something like that?"

"Uh-huh," Jonathan replied.

"He's talking about all of us, everyone in the country, but he mostly meant you guys," Stan mused. "You guys who all came back from the war, and also the other guys who will be coming back soon. All of you guys stood up to Hitler and Tojo and faced your fears, and then you won the war. Now you get to…I dunno, move on to the future because whatever is ahead for you boys, it ain't gonna be nothin' like the war was."

Stan looked over at his nephew once again.

"You get what I'm sayin'?"

"Sort of," Jonathan replied. Stan Walker was having difficulty putting what he wanted to say into words, but Jonathan was still able to grasp the overall spirit of what his uncle wanted to say.

"Let me ask you something, Uncle Stan," Jonathan said. "You know how last week at dinner you were telling everybody about Marty going to Pitt and then Ma said that I should do the same thing?"

Stan Walker uttered a quick "uh-huh," almost certain what Jonathan's question would be; what his predicament was.

"Well, Francine wants me to buy a house as soon as possible after the wedding, and to go find a job…"

"I'm sure she does," Stan interrupted. "And she probably thinks college is a foolish idea for you because you're getting married and will have a family to take care of. And you feel like you're caught in the middle between Francine and your Ma, right?"

"Yeah, exactly!" Jonathan's tones indicated gratitude that his uncle immediately grasped the predicament that Jonathan felt.

"I know it's different for you than it is for Marty," Stan responded. "And now for Joey and Tommy too, it sounds like. You know, with you getting married and all, unlike Marty and your brothers. You got a wife to support, and trust me, I know that's a big responsibility. Remember when I was out of work for all those years and if it hadn't been for my sister and your Pop letting us live with all of you, I don't know how I woulda done it for my family."

Stan paused for a few seconds, trying to decide the best words to use to convey to his nephew what he thought was so important for Jonathan to comprehend.

"Even though you need to start supporting Francine right away, you also need to think about how things will be down the road. You know, in five years when the two of you will probably have a coupl'a kids, and then in ten years and then even after that. You done any thinkin' about the kind of job you would go out and try to get right away?"

"Nah..." Jonathan started to reply, but then he corrected himself.

"Well yeah, sort of," he continued, "but I haven't come up with any good ideas yet. I've looked in the *Press* and the *Post-Gazette* in the 'Male Help Wanted' section of the classifieds and there's jobs in there for night watchmen and dishwashers; you know, things like that where I might get a job right away. But there's not a whole lot of jobs listed, and most of the them anyway are for pipefitters and plumbers and draftsmen. Oh yeah, tool and die makers too, I saw a couple of those in Sunday's paper. But I don't know how to do those jobs since I was a pilot, not a mechanic or anything like that. Besides, I figure there's gonna be a million guys coming back who *were* mechanics in the Army or Marines, or pipefitters in the Navy; and they'll wind up getting those jobs, not me, because they already know how to do all that stuff. Which is how it should be, I guess."

"I agree," Stan nodded, then continued.

"Look, I'm luckier than I am smart, and I'm sure your Pop will gladly agree that there's a whole lot I don't know…"

Jonathan winced as his uncle continued. He knew full well that Gerald Coleman wasn't particularly fond of his brother-in-law; he just hadn't realized that Stan Walker was fully aware of how Gerald felt about him. He began to object but out of the corner of his eyes saw his uncle raise his right hand; that "don't bother" gesture.

"It's okay, we're all family. It doesn't really bother me because we all get along for the most part and have supper together and all that. It was probably that way in your unit during the war, right? You probably flew right alongside some guys that you really didn't like all that much on the ground. Marty told me about a coupl'a guys on the ships he was on that if he coulda thrown them overboard and not gotten caught, he probably woulda; but when they were in action he forgot all of that. Anyway, we're all family and it's okay if your Pop thinks that. After all the years we lived with all of you, he has the right to think anything he wants."

Jonathan was increasingly uncomfortable with his uncle's prescience, but fortunately Stan Walker changed the subject back to Jonathan's predicament.

"Anyway, here's how I see it. There's millions of you guys coming home from the war all of a sudden. You remember how hard it was to find jobs during the Depression? I don't think it will get quite that bad again but for a coupl'a years jobs are gonna be hard to find and I think the economy isn't gonna be so good because of lots of guys looking for work. But that's only gonna last two or three years; maybe four. Why not take advantage of that time to let Uncle Sam pay for you to get a college degree so when things get going full steam by the end of the '40s, you will be all set for some fancy job that pays you a hell of a lot more than the kind of job you could get right now? And that's if you could even find one right away that pays more than what a dishwasher can make."

Jonathan paused to contemplate what his uncle was saying. Intellectually he understood and sort of agreed with Stan Walker's advice, however…

"But what about Francine?" Jonathan asked. "You know, her wanting me to get a job now so we can go buy a house now. If I tell her what you told me she's just gonna say 'you can go to night school in a couple of years after we get a house and we're settled' or something like that."

Stan Walker sighed. Life was definitely much simpler for his own son than it was for his nephew.

"Maybe you would do that," Stan said, "but you know what? I got a hunch that you probably would never get around to it. Or maybe you will, but you'll be working such long hours that after a year or so of trying to do night school also, you won't want to finish it. Maybe it would work, but it would be a lot harder for you than goin' to school right now, that's for sure."

Stan's Buick was now approaching the three-way intersection with Penn Avenue and 34th Street. Jonathan suddenly recalled what Joseph had let slip about his and Tommy's near-miss at this very intersection last week, and made a mental note to follow up on that matter that he had let slide back at the bar.

Aware that they were now within about five minutes of the Coleman house, Stan knew that he had to wrap up this unprecedented, deeply personal conversation with his nephew.

"Look, Jonathan, I know exactly the situation you're in. You got a big decision ahead of you, and whatever you decide to do affects not just you but Francine also. What did your Pop say about what you should do?"

Jonathan shrugged.

"I haven't really talked this over with him yet," he said sheepishly. Suddenly, Jonathan felt uneasy having such a personal conversation with his Uncle Stan when he had yet to approach his very own father for advice. For years, until he headed off to Air Corps training way out in Arizona, Gerald Coleman had always been there with just the right advice for his eldest son. And even later, during that Thanksgiving furlough when Jonathan was not only uncertain about whether he should ask Francine to marry him but also fearful of his mother's reaction if he did so, he had talked over that dilemma with his father. Gerald Coleman had listened patiently and Jonathan could still recall his father's exact words: "Don't worry about that. If you decide that after all that has happened Francine is the one for you, then I'll talk to your Ma. Okay?"

"Well you need to talk to him," Stan quickly responded. "Like I said, your Pop thinks I'm a windbag and maybe he's right. And I know my sister thinks that I think I'm Gatsby, moving my family all the way out to Fox Chapel. But if I've ever been sure of anything in my life, it's what I've been telling you."

Stan paused for a second as the Buick fishtailed a touch. Once he was out of the skid, he continued.

"Of all of you guys – both your brothers and Marty too, and then you – you're the smartest one. I never said nothing to your Ma or Pop because it wouldn't have made no difference, but when you graduated from Schenley I thought it was a shame that there was no money for you to go to college back then. You were lugging produce boxes at *Weisberg's* and you shoulda been at Pitt. But back before the war, college was mostly for the sons of rich men who could still afford to send their boys there even during the Depression. But now, with Uncle Sam paying all of the school bills for all you guys, plus giving you that living money too…that's the least the government could do after everything you guys did during the war."

Just before he made the final turn onto the Coleman's street, Stan Walker eased over to the curb and slowed his Buick to a crawl so he could finish what he was saying.

"For every single one of you guys, it'll be a waste if you don't use Uncle Sam's money to go to college or at least trade school. For you, though, as smart as you are, it'll be an even bigger waste. I know you're gonna have a wife to support in less than a week. So you take the government's seventy-five dollars a month of college living money and you use twenty-five or thirty bucks of that to get a decent enough apartment close to Pitt. Francine cooks a lot of meatloaf and spaghetti, plus the two of yins go over to your Ma's for supper a couple times a week and over to Jack Donner's house a couple other times. You make Uncle Sam's money go as far as you can. Tell Francine that there will be plenty of houses waiting for her in '49 or '50, and what's even better is that after you get your fancy college degree job you will be able to buy her an even nicer house than you could afford right now."

Just then, Jack Leonard's Hudson made its way past the Buick followed ten seconds later by the Colemans' Packard, with Marty Walker honking the horn as he drove by when he recognized his father's car. Stan eased down on the accelerator and the Buick again fishtailed as the whitewalls tussled with the slushy Polish Hill streets for control over the car's destiny.

"Talk it over with your Pop like I said; your Ma, too. If you want, tell them what I told you. I didn't tell you nothing that I wouldn't say directly to my sister's face."

"Okay, Uncle Stan," Jonathan sighed.

"I'm just thinking about what's best for you; for all of you boys," Stan said, his right index finger pointing ahead at the same time to indicate "all of you boys" meant every single one of the occupants of the other two cars as well; even Jack Leonard. "You got that, right?"

This time, Jonathan just nodded as his Uncle eyed an open parking spot two doors past the Coleman's house and glided the Buick into the slushy mess alongside the curb.

All six men entered the Coleman house together. Gerald was the only one in the living room at the moment; Irene and her daughters were in the kitchen preparing the special *Wigilia* supper. Irene stuck her head out of the kitchen doorway when she heard Thomas and his rescuers begin to cross the threshold. Satisfied with her own eyes that Thomas was alive and well, she eased her way back into the kitchen. This was Gerald's matter to handle, at least at the outset, just as a similar situation with one of her daughters would be hers to initially deal with.

Gerald Coleman rose as soon as everyone was inside, but before he could say anything Jonathan caught his eye and nodded to his right, indicating that he wanted a word with his father.

Gerald walked over to the side of the room where Jonathan began heading. Jonathan lowered his voice but he knew that everyone, Tommy included, could most likely hear what he was saying...which was just fine with him.

"Don't go too hard on him, okay Pop?" Jonathan said. "We all talked to him there for a while. He knows it was a stupid thing to do and he won't do it again. But especially being Christmas Eve and all...remember four years ago what I put you and Ma through on Christmas Eve, right? Just take it easy on him, okay?"

Gerald thought about what Jonathan had just proposed, and couldn't help but think about how mature his eldest son had become. For many years, Gerald would have been the sole decider as to how much punishment any one of his sons – Jonathan included, his own Christmas Eve disappearing act four years ago fresh in Gerald's mind – would receive for a stunt such as this one. But here was Jonathan, effectively preempting his own father in that role…or at least attempting to do so. Even more so, what Jonathan requested of his father was no different than what Gerald would have done anyway. All of this made Gerald proud of Jonathan, but of course a little bit sad as well since here was yet one more reminder that time had still marched ahead with precision even while his two oldest boys had been away at war.

Mild pleasantries were exchanged with Stan and Marty, but the Walkers were in a hurry to get back home to Fox Chapel so they stayed at the Coleman house less than five minutes. As goodbyes were said all around, Stan Walker caught Jonathan's gaze with a look that clearly reminded Jonathan: "talk to your Pop."

❄ ❄ ❄

The Polish Christmas Eve tradition of *Wigilia* had been embraced by the Coleman family for years. During the Depression years, the traditional meatless supper was relatively easy to observe given the mealtime sacrifices most families needed to make anyway to get by. But Gerald and Irene didn't think in those terms, and they made sure that each of their children was aware that tradition, not austerity, dictated the spread of fried carp, herring, Borscht, and the rest of the Polish delicacies that made their way to the Coleman's table on Christmas Eve.

Fortunately for Thomas, the dinnertime conversation was steered away from his disappearing act and instead focused on the sudden news from earlier in the day about his impending discharge day, as well as Joseph's. Thomas forced cheerfulness into his responses to any questions directed his way, but for the most part the conversation focused on Joseph's sudden good fortune.

Because Jack Leonard's afternoon pie-and-coffee date with Charlene had been interrupted, he wound up joining the Colemans for their *Wigilia* supper feast. A week earlier, Charlene would have been astonished to hear her mother suggest to any suitor of Charlene's: "We would love to have you stay and celebrate Christmas Eve with us; would you like to?"

Charlene realized that her mother somehow saw Jack Leonard as the "anti-Hollywood"; someone whom she reckoned could draw Charlene's interests and passions away from acting and entertaining back towards…well, towards "regular life" as Irene Coleman saw it. But what Charlene knew her mother hadn't counted on, though, was that at this very moment Charlene was wrestling with how passionate she actually was about her acting and entertaining. The disinterested way in which her latest movie role had been cast – not to mention that role being such an insignificant one – had left a sour taste in her mouth about the entertainment business and the studios during the entire train ride back to Pittsburgh. And now, this powerful attraction to one of the neighborhood boys turned Marine hero had provided such a enchanting distraction from those troubles ever since she had met Jack Leonard…

All in all, supper was a pleasant affair. Following the meal, though, Jack Leonard did need to return home to his parents' house, and Charlene quickly put on a jacket and accompanied him out onto the Coleman's front porch to say goodnight. The front window shades were drawn, giving Charlene and Jack a modicum of privacy. The temperature had once again dived into the upper teens, but Charlene could only feel the delicious warmth of being in Jack Leonard's company.

"Sorry again about earlier," Jack apologized. "Tommy was kinda in bad shape when we got there, so…"

"It's alright," Charlene cooed. "Thank you for going to get him."

"You should keep an eye on him for a coupl'a days, too. You know, make sure he's acting normal and doesn't decide to take your Pop's car again. Jonathan and Joey are gonna watch out for him, but you should also."

"I will," Charlene promised.

"I'm gonna take him down to the discharge station with me on Thursday since I'm getting out the same day, so I can keep an eye on him also."

"Thank you," Charlene said again, finding herself just a touch irritated that Jack was still talking about Tommy. As if reading her mind, he reached out and folded both of her bare hands into his gloved ones and locked eyes with her.

"I can't wait to see you tomorrow at Mass," he said before lowering his eyes slightly. "I wish I could hang around here with you but my folks really want me to spend Christmas Eve at home with them; you know, first Christmas back home after the war and all that."

"I know," Charlene nodded. "Same here. I would love to come over to your house with you but you know how my Ma is, and right now she's not giving me any trouble about Hollywood and the movies and all that. So I don't want to make her mad by not being home."

Charlene smiled and felt an involuntary shiver as the cold was starting to get to her.

"But I can't wait until Christmas tomorrow," she added, "when we get to spend at least part of the day together."

"Me too," Jack agreed. "Look, you better get inside before you get sick."

He leaned forward at the same time that Charlene did. Their goodnight kiss lasted a good ten seconds.

"Good night," Charlene murmured when they finally broke away from their kiss, only to find her lips seeking his once again. Another ten seconds or so passed, and this time when the kiss ended Jack summoned the will to offer his own "Good night, Charlene" and head down the front stairs out to the sidewalk. He looked back just as he opened the door to his Hudson and Charlene was still standing on the porch, smiling at him. When she saw him look back she blew him a kiss, bringing a smile – a melancholy smile – to his face as he got into his car.

Back in the Coleman's living room, all eyes were on Charlene when she finally hurried back inside.

"He's a very nice young man," Irene Coleman said as Charlene shed her coat and walked over to the coat closet to hang the garment.

"It's okay, Ma," Charlene replied, smirking as she looked back over her left shoulder as she opened the closet door, "you don't have to keep selling him to me."

"He's not one of your movie star friends," Irene countered, "so maybe you didn't notice what a nice boy he is. I just wanted to point that out to you, that's all."

Charlene wondered what her mother's reaction would be if she spun in place at this very moment and spelled out the details of the two exceptionally lovely goodnight kisses that had just taken place on Irene's front porch. Or maybe if Charlene locked eyes with her mother and said something like: "Well, Ma, let me tell you how nice I think he is, and what I would like to do with him if we could get a little privacy somewhere; would you like me to go on?"

Instead, Charlene just smiled at her mother – that sweetly seductive Carla Colburn smile, offered up for just this occasion – and walked wordlessly over to the sofa to sit next to her brother Joseph.

The rest of the evening was spent listening to Christmas music coming from various radio stations as Tommy again manned the Philco's dial. The entire Coleman family – all seven of them – relaxed through the evening. Throughout the evening, Bing Crosby's *I'll be Home for Christmas* must have been played a dozen times. The past two Christmas seasons, that very song had brought tears to tens of millions of Americans on the Home Front and overseas. Tears still flowed this year for many, including Irene Coleman the first three times the song came forth from the Philco's speaker. But now for Irene the tears were ones of relief rather than worry and sorrow. Still, Irene knew – each one of them knew – that all across the country on this very evening, men and women and children were hearing this song and weeping for a lost son or father or brother who would never be coming home.

❄ ❄ ❄

Until two years before Ruthie was born, Irene Coleman would shuffle her children off to the traditional Midnight Mass at Saint Michael's. But on Christmas Eve of 1933, both eight-year old Charlene and six-year old Thomas were both dreadfully sick with a strain of influenza that had quickly made its way around Pittsburgh starting just before Thanksgiving. Both children were far too sick to attend Midnight Mass, and Irene fretted her way from one bedside to another for the second day in a row as the clock ticked down until the midnight hour that would usher in Christmas.

Irene's intention had been all along that Gerald would take eleven-year old Jonathan and nine-year old Joseph to Saint Michael's by himself while she stayed home with the younger two, but the sudden sneezing fit on the part of Joseph just after 10:00 that evening put a halt to those plans. For the first time, the entire Coleman family stayed home from Midnight Mass.

Miraculously, both Charlene's and Thomas' fevers broke sometime in the middle of the night and by morning both felt well enough that Irene shuffled them off along with the rest of the family to Saint Michael's for Christmas Morning Mass. The entire clan returned home, opened their Christmas presents, and a wonderful Christmas Day – despite the Depression – was enjoyed by every member of the Coleman family that year.

Sometime before the next Christmas, Irene went to Saint Michael's to visit with Father Nolan. For all of those years when she and Gerald had herded their children to Christmas Eve Midnight Mass, the following Christmas Day was usually overshadowed by the intense fatigue felt by the children from having stayed awake until past 2:00 in the morning. While at Saint Michael's, Irene and Gerald spent most of their time anyway nudging one child after another awake as the youngsters were powerless to stay awake.

Midnight Mass was as much a part of Polish-American tradition as *Wigilia* was, Irene Coleman acknowledged to Father Nolan; but for a family such as the Colemans that had so many small children, would it be such a terrible sin to trade bleary-eyed attendance at Midnight Mass for far more attentive attendance at Christmas Morning Mass?

Irene Coleman's request was far from the first one of its kind that had made its way to Father Nolan, and he quickly put her mind at ease that not only was Irene's proposal acceptable to him, he was fairly confident that the Almighty Father in Heaven understood as well. And from that point forward, through the rest of the Depression years and through the war years, the Colemans would attend Mass at Saint Michael's on Christmas morning.

This year would be no exception, and by 11:00 that night, every single member of the family was tucked away in an upstairs bedroom. Ruthie quickly fell asleep, but sleep was elusive for her sister and each of her brothers.

Charlene wished that Jack Leonard was with her at this very moment and that they could usher in the very first seconds of Christmas, 1945 together.

Jonathan's mind raced with one imagined conversation after another with his fiancé, hoping to find the one script that would not result in tears or harsh words.

Thomas did his best to digest the words that Jack Leonard had offered earlier this afternoon – "Tommy, you're one lucky son of a bitch, you know that?" – and tried as hard as he could to believe that sentiment to be a true one.

Joseph fought against the sleep that threatened to overtake him, certain that his nightmares were once again waiting for him.

6 – Tuesday, December 25, 1945

Gerald Coleman was certain that Saint Michael's had never been this packed. With twenty minutes left until Christmas Morning Mass began, not a seat remained unfilled. Latecomers (who, on an ordinary Sunday or even at Christmas Mass in some past year, would not have been latecomers at all) began finding spots to stand along the sides and the back of the nave…the main seating area of Saint Michael's.

Uniforms abounded among those present, including Gerald's three sons. At his request, Jonathan, Joseph, and Thomas each dressed for Mass in their respective service dress uniforms. This coming Saturday at Jonathan's wedding each would wear his uniform once again – even Thomas, his upcoming discharge this Thursday notwithstanding – but the time was drawing to a close that the Coleman boys would be proudly seen in the uniforms that they had willingly donned to defend their country and their family. If pressed, Gerald would not have been able to put into words the reason he wanted his boys to wear their uniforms; he just did, and of course they complied.

Francine Donner's family had rendezvoused with the Colemans outside Saint Michael's shortly after 7:30 that morning, with an hour left until the beginning of Christmas Mass. Both Irene Coleman and Sally Donner were certain that seating would be at a premium this morning; and since Jonathan and Francine would of course want to sit with each other, seating the two families astride from one another prevented any hurt feelings from Jonathan abandoning his family to sit with Francine's, or vice versa. And to do so required an extra-early arrival by both families.

Also in the vicinity was Jack Leonard's family, for the very same reason. Antoni and Beatrice Leonard were only casual acquaintances of Gerald and Irene Coleman, but the families did know each other. Just as Jonathan sat to the extreme left of his family in the long center row and Francine sat to the extreme right of hers, Jack and Charlene did likewise on the other side of the Coleman clan to link their two families together this morning.

Gerald's thoughts were still wandering as the morning Mass began. Even when the standing and kneeling and praying was well underway, Gerald's thoughts were elsewhere, at least in part. His mind time-traveled to Christmas mornings past, and even to future Christmas mornings that had yet to occur. He saw his children as toddlers, but also as parents the same ages as Gerald and Irene were this very morning in the present day of 1945. He could see images of grandchildren yet to be born, as vividly real as if they were also squeezed into the family's row at Saint Michael's this morning. And, as Gerald's thoughts took flight back and forth through time, omnipresent feelings of gratitude and thanksgiving went along for the ride.

"I would like every young man here today who has served our country in this time of war to please stand."

Father Nolan's departure from the traditional progression of Christmas Morning Mass about twenty minutes into the Mass brought Gerald back to the present day. He looked to his right to see if Thomas was rising in place. He half-expected his youngest son to remain seated, given the reason for yesterday's disappearing act, and for a second or two it appeared that was exactly what Thomas planned to do. But he eventually did rise – albeit with an audible sigh that Gerald could hear four seats to Thomas' left – joining both of his brothers, Jack Leonard, and about two hundred other men of ages ranging from Tommy's eighteen up to men of Gerald's age, perhaps even older. Most were in uniform, but perhaps thirty or so of the men who were now standing were wearing civilian clothes.

Father Nolan gave enough time for everyone who was going to stand to do so, and then he continued.

"Our Father in Heaven, we thank you for watching over these brave men as they took up arms to defend our country in its darkest hour. Four long years ago, most of us who are gathered here today were also present as we gathered to not only celebrate the birth of Your Son but also to beseech you to deliver us from the aggression of our enemies who meant us grievous harm. We asked you then to bestow upon the men of Saint Michael's; and upon the men of Pittsburgh; and upon the men from all across our great nation the courage they would need to achieve victory."

The priest paused for a moment as his gaze moved slowly from his left to his right, then he continued.

"Our Father in Heaven, you answered our prayers to you from that blessed morning, and for that we are forever in your service. Many of these men you see standing here bravely faced the horrors of war, and through your loving mercy have returned home to their families. Many other men among those here were spared the terrible tragedy of combat but they are also heroes, for they would willingly have braved those same horrors if they had been called upon. Through your loving mercy you brought an end to those long, terrible years of war before any one of these men standing before you was called upon to make the ultimate sacrifice."

Father Nolan took deep breath – a necessary deep breath – before continuing.

"There are others from among our families gathered here today whom you did call upon to make the ultimate sacrifice. We are mere mortals and so we are powerless to avoid asking the inevitable question of you: Why, Lord? Why were some of those from among your flock here at Saint Michael's, and so very many from your flock all across our city and our state and our nation called home to you during these long years of war? We ask those questions knowing that the only answer we can ever know for certain is the one with which we must be content: because it was Your will."

Father Nolan always displayed an uncanny memory for recalling precisely where he had spotted families sitting during any given Mass as the service got underway, and this morning was no exception. During this last part of his sermon his gaze found Lukas and Paulina Jaskolski; and then Martin and Stella Bonnaverte; and then Carl and Bessie Kozlowski; and then Karol and Margaret Rzepecki, whose son Paul had been the very first casualty from the Saint Michael's family, killed in the attack on Pearl Harbor...

As Father Nolan spoke, both Jonathan and Joseph found themselves gazing around Saint Michael's at the many familiar faces among those standing. Both brothers recalled doing much the same thing at Father Nolan's request during Sunday Mass back in November of '42, only an hour or so after arriving back in Pittsburgh for that all-too-brief Thanksgiving furlough. So many of the faces each brother recalled seeing that Sunday morning were back here again today, but others – like Tommy Bonnaverte – were gone forever. Others, like Jack Leonard, had already been off to war by that time.

So much had happened in three years that had passed since that morning back in '42, both Jonathan and Joseph were thinking to themselves at almost the exact same instant – though neither knew about the other's contemplations, of course – and now, it was all over. Just as they had both tried to convince Tommy yesterday afternoon, the future was what mattered now, not the past.

❄ ❄ ❄

Exchanging presents back in the Coleman living room after Mass was a joyous event. In years past, when the children were younger, gifts were exchanged in the earliest hours of the morning before Irene would shuffle her family off to Saint Michael's. Now, though, with everyone – even Ruthie – old enough to be patient enough to wait until after Mass for their presents, that was exactly what transpired this morning.

Civilian clothes were the overwhelmingly popular choice for the Coleman boys: sweaters galore, flannel shirts, a pair of handmade boots for each son courtesy of Gerald Coleman's skilled cobbler's hands...even socks and undergarments were among the gratefully accepted gifts. Gerald was the grateful recipient of a new cigarette lighter (his current one had been a gift from Ruthie during the last Christmas the family had spent together, four years earlier); a new pipe; and from all of his sons together, a shiny new set of cobbler's tools to replace the aging ones he had used for years.

The boys — Charlene also — all chipped in to buy their mother a new set of pots and pans since so many of those in Irene's current inventory challenged Gerald's tools in the longevity department.

Francine's gift to her soon-to-be mother-in-law and father-in-law was a beautiful painting of the Allegheny Mountains in central Pennsylvania at sunset, with the rich reds and oranges and yellows majestically intertwined with the rich dark greens of the dense forests. Jonathan had helped her pick out that painting, and made sure that his name was on the tag along with Francine's. Hopefully his mother would adore what Francine had selected to fill that one stubbornly blank wall in the house's dining area near the table. But just in case Irene would find herself of the mind that no gift from Francine Donner could be a satisfactory one, Jonathan being part of the equation would hopefully temper any impertinent grumbling later on.

The previously gift-wrapped packages all open, one and all assumed that the exchanging of Christmas gifts had now concluded when Gerald rose from his armchair and walked over to the coat closet. He opened the closet door, reached inside as if fishing in a coat pocket for something, and a moment later shut the closet door as he walked over to the sofa where Jonathan and Francine were sitting.

"This is another present from your mother and me," he said to Jonathan as he handed him an envelope. "For you and Francine."

Jonathan looked quizzically at his father as he hesitated for a second before reaching forward to take the envelope from Gerald. He looked to his left at Francine, his face indicating both puzzlement and apprehension.

"Go ahead and open it," Gerald said as he walked back to his armchair and eased himself back onto the cushioned seat.

Jonathan looked over at his mother, standing behind one of the other armchairs where Charlene was seated, and then did as his father asked. The envelope had been glued shut so Jonathan slid his right index finger into a small unglued opening on one side and carefully opened the flap, breaking the glue's seal a little bit at a time. Even before the envelope was fully opened he could tell that it contained a small stack of cash and also several pieces of different colored cardboard.

Realizing that Jonathan now had an idea of the envelope's contents, Gerald said:

"This is for your honeymoon, so you can go to Florida where it's warm instead of you and Francine freezing over in Washington. All the railroad tickets you need are there for you to leave next Wednesday, just in case something takes longer with your discharge on Monday and you need an extra day. The money is for hotel rooms and your meals for seven days…"

"Pop, you can't! This is so much money!" Jonathan protested.

Gerald held up the palm of his right hand to silence his son's objections.

"Your mother and I saved this money for a long time during the war just for this," Gerald explained. "We're thankful you're home safely and we want you and Francine to get off to a good start after your wedding…"

"Ma!" Jonathan interrupted, looking over at Irene Coleman this time. "This is too much!"

"Nonsense," Irene rebutted. "Just like your father said, we're grateful that we have the opportunity to be able to give you this present, because after all…"

Her voice trailed off, leaving the sentence unfinished; but everyone in the room knew what Irene had been thinking and would have said: "because after all, you might not have come back from the war."

Now it was Francine's turn to protest.

"Mrs. Coleman, really we appreciate…"

Gerald was the one who interrupted her.

"Francine, you're about to be part of the family. This present is for both you and Jonathan so you can have a honeymoon that you will remember, especially after all those years you two spent apart during the war."

Sighing, Jonathan realized that objecting any longer would be a futile effort and would soon begin to infringe on ingratitude.

"I don't know what to say, Pop," he said to his father as he rose and walked the short distance to his father's chair. Gerald had also risen, and father and son embraced. Jonathan walked over to repeat the gesture with his mother as Francine rose and accepted a hug from her future father-in-law. All eyes in the living room, even Ruthie's, were next on Francine and Irene to see what would transpire. Alas, no drama; Irene embraced her son's fiancé with the same warmth she had bestowed on her son.

The thank-you embraces now concluded, Francine decided one more was called for. She smiled at Jonathan as she hugged him tightly, and then excitedly said as she leaned back from the embrace:

"This is so wonderful! We get to go to Florida for our honeymoon after all!"

❄ ❄ ❄

"This is for you," Jack Leonard stated the obvious as he handed the exquisitely wrapped small package to Charlene. The clock had ticked past five o'clock. The Coleman's Christmas Day feast had concluded shortly past 3:30, which made for perfect timing since the Leonard family's tradition called for a lighter meal earlier in the afternoon with their Christmas Day bounty taking place during the normal supper hour. Charlene of course had been invited to the Leonard home so she could share at least part of Christmas Day with Jack, reprising but reversing how they had stolen a few hours together on Christmas Eve.

Jack and Charlene were alone in the small enclosed dining room area. Beatrice Leonard was fussing about the kitchen, working on the finishing touches to tonight's Christmas supper, while Antoni Leonard was plopped next to their family's Zenith, accompanied in the living room by Jack's older brothers and sisters and their spouses and families, listening to Christmas music. With Jack and Charlene temporarily absent, whispers flew back and forth across the living room about the surreal experience of having Carla Colburn not only accompanying Jack to Christmas supper at the Leonard home but also dating him!

"Oh, Jack," Charlene cooed. "The wrapping paper alone looks beautiful!"

Indeed, unlike the drugstore Christmas wrapping paper that had adorned each and every gift at the Coleman home earlier – reds and greens with printed Santas or Christmas bells or evergreens encased in snow – this paper was a rich red in color, ornamented with the slightest embossed lines, but nothing else.

"It's from Boggs and Buhl," Jack felt compelled to explain. Two days earlier he had traveled by streetcar to the north side of the Allegheny River, across from downtown, to the area that had once been known as Allegheny City. The area that had once encompassed its own "Millionaire's Row" district along with that of Pittsburgh had lost much of its 19th century luster. Still, the upscale Boggs and Buhl department store remained intact, and anyone in Pittsburgh who wished to send a message of "you are extra-special" along with a present scraped together the extra dollars necessary to secure such a purchase. Jonathan had purchased Francine's engagement ring in the Boggs and Buhl jewelry department back in '42, but given the financial tightness of the Depression years followed by the sacrifices of the war years, that engagement ring remained the only gift either purchased or received from the store by any member of the Coleman family...until now, apparently.

"I wanted to get you something extra-special," Jack continued.

"Can I open it?"

"Sure," was the inevitable response.

Charlene carefully opened the exquisite wrapping paper to reveal a white rectangular box, adorned on one side with an oval surrounding a drawing of the top of an

Asian temple along with the words "SUMATRA BY TUVACHÉ."

"Perfume! I love it!" Charlene squealed.

"You do?" Jack's voice was apprehensive and hopeful, both at the same time.

Charlene looked up from the perfume box at him.

"Of course!" she replied. "Why wouldn't I?"

Jack shrugged nervously.

"Well, I wasn't sure what to get for you Christmas because...well, you know..."

Charlene cocked her head.

"No, I don't know," she said, but actually she had a good idea what Jack wasn't blurting out. Still, she felt this was a good time to get this particular issue out in the open.

"Tell me," she continued...not confrontationally or nastily, but as pleasantly as possible demanding an answer.

"Well, with you out in Hollywood and everything," Jack said hesitatingly, almost certain that whatever he said would wind up causing a quarrel with Charlene. "You know, I'm sure you get fancy Christmas presents all the time..."

Charlene fought the bubbling irritation.

"Not at all," she responded, forcing a smile as she answered. "Last Christmas I went to a party at an MGM actor's house" – then she quickly added "and his wife's" before continuing.

"There were maybe twenty people there, and everybody bought a small grab bag present for a gift exchange, along with a $100 War Bond that we all donated to one of the veterans' hospitals. I wound up with a set of very nice earrings, but by no means are they extravagant."

Suddenly Charlene remembered:

"You know those earrings I had on last Saturday night?"

Her eyes were immediately mischievous as she lowered her voice to barely above a whisper.

"You must have noticed them when you were kissing my ears when we were necking..."

Jack immediately blushed at Charlene's brazen, personal words.

"I know it was dark in your car," she continued, "so maybe you didn't notice them after all."

Her voice went back to its normal volume.

"Anyway, that's what I got for Christmas last year. Well, that and a nice blouse that my Ma and Pop mailed out to me that they bought right here at good old Joseph Horne."

Charlene reached out to take Jack's hands.

"I love the perfume," she smiled, "and the fact that you went all the way over to Boggs and Buhl to get it for me. Honestly, it's the sweetest Christmas gift I've ever received. Please don't give all this 'Hollywood starlet' business another thought, especially at Christmas when I'm with you. It's not like Clark Gable bought me a Christmas present, right?"

"I guess so," Jack nodded, certain that Charlene was doing her best to ease his apprehension but feeling a little more at ease because she was actually making the effort to do so.

"I have a present for you, too," Charlene released Jack's hands and turned to retrieve her purse from the chair where she had placed it. She reached in and took out an identically wrapped package, albeit smaller in size than Jack's perfume gift.

"I'm surprised I didn't run into you at Boggs and Buhl," Charlene laughed. "That would have been something, huh?"

For the first time since the gift exchange had begun, Jack Leonard finally felt at ease. He chuckled.

"Yeah, it would have, that's for sure," he agreed.

"Go ahead, open it," Charlene urged.

Jack opened the wrapping paper as carefully as Charlene had done with her present, revealing a small cream-colored box. He eased the lid of the box upwards to reveal an elegant set of gold-colored cuff links, a tie clasp, and a collar pin.

"They're real gold," Charlene blurted out. Moments earlier in light of Jack's uneasiness she had decided that she would avoid pointing out this particular attribute of her present, but then she thought to herself: *what better way to tell this man how crazy I am about him than to make sure he knows I picked out solid gold jewelry for him, even thought we just met?*

Jack's mouth dropped open.

"Charlene…" His voice trailed off.

Charlene stepped forward and placed her arms around his neck, standing on her tip-toes to bring her mouth roughly to the same height where Jack's was. She stepped in but paused a few hairs away from bringing her lips to his.

"You're the most special man in the world to me, and I wanted to give you the most special gift I could think of for Christmas," she murmured, a sad smile coming to her lips as she spoke.

❄ ❄ ❄

All the while Jonathan Coleman was walking home from Francine Donner's house, he felt that for the first time since his return home all was right with the world. He had done much the same thing that his sister had – gone to Francine's for yet another Christmas feast only hours after stuffing himself on his mother's cooking – and had spent the next couple of hours with Francine's family. Jack and Sally Donner had bought their future son-in-law a small Christmas present – a pen and pencil set, with both writing instruments engraved with Jonathan's full name – and fortunately Jonathan had come to the Donner home prepared. He presented Jack Donner with a brand new Ben Wade pipe, and Sally Donner with a sewing and mending kit from Kaufmann's that Francine had indicated her mother had had her eye on for years.

The evening at the Donners' was a peaceful one, with both of Francine's parents doing their best to make Jonathan feel as if he was already part of the family. Jonathan had spent enough hours at their house during the past week since arriving back in Pittsburgh, but most of that time had been devoted to finalizing plans for the wedding and reception. Tonight, however, was simply a night for relaxing and enjoying the glorious peace of the first Christmas after the end of the war.

Tomorrow, however, would be a very different day for Jonathan Coleman.

7 – Wednesday, December 26, 1945

"It's for you," Joseph Coleman held the telephone towards his older brother. "Francine," Joseph added, though Jonathan knew with all the certainty in the world who was telephoning him at 8:30 this morning.

Jonathan got up from the breakfast table and walked out to where Joseph had risen a moment earlier to answer the ringing telephone.

"Hello?"

"Jonathan, it's me!"

"Hi Francine…" was all Jonathan was able to say before Francine excitedly interrupted him.

"Did you see the *Post-Gazette* this morning?"

"Um…yeah," Jonathan replied, his mind immediately recalling what he could of this morning's newspaper and trying to determine what it might be that Francine was so excited about.

"Isn't that news wonderful?" If anything, the excitement level in Francine's voice was growing with every statement she made.

"What news? You mean about the draft and the additional discharges?" A front-page story related how, with the war now over, only single men would be subject to the draft as well as noting that discharges from the military would soon be coming at even a faster rate than the frantic pace since shortly after V-J Day.

"Not that! About the houses!" Francine's voice now carried a touch of irritation that Jonathan apparently wasn't on the same wavelength with her.

Jonathan sighed. There had been something on the front page about…

"All of the new houses next year are being set aside for veterans! It was the headline story; I have it right here: 'VETS TO GET ALL NEW '46 HOMES.' And they're going to be building lots of them!"

"Francine…"

Francine continued as if she hadn't even heard Jonathan begin to speak.

"The article says that more veterans will be looking for houses in '46 than the number of houses that will be available, so maybe there will be a list or something for you to sign up…"

"Francine…" Jonathan's voice was louder and more insistent this time, but still to no avail.

"…and maybe we can get one of the first ones and not have to wait as long…"

"Francine!" This time, Jonathan actually yelled her name, finally derailing Francine's excited narration.

"Francine," Jonathan continued, his voice's tone switching from angry to frustrated, "I don't think buying a house is a good idea right now, even if I could afford it…which I don't think I can."

Jonathan paused for a split second, wondering if he should relate the highlights of his Christmas Eve conversation with Stan Walker to Francine. He decided that he would, hoping that Francine would give some weight to the words of someone who wasn't Jonathan himself, nor someone from his immediate family.

"I was talking with my Uncle Stan about houses and jobs and college and everything, and he really think that the best thing for me – for us – right now is for me..."

"Let me guess," Francine interrupted angrily. "He thinks you should go to college like your mother says you should and...

Now it was Jonathan's turn to angrily interrupt once again.

"This has nothing to do with my mother," he said through clenched teeth, lowering the volume of his voice because of his entire family – including Irene Coleman – gathered around the kitchen table barely twenty feet away on the other side of the wall. He walked as far into the Coleman living room as the telephone cord would allow him to do, wishing that the Colemans somehow had another phone in the house, in a different room, where he could be afforded some privacy.

"This is about what's best for you and me in the long run," he continued, raising the volume in his voice slightly but with his words still dripping with barely controlled fury. "If I go to college now so I can get a really good job in a couple of years, we will be able to buy a really nice house then..."

The interruptions continued.

"There are plenty of jobs!" Francine protested.

"No there are not!" Jonathan countered. "Take a look in the 'Male Help Wanted' section and you'll see that most of the jobs are for mechanics and draftsmen, which I don't know how to do, or otherwise they're for dishwashers and night watchmen."

"Well how about all of this house building?" Francine suggested. "You could get a job building houses."

"Francine, I don't know anything about building houses!" Jonathan's exasperation was in high gear now.

"Well what about…"

Finally, Jonathan exploded.

"Damn it, Francine! You think that I can just go downtown and walk in someplace and then come out with a job as…I don't know, a bank manager! Hell, about all I'm qualified to do right now is work behind the soda fountain at Grant's 5 & 10! Or maybe go back to *Weisberg's* and get up at 3:30 every morning to lug produce boxes! I'm trying to do what's best for us in the long run! Why the hell can't you see that?"

"Don't you curse at me, Jonathan Coleman!" Francine's voice was now every bit as angry as Jonathan's. "I'm not one of your Air Corps sergeants that you can order around because you're an officer and then have to do everything you say!"

Realizing that he had crossed the line with his curse words, Jonathan attempted to mollify the situation.

"Look, Francine; I'm sorry I cursed. But I've been doing a lot of thinking about all of this and I'm trying to do what's best for us, like I said. How about all the way down to Florida on the train, and then during the honeymoon, we sit down together and talk this over…"

One final interruption.

"Maybe there won't be any honeymoon!" Francine Donner snapped as she slammed down the telephone, abruptly and furiously hanging up on Jonathan Coleman.

❄ ❄ ❄

There would be no hiding what had just transpired as Jonathan slowly shuffled back into the kitchen. All eyes were on him. Even though he had tried to keep his voice low, and even though only his half of the telephone conversation could be heard, everyone – even little Ruthie – knew that he and Francine had just had a terrible fight, as well as what that fight was about.

Sighing, he plopped himself into his chair, staring morosely at the cooling cup of coffee in front of him. His eyes glanced over at the pack of Chesterfields sitting between his coffee cup and Joseph's, but to Jonathan the very act of reaching for a cigarette at this very moment felt like far too monumental of a task.

"Come on, let's take a walk down to my shop," Gerald Coleman said to his eldest son as he rose stiffly from his own chair, crushing out his cigarette into the ashtray as he did. Jonathan didn't budge, though, and after about ten seconds Gerald walked over and placed his left hand gently but firmly on Jonathan's right shoulder. Jonathan looked up at his father, Gerald's earlier declaration finally sinking in, and with another deep, mournful sigh he finally stood.

The entire walk to Gerald's shop was a silent one, with both father and son lost in their respective thoughts as well as fighting off the bitter December morning cold. Once inside the shop Gerald and Jonathan shed their coats and gloves and each immediately lit a Chesterfield, hoping the warmth of the inhaled cigarette smoke would radiate through their bodies.

Jonathan half-expected his father to begin working on one of his backlogged projects and then ease into conversation with his son, but instead Gerald immediately asked Jonathan, even as he was lowering himself onto his workbench:

"So what were you and Francine fighting about?"

Jonathan let out a deep breath. He knew his father had a pretty good idea about what the problem was, if not of all the specifics. Rather than start at the beginning, Jonathan decided to start at the end.

"When she hung up on me, she said something about 'Maybe there's not going to be a honeymoon.'"

Gerald raised his eyebrows slightly, then looked at Jonathan.

"She was just saying that because she's mad. I'm sure she doesn't mean that."

"I don't know, Pop. It's more than her just saying that. It feels like we're…I don't know…"

Gerald waited a few seconds for Jonathan to articulate what it was he was trying to say, but when no other words followed he offered his own thoughts.

"You were away for so long, and you've only been back for a week. You both are getting used to each other again, and have so much…"

"It's more than that, Pop," Jonathan interrupted. "Francine is so…I mean, the only thing she talks about is buying a house right after we get married, and me getting a job right away, but the jobs that are out there right now…"

Jonathan sighed before continuing.

"You know the other night, on Christmas Eve, when we went out to Fox Chapel to get Tommy?"

"Uh-huh," Gerald nodded.

"Well, I drove with Uncle Stan on the way back, and we were talking about jobs and college and houses and all that."

Jonathan proceeded to give his father a summary of what he had discussed with his uncle, along with what Stan Walker had urged Jonathan to do. Gerald listened patiently to his son's narration of the Christmas Eve discussion with his brother-in-law.

"Well," Gerald finally said after Jonathan had finished, "I think Stan is right about this. But you also need to keep your wife happy; that's what marriage is all about. Sometimes she has to get things that she wants even if you think differently."

"I know that, Pop," Jonathan said, casting his eyes downward, his shoulders slumping. "But the way Uncle Stan talks, this isn't a small decision like what kind of lamps to buy for the living room, or deciding between a Philco or Emerson for what kind of radio to get. He thinks that going to college now means a better life for Francine and me, a better house for her later on…all of that."

"I know," Gerald nodded. "And I agree, but Francine is a woman and she's not thinking about things like that. She waited for you for three years and she wants to get your life together started now, not in three or four more years."

"Yeah, but what about what Uncle Stan says about jobs and all that? It's not like I could go get a war plant job that pays really good. All those plants are shutting down or cutting way back now that the war is over; the stories are in the newspaper and on the radio every day. And the way Uncle Stan tells it, it's gonna be sort of like the Depression; maybe not as bad, but not real good, either."

Gerald crushed out the remnants of his Chesterfield and reached for his trusty old Army & Navy brand pipe that he kept in his office. His brand new Christmas present pipe – still unsmoked – was back at the house. He began slowly, contemplatively packing tobacco into the pipe.

"I just don't know," Gerald finally responded. "I'm sure that like Stan says, that with all of you boys coming home and the war plants shutting or scaling down, that it will be tough to find jobs for a little while. Maybe he's right, that after a couple of years everything is going to be really good, and using the time until then to go to college is the smart thing to do. So maybe that is what you should do."

"Yeah, but what about what you just said before? About doing things to keep my wife happy? You know, 'that's what marriage is all about' and all that?"

Gerald slowly, sadly shook his head.

"I know," he replied. "And sometimes in a marriage you feel like no matter what you decide to do, it's the wrong decision for one reason or another. But the good thing is that almost all the time, even if she gets mad at you or you're mad at her, it all settles down sooner or later."

Jonathan absorbed his father's words as he reached for another cigarette.

"Yeah, but what about what Francine said right before she hung up? That part about maybe there won't be any honeymoon?"

Gerald shook his head again.

"She was just mad; I'm sure she didn't mean that."

❄ ❄ ❄

Francine Donner had indeed meant exactly what she said.

"I don't want to get married anymore," she tearfully proclaimed to her mother. "He doesn't care at all about what I want…"

Francine went on for a good thirty seconds with a recitation of Jonathan Coleman's heartlessness and uncaring nature. Sally Donner listened to her daughter without interrupting. Finally, Francine ran out of steam as a fresh batch of tears sprung forth.

"You don't really mean that about not wanting to get married," she finally said. Jack Donner was already off at work, meaning mother and daughter were alone in the Donner house this morning, sitting at the kitchen table.

"You also don't really mean any of what you just said about Jonathan," she added. "About not wanting to get married…"

"Yes I do!" Francine retorted. "He's so different now since he's home…"

"Francine, that's not true at all!" Sally Donner interrupted. "How could he possibly be different if you haven't seen him in more than three years?"

"But we wrote all those letters back and forth about what we would do after the war when he came home and we got married. I wrote to him over and over about us buying a nice little house and what it would be like…"

"And I'm sure you will," Sally Donner interrupted, trying her best to inject soothing tones into her voice. "Maybe not right away, but I'm sure you will. Maybe Jonathan is right about taking advantage of that government money to go to college so he will make a good living for you and him and your children."

Sally reached for the pack of Pall Malls sitting in the middle of the kitchen table.

"You honestly don't think he's telling you that just because he doesn't want you to have a house and doesn't want to go get a job, do you?"

Sally's pause demanded a response from her daughter, but none was immediately forthcoming.

"Do you?" she repeated.

"I don't know," Francine muttered, reaching for her own Pall Mall right after her mother laid the pack back onto the kitchen table.

"Francine?" Sally Donner would not let this one slide by. She loved her daughter with all her heart, but over the years Francine had often displayed the tendencies of a spoiled child…which she most certainly had not been, at least in the Donner household. Francine would often pout when she didn't get her way about something, especially when it came to her boyfriends over the years. With Donnie Yablonski, Francine had been especially keen on getting her own way about everything from which movie they would go see to which drugstore's counter they would visit for ice cream sodas. Sally Donner often wondered – though she of course never shared this particular musing with her daughter – if the manner in which Donnie had taken advantage of Francine shortly before leaving for basic training was a revenge of sorts for

Francine's demanding nature while the two of them had dated.

Jonathan Coleman had tamed much of that demanding nature when the two of them began dating. Whereas Donnie had been meekly compliant, apparently willing to go along with Francine's demands in exchange for dating such an attractive and popular girl, Jonathan had been far more forceful with her. Not in an unpleasant way, of course; but he seemed immune to Francine's pouting and temper, and over time Francine seemed to grow to appreciate the occasional assertion of Jonathan's self-assured nature into their relationship.

Perhaps, Sally Donner thought to herself, that Jonathan's three-year absence had brought about the unfortunate consequence of allowing the tiny remains of Francine's spoiled nature to take root and once again flourish. Sally only had her daughter's side of the story, but even taking Francine's slanted perspective into account, Jonathan didn't seem unreasonable in what he was proposing.

If only the two of them hadn't rushed into setting a wedding date so soon after Jonathan's return! Even if they had decided to wait a few months, the same pressures would still be facing the two of them: where to live, job versus college, all of that. But at least they wouldn't have this furious deadline of a wedding date only three days from now hanging over their heads while they sorted out all of this business.

"So you think Francine is really gonna call off the wedding?"

Joseph and Thomas Coleman were walking down Herron Avenue to Slovatski's Market to grab a couple of sandwiches for lunch. The temperature had climbed above the freezing mark and the winter Pittsburgh skies were not only cloudless today but also somewhat free of the pervasive layer of industrial soot that always seemed to be hanging over the city. As a result, this day after Christmas, as this incredible year of 1945 wound down, felt almost spring-like to the Coleman brothers...almost. They still would have rather been driving their father's Packard rather than walking even this easy half mile, but as Jonathan had predicted in that Fox Chapel bar on Christmas Eve, Thomas' driving days were indeed over for a while; at least until he got his driver's license and got out of the doghouse with his father.

Joseph looked over at his younger brother.

"Nah," he answered Tommy's question, then added: "At least I don't think so. Not with only three days left."

"I don't know," Thomas wasn't as certain as his brother seemed to be. "I could hear her yelling at Jonathan through the phone and we were all the way in the kitchen. She seems dead-set on having Jonathan get a job and buy them a house."

Joseph shrugged.

"It's not just the house and Jonathan getting a job," Joseph countered, contemplating his brother's statement even as he was replying. "I sorta understand how she feels. She's waited all this time for Jonathan to get back. They're both twenty-three now and if the war hadn't happened and they had gotten married a couple years ago, she would probably have at least one kid by now; probably two."

Joseph looked over at his brother as they crossed the street.

"I'm not taking her side or anything," he continued. "I'm just trying to understand why she is so mad at Jonathan and why she's so stubborn about this."

Joseph paused for a second, wondering if he should continue with what had just come to his mind. Aw, the hell with it, he thought.

"If Abby were still around and I just came back – you know, if she had waited for me for three years – I would expect her to do the same thing. You know, want us to buy a house right away and start a family and all that. Me goin' to college wouldn't be all that important to her."

"I guess," Thomas shrugged.

"Jonathan understands her also," Joseph added. "If there were a whole lot of good jobs available right now, like right after the Depression was over and then during the war with all of the war plants and everything, I think he would go right out and get a job and buy a house and everything. That's what he was planning to do anyway. But after listening to Marty and Uncle Stan, I think he's changed his mind and is thinking of things down the road for them."

"So why won't Francine do the same thing? Change her mind?" Thomas asked.

Joseph shrugged.

"Who knows," was his response to his younger brother's question. "Girls think differently than we do. And once they're out of high school, they think even more differently, if that's possible. Now that you're home to stay you'll find that out soon enough."

"Yeah, I guess," Thomas replied before turning the conversation back to their older brother's predicament.

"I hope Jonathan and Francine get over this fight pretty soon," Thomas said. "There isn't a lot of time left, and the closer it gets to Saturday, if they're still fighting, I don't know what's gonna happen."

Joseph nodded as he simply said:

"Yep."

❄ ❄ ❄

"Let's let them settle this," Gerald Coleman said to his wife.

"Someone needs to talk to her," Irene stubbornly insisted. "And him, too. I can't believe three days before their wedding they are fighting like this, and she's saying things to him like 'maybe there won't be a honeymoon.'"

Irene looked over at her husband across the kitchen table.

"I think Sally Donner and I should sit down with the two of them, or maybe just Francine, and tell them to postpone the wedding until springtime like they should have done in the first place. This way…"

Gerald Coleman only rarely interrupted his wife mid-sentence, but this was one of those rare occasions.

"Let's let them settle this," he said again, this time more forcefully than a moment earlier.

"Maybe they won't be able to," Irene Coleman fretted. "And then the whole wedding will be called off!"

Gerald shrugged.

"If that happens, then that's what was meant to be," he said in even tones. Then he looked piercingly at his wife.

"Isn't that what you would want to happen anyway?" he challenged.

Irene felt herself redden with anger.

"That is *not* what I want to happen!"

Gerald maintained his steely-eyed gaze.

"Well, maybe before," Irene muttered in response to her husband's demanding look, "but not now. I *would* be happier if they postponed the wedding until springtime so they can get all of this sorted out. We could tell everybody…"

A second interruption from Gerald, so soon after his previous one, signified that this was not a normal discourse and he was most certainly putting his foot down.

"We will stay out of this," he said in even, commanding tones. "I'm sure they will work things out but if they don't, then that's how it was meant to be."

❄ ❄ ❄

In the end, it was Jack Donner who saved the day, so to speak; with a little help from Francine's sister Julia.

He arrived home from work at 4:30 that afternoon and was greeted by his worried-looking wife. Sally Donner told her husband all that had transpired since this morning. Jack absorbed the entire tale and walked upstairs to his daughter's bedroom, where Francine had sequestered herself since early that afternoon.

He knocked lightly on the closed door and upon hearing a muffled "come in" he turned the doorknob, eased the door open, and walked inside. Francine was sitting on the side of her bed, morosely staring downwards. Jack Donner reached for the small wooden chair from Francine's dressing table, pulled it over until it was a couple of feet away from Francine's bed, and sat down in front of her.

"Tell me what is going on," were his gentle but firm words.

"Nothing," Francine instinctively responded, realizing even as that single word was escaping from her lips it was the wrong response.

"'Nothing?' Your mother tells me that you might not want to get married now, and your answer is 'nothing'?"

Francine rolled her eyes and let out a deep sigh.

"Okay, not 'nothing' but I don't want to talk about it, okay?"

Jack Donner blew out a breath.

"Well, we *will* talk about it since you're the one who brought this up to your mother in the first place."

Francine's eyes narrowed.

"Fine," she retorted, more tersely than she normally would dare to address her father. Francine proceeded to give her father an even more abbreviated version of her stalemate with her fiancé than she had related earlier to her mother. Jack Donner listened to his daughter's recitation without comment. When she finished he nodded a couple of times and appeared to be mulling over what he had just heard.

"So this is all about whether Jonathan should get a job right away or take the government money and go to college," he finally said.

"No it isn't!" Francine retorted. "It's about him not wanting to buy a house like we had talked about, so we can start our life together!"

Jack Donner shook his head.

"No," he said, rebutting his daughter's assertion. "Jonathan can only buy a house if he goes and gets a job – a good job – right away. But if he uses his G.I. Bill to go to college, then he doesn't get a job and therefore won't be able to buy a house."

"Fine, Pop," Francine responded in exasperated tones. "If you want to put it that way…sure."

"Okay," Jack Donner nodded. "Now we're getting somewhere."

He rocked his chair backwards for a second and then brought it forward once again before continuing.

"And you don't think it's important for Jonathan to go to college for free now, so the two of you can have a better life for years to come?"

Jack Donner could tell that he had hit a nerve by the way Francine lowered her eyes and refused to look directly at him as she reluctantly answered.

"Well…maybe," she hesitated. "But we've waited so long while he was away, and we lost a whole year before we get engaged. If we have to wait three or four more years, we'll both be twenty-seven years old! I want us to get a house *now* and start a family!"

"I'm sure you do," Francine's father said soothingly. "But let me tell you what would probably happen if Jonathan did things your way."

Fire shot into Francine's eyes when her father used the phrase "did things your way" but she decided to let the words go unchallenged.

"There aren't a lot of jobs to go around now and it's going to get even rougher…"

"Why does everyone keep saying that?" Francine interrupted. "Everyone talks like we're still in the Depression, or that it's about to start again. You did just fine supporting us through the Depression and during the war, and you didn't go to college!"

"Francine," Jack Donner sighed. "You don't realize it, and I'm not even sure that Jonathan fully realizes it, but he's trying to give you a better life - an easier life – than your mother and I had, or that his mother and father had. I'm sure he doesn't look forward to the idea of going back to school for four more years and doing all of that book work…"

Francine interrupted her father once again, her mind still mulling over the first part of what he had just said.

"What do you mean a better life than you and Ma? We always had food on the table, and you were never out of work, even during the Depression."

"That's true," Jack Donner admitted. "But you were a little girl, and you weren't aware that every single month since your mother and I got married we would wonder if the money I made would last for the entire month. It wasn't until the past couple of years during the war that things got a little bit better with the money, but even then with the wartime wage controls in place we couldn't get even a couple cents an hour raise. I was fortunate enough to put away enough for your wedding, but..."

Jack Donner paused and for a second Francine thought her father was about to begin sobbing. Finally, he continued in subdued tones.

"You know that I always wanted a special wedding day for you with a fancy reception at Webster Hall after the ceremony, but we just can't afford it. The best your mother and I can do is the banquet in the basement at Saint Michael's. I know it's difficult for you to look so far ahead but what Jonathan is trying to do is make sure that when your daughter gets married someday you can give her a fancier wedding than your mother and I are able to do for you. Or that you and Jonathan can take summer vacations with your children like your mother and I were never able to afford to do with you and Julia and Albert."

Jack Donner had been looking away from Francine as he talked, as if ashamed to admit that he hadn't been able to give his wife and children all that he would have liked to. Now, though, he looked back at his daughter.

"Francine, I can't tell you to get married this Saturday if you really don't want to. But I can tell you that you will be making a terrible mistake if you call off the wedding. You know that for a while I didn't much care for Jonathan, and you know the reason for that."

He paused and peered hard at Francine, who shamefully dropped her eyes in response to what her father had said. For nearly a year after her drunken dalliance with Donnie Yablonski she had let her father believe that the reason for her abrupt breakup with

Jonathan was something that Jonathan had done. Not until the following Thanksgiving when she reunited with Jonathan did Francine's mother spill the beans to Jack Donner about Francine being at fault for the breakup, not Jonathan. Until then, though, Francine's father had blamed the Coleman boy for…well, for something he had done, whatever it might have been, that had hurt his little girl.

"I can't think of a better husband for you than him," Jack continued. "I'm sure he survived all kinds of things during the war that he doesn't want to talk about, but he also grew to be a fine young man, too. He's been over here nearly every day since he came home and it's easy to see that he would do anything in the world for you, including going to college with all of that hard studying and everything, so you can have a good life."

Jack Donner rose from the wooden chair, carried it back to Francine's dressing table, and turned to face his daughter one more time.

"You need to tell Jonathan – and your mother and me – what you are going to do…very soon."

❄ ❄ ❄

Francine wanted desperately to make up with Jonathan this very evening. The only thing holding her back was the faintest hope that if she held out long enough, Jonathan would come around to her way of thinking about a job and a house rather than college and a small apartment near Pitt. Maybe he would be so afraid that Francine would call off the wedding that he would drop this idea of college that Francine still thought was so silly, despite what her father had just told her.

After supper, Francine went over to her sister Julia's house, about ten minutes away, to talk over this whole predicament. Surely her sister would turn out to be the one sympathetic ear she had been seeking all day. Julia's husband Phil was down at Leo's grabbing a couple of beers, and Julia was home alone with her daughter Stella.

"Phil is worried about getting laid off," was the first thing Julia blurted out as soon as she and Francine settled around the kitchen table and lit cigarettes. This was news to Francine; nothing had been mentioned about any possible job loss yesterday when the Donner family had gathered for Christmas supper.

"He just got word today," Julia explained. Her husband worked at a Westinghouse plant on the outskirts of the city that made gyroscopes for tank guns. With the end of the war, rumors had been swirling for months that cutbacks and layoffs were in the wind, though the plant's management insisted that the facility would be converted to civilian production and the workforce would be unaffected. Now, only one day after Christmas, the official word had changed: civilian production was indeed in the plant's future, but with a reduced workforce manning the plant.

"If that happens, I don't know where he's going to find work," Francine's sister continued as she kept an eye on Stella in her high chair. "It would be different if he had a college degree and knew how to do something other than work on an assembly line…"

By the time she left her sister's house shortly before 9:00 that night, Francine's perspective about her future with Jonathan had changed. She didn't intend to apologize to Jonathan for her outburst this morning; after all, she wanted him to realize that she was giving in and postponing for several years her dreams of what their life would be like. Still, she now reluctantly agreed with Jonathan, his Uncle Stan, Irene Coleman, her own father, her sister – it seemed like everyone else in the world other than Francine – that four years at Pitt, courtesy of Uncle Sam, was indeed the best course of action for the future Mister and Mrs. Jonathan Coleman.

Still, she would wait until tomorrow morning to talk with Jonathan for that last hope that he would still change his mind about college for fear of her calling off the wedding, despite all evidence to the contrary. Francine went back home and shortly after walking into the Donner living room, the telephone rang. Sally Donner answered it and a few seconds later held out the handset and said:

"Francine, it's for you."

8 – Thursday, December 27, 1945

Francine's phone call to Jonathan came shortly after 7:00 this Thursday morning. Jonathan was already awake after a mostly sleepless night. Several times throughout the night he felt like either calling Francine or even going over to her house. His frantic desire to resolve this terrible schism with Francine was trumped by his fear of how Sally and Jack Donner would react in the face of a midnight phone call or a 2:00 A.M. visit by Jonathan, so he suffered through the night.

Even as he was reaching for the telephone while the bell continued to clang, Jonathan told himself to remain calm and – if at all possible – stand his ground with Francine. Just like flying into combat, he told himself; there might be a fierce battle ahead but courage and steadfastness was called for.

"Can we meet for coffee? You know, where we can talk privately?" Francine asked after they exchanged hesitant hellos.

"Sure," Jonathan said, extrapolating from the manner in which Francine's request was worded that perhaps she had finally come around to his way of thinking. He briefly thought about pressing for a clue or two over the phone, but then thought better of the idea. Let's see what she has to say, he told himself as they agreed to meet at Slovatski's in about a half-hour.

During the ten-minute walk to the market, Jonathan fought off the morning's frigid air by rehearsing his conversation with Francine over and over, trying to envision every possible twist and turn the discussion might take. He reminded himself to keep his cool, even if

Francine blurted out any unfounded, nastily worded accusations.

In the end, Jonathan's rehearsals were for naught. Francine told him that despite what she so fervently wanted, and what she insisted the two of them had agreed to during hundreds of letters written back and forth during the war, that she was willing to be patient and be supportive of Jonathan's newfound desire to use the government money to go to college. She made sure to relate what her father and sister had told her so Jonathan would be aware that she wasn't simply bending to his will because he would soon be her husband. This coming Saturday Francine might be promising to love, honor, and obey Jonathan for the rest of their lives, but she wanted him to know that the last one of those promises didn't necessarily mean absolute blind obedience of his every wish and whim.

In response, Jonathan promised that if the opportunity presented itself a year or two down the road to somehow buy a house anyway – maybe by taking on a part-time night job once he got accustomed to the demands of college academics – that he would do everything in his power to accelerate the timeline and get them into a house sooner than three or four years down the road.

Détente is often a fragile exercise in diplomacy, with neither side fully getting what it wants yet somehow finding enough common ground to put aside differences – often strong differences – and forge ahead. And that is exactly what transpired this Thursday morning at a table in a dark Polish Hill market: détente, not surrender.

With this matter finally – hopefully – behind them, Francine looked at Jonathan and said:

"There's something else I need to tell you about. I got a phone call last night right when I got home from my sister's house..."

❄ ❄ ❄

Getting discharged from the Marine Corps was almost as trying of an exercise as arriving at Parris Island...without the abusive yelling of fearsome drill instructors, of course. A discharge physical instead of an arrival physical; turning in gear instead of being issued gear; signing as many, perhaps even more, government documents; and, of course, shuffling from one line to another for hours on end...

But by 11:00 that morning, five hours after arriving as ordered at 6:00 AM sharp, both Jack Leonard and Thomas Coleman were no longer active duty Marines. They would always be Marines, as Jack had reminded Tommy on Christmas Eve at Lou's, but their days in uniform were apparently over forever.

"Come on, let's go get lunch and I'll buy you a beer; out at that bar in Fox Chapel," Jack Leonard said as they walked out of the Marine Corps station on Forbes Street in the city's Oakland section, not far from the University of Pittsburgh.

"Yeah?" Tommy was surprised; he figured that Jack would want to find Charlene as soon as possible, given how few days they had left together until she headed back to Hollywood.

"Yeah," Jack responded, heading towards his car parked a few buildings down the block from the Marine

Corps station. "One Marine to another; let's celebrate our first hour or two of being civilians again."

"Sounds good to me," Tommy said, grateful that this older staff sergeant who had survived Guadalcanal, Tarawa, Saipan, and Tinian was going out of his way to buffer Thomas Coleman's abrupt, unexpected – and not entirely welcome – departure from the United States Marine Corps.

❄ ❄ ❄

The clock had ticked just past noon when Jonathan finally located Joseph, who earlier had grabbed a streetcar headed towards downtown just after Jonathan left to meet Francine. Joseph didn't have any particular reason to head downtown; he was just feeling claustrophobic in the house and felt like enjoying the chilly air and the bustle along Wood Street and Fifth Avenue and Liberty Avenue. Besides, after yet another troubled night's sleep filled with horrific dreams of Nazi prison camps, Joseph felt an overpowering desire to get away from the house, at least for a little while.

Finally, around 11:30 he decided to head back home and see if Jonathan was back from his tête-à-tête with Francine, and if Tommy had finished up with his discharge. Maybe the three of them could go see a movie this afternoon. He walked from the streetcar stop to the house, and as soon as he stepped inside he saw Jonathan sitting in the living room, listening to the Philco with a pensive look on his face. Joseph immediately assumed that the conversation with Francine hadn't gone well at all, and perhaps the worse had indeed happened and the wedding was called off.

"How'd it go with Francine?" Joseph asked hesitatingly.

"Good," Jonathan quickly replied. "Pretty good. I don't think she's too happy but I guess her father talked to her last night, and also her sister, and everyone is telling her that the smart thing to do is for me to go to college so I can get a better job later on...you know the whole story."

"So the wedding is on?"

"Yeah," Jonathan nodded. "I don't think Francine was serious about calling it off. I mean, she never exactly said that; it was more that thing about maybe there wouldn't be a honeymoon, or whatever it was that she said."

Joseph could tell that his brother was now downplaying what Francine had yelled at him a day earlier, as if he wanted to sweep all of that unpleasantness under the rug so nobody in the Coleman family would be upset with her...especially with the wedding only two days away now. Joseph was fine with that; his own displeasure with Francine had been laid to rest years earlier and he saw no merit in resurrecting any new hard feelings towards her.

"There's something else," Jonathan said, looking at his brother as he rose from the chair next to the Philco. *It's Been a Long, Long Time* began to play at that very second.

"Yeah?"

"Francine told me that last night, Abby called her."

❄ ❄ ❄

"Well if it isn't our Marine friend from Polish Hill," Lou the owner and bartender said when he saw Tommy walk through the door of the bar. "Getting to be a regular out here, huh?"

Noticing that the other guy accompanying Tommy wasn't Marty Walker, Lou asked:

"Where's your cousin?"

Tommy shrugged.

"At home, I guess. I didn't stop by…I mean…"

Tommy began stammering, nervous that without Marty present Lou would kick him out of the bar.

"We both just got discharged from the Marines today," Jack stepped into the conversation, "so I brought Tommy out here to celebrate. Just the two of us Marines, not his cousin who could only get into the Navy, you know?"

Jack's tone contained enough levity that Lou knew this other guy was only joking about Marty's naval service "shortcomings."

"Yeah, okay," Lou said. "You guys made us proud."

The bartender looked at Tommy.

"You too, like I said before. You were as ready to go fight on those islands as the rest of the Marines."

Lou recognized this other fellow accompanying Tommy Coleman from Christmas Eve, but realized that he didn't really know anything about him.

"So what about you? You fight on those islands?"

Jack hesitated for a moment before answering.

"Yeah," was his single-word response.

Instantly recognizing that Jack Leonard wasn't particularly inclined to go into any details about what he had done – what he had endured – during the war, the bartender let the questioning drop away.

"I'm buying lunch and a coupl'a beers for the two of yins," Lou pronounced. "Like I said, you boys done us proud."

"Thanks a lot," Jack said, with his gratitude echoed by Tommy a split second later.

They ordered burgers and fries right after Lou laid down a couple of Fort Pitts in front of them. As soon as Lou left Jack raised his glass towards Tommy, who did likewise.

"Semper Fidelius," Jack offered as a toast, using the complete phrase of the Marine Corps' motto rather than the more common shortened version.

"Semper Fidelius," Tommy repeated.

Silence followed as both Jack Leonard and Tommy Coleman stared at their beer glasses after taking their first swigs. Finally, after close to a minute, Jack Leonard said, still gazing forward:

"I think it just hit me this second that it's really all over."

❄ ❄ ❄

"She's not engaged any more," Jonathan said to his brother. "Abby told Francine she broke off the engagement in late August, I think, but she went to go visit her cousin or something out in Cincinnati."

"Did Francine say why?" Joseph asked.

Jonathan shook his head.

"I asked. I don't know if Abby didn't tell her, or if she did but Francine wouldn't tell me. All I know is that Abby got back in town last Saturday and just found out that Francine and I were getting married. So she called Francine…"

"Did Francine tell her anything about me?" Joseph interrupted.

"Yeah," Jonathan sighed. "Probably too much, it sounds like."

"Whaddya mean too much?"

"I dunno," Jonathan backtracked a little bit. "Abby knew you had been shot down and all that, so I guess…I dunno…"

Joseph's eyes narrowed.

"Did you say anything to Francine about…I dunno, what I said about me still being stuck on Abby? Or me thinking about her the whole time I was a prisoner?"

Jonathan's lack of an immediate response, along with his looking away from his brother, gave Joseph his answer. Before he could protest, Jonathan offered:

"That's not really bad, right? I mean, maybe if Francine told that to Abby she'll think that maybe she should try again with you…"

"You're joking, right?" Joseph's eyes widened as he considered what his brother had just said. "She was *engaged* to another guy, and she was gonna dump me with a Dear John letter while I was over in England; Tommy told me that's what Francine told him. Why the hell would I even think about getting back together with her?"

Jonathan just stared at his brother without answering the question. After nearly a minute of silence, Joseph shook his head and turned towards the door.

"I gotta get out of here," he muttered.

"You just got back," Jonathan eyed his brother.

"Yeah, I know, but after what you just told me…I just gotta get outside and walk around."

"How 'bout I come with you?" Jonathan said quickly.

Joseph shrugged.

"Sure," he answered noncommittally. Joseph didn't specifically want his brother's company, but he wasn't averse to it. The brothers both grabbed their flying jackets and gloves and headed outside. The forecast called for snow later in the day, but for now the weather outside was even slightly warmer than yesterday's when Joseph and Tommy had walked to Slovatski's Market for lunch. The thermometer had climbed close to forty degrees and this morning's *Post-Gazette* called for the temperature to cross that mark by two o'clock. They headed down Herron Avenue but instead of turning at Webster to stop at Slovatski's Market, Jonathan took the lead and they kept walking straight on Herron.

"I just realized something," Joseph said.

"What's that?"

"This is the longest I've walked in the winter since the Nazis marched us out of the Luftstalag the first time back in January."

Jonathan didn't know how to respond, so he remained silent.

"I swear," Joseph said somberly, looking over at his brother, "I thought I was gonna buy it that first day. All I could think of was the Bataan Death March and with the Krauts getting so close to losing the war, I thought they were going to kill us all. Especially when I got pulled for that work detail…"

Joseph shook his head and looked over at Jonathan.

"I keep having really bad nightmares," he blurted out. "About being a prisoner. Sometimes the tanks are coming back again but they're Panzers, not ours, and they start blasting us all. Last week right after I got home – that day Tommy and I went to Schenley – that night I dreamed that we were all there, at Schenley, and the Panzers were rolling right down Bigelow Boulevard to come kill us there."

Joseph paused.

"You know what? I just remembered that in that dream – the one where we were all at Schenley – that we were there for Abby's wedding. That's really strange, just finding out she's not engaged anymore…ya think?"

Jonathan shrugged.

"Yeah, I guess. But if your dreams are anything like mine, they're all jumbled up and after I wake up, if I can remember anything from them at all it's really strange and don't make any sense."

Joseph nodded.

"Yeah, mine too. I remember that Tommy Bonnaverte was there in that dream too, but that's probably because we had just been talking about him with Sadowski earlier."

Joseph paused for a second.

"Anyway, these nightmares are really getting to me; every night. I guess I'm sleeping – you know, because I'm dreaming – but it doesn't really feel like it. I'm always tired and it's getting to the point where I'm almost afraid to fall asleep."

"Why didn't you say anything about this last week when we were sitting at Leo's?"

Joseph shrugged.

"I dunno; I guess I was hoping the nightmares would go away after being home for a few days, but they're still there."

Joseph looked over at his brother.

"What do you think I can do?" To Jonathan, Joseph's voice as he asked that question sounded the same as it had before Joseph even entered high school: soft-pitched, high-toned, and hesitant.

"I don't know," Jonathan shook his head. "I guess you have to hope they go away after a while."

"Yeah, I guess," Joseph replied.

Ever since bringing up his nightmares, Joseph had simply been following his brother's lead in their trek, not paying attention to where they were headed. Suddenly aware of his surroundings, he realized that they were almost to the corner or Forbes and Atwood in the Oakland section.

"Where we going?" Joseph asked.

Jonathan paused a few beats before replying.

"I thought we'd go to Jack Canter's for roast beef sandwiches."

Joseph looked over at his brother, uncertain whether to be angry or laugh.

"You do that on purpose?" Joseph asked.

Jonathan shrugged.

"Yeah," he admitted. "That's a pretty good place to talk about Abby, right?"

❄ ❄ ❄

The last time either of the Coleman brothers had been at Jack Canter's delicatessen was during their brief Thanksgiving furlough back in '42. They had been sitting at the counter when Francine Donner and Abby Sobol walked in. That chance meeting had been the spark that had reunited Jonathan and Francine, and also the occasion that had launched Joseph's shooting star romance with Abby. Maybe Jonathan was right: what better place to contemplate this revelation of Abby Sobol no longer being engaged?

Jonathan and Joseph headed to the counter, grabbed a couple of seats, and each ordered a roast beef sandwich and a cup of coffee. Jonathan reached for a Chesterfield and handed it to his brother, then took one for himself. He flicked open his Zippo, lit Joseph's first then his own. If some force out there in the cosmos could have shown the brothers a movie from their visit to this same lunch counter back in November of '42, Jonathan's and Joseph's movements with the cigarettes and the Zippo this very moment would appear to be an intentional mimicking of their very same actions three years earlier.

"So what do you think?" Jonathan said after he took a deep drag of his cigarette.

"I dunno. What am I supposed to think? Sounds like she broke off her engagement, so that's that for whoever that 4-F guy was."

"Yeah, but what about you? You and her?"

Joseph's eyes narrowed.

"She was *engaged* to that guy," Joseph said tersely. "That means that she probably…you know…"

Jonathan shrugged.

"Maybe not," he said. "But even if she did, so what?"

Joseph's eyes widened.

"You're kidding, right?"

A sardonic smile appeared on Jonathan's lips, and Joseph immediately grasped the meaning.

"I know," Jonathan nodded. "I remember how I felt when I found out about Francine and Donnie. It took me almost a year to get over it – as much as I could anyway – and I almost didn't."

Jonathan paused to take a sip of his coffee.

"I don't like to think about that whole business; you know that. Especially with us getting married in two days. But you know what?"

"Huh?"

"I'll probably never totally forget about…it, but as time has passed since then I figure it was just one of those things. Even though it was right after the war started, it still was because of the war – you know, with Donnie shipping out."

"I don't follow you," Joseph scrunched his eyes as he took a sip of his coffee.

Jonathan sighed.

"You remember how Francine and I started talking right here at this counter and we decided to go see *Thunder Birds*, just like you and Abby?"

"Yeah," Joseph nodded. "How could I forget?"

"Well, before we went to see the movie I was talking with Pop," Jonathan said, looking away from his brother to stare reflectively at the cup of coffee in front of him. "I told him that I was real nervous about going out with Francine after…after what happened with Donnie, then me and her not even talking to each other for an entire year, other than that one bad argument we had before you and I left for Thunderbird. Pop started telling me about back when he was in the Great War…"

A shocked look came to Joseph's face at the mention of their father.

"Nah, nothing like that," Jonathan quickly changed course. "He wasn't married to Ma then, even though he was already courting her. Anyway, he started telling me about some other fellow in his unit who was engaged to a girl back home here in Pittsburgh. But when they were at Camp Grant for basic training Pop's friend found out she had been with another guy while they were at basic training. The guy broke off the engagement but Pop ran into him a couple years later, and the guy starts crying about how he should have forgiven her and married her anyway, because the woman he did marry wasn't very nice…something like that."

Jonathan paused to take another sip of coffee and light another Chesterfield.

"Pop was telling me that maybe I should forgive Francine and give her another chance. Well, not exactly telling me to do that; more like that I shouldn't automatically forget about the idea, that I should be open-minded, you know?"

Joseph nodded as he lit his another cigarette of his own.

"Anyway, Pop started telling me that once the war began – our war, not his – people probably started doing things they normally wouldn't do, especially with things going so bad out in the Pacific at the beginning. Almost like the end might be coming, so what the hell, right? He was saying that maybe with Francine and Donnie it was just one of those strange things that wouldn't have happened before the war, and maybe I shouldn't be so quick to write off things with Francine now that we were talking again and going to a movie together that night."

Jonathan sighed.

"Jeepers, I don't know why I'm talking about that business with her and Donnie two days before I'm getting married. I've spent four years trying to forget about it, but I guess…"

Jonathan looked over at his brother.

"Maybe things with Abby will wind up like that; you never know. Now that she's not engaged anymore, you and her will probably talk at the wedding and…"

Joseph interrupted:

"Yeah, but like I said before, if she was engaged to that guy, then she probably…you know…"

Jonathan shrugged.

"Well after you got to England, didn't you…you know, with any of those British girls? Or any of the WACs?"

Joseph blushed as he looked away.

"That's different," he muttered.

Jonathan let out a short, melancholy chuckle.

"When you said that I just remembered that when I was talking to Pop that day about Francine, he asked me if I had been with any girls out there in Arizona. You remember when a bunch of us went to that one…house where those girls were?"

"You told Pop about that?" Joseph asked incredulously.

Jonathan shrugged.

"Not exactly," he answered. "But it kinda slipped out. I told him that it was different with me because I was a man, plus Francine and I weren't engaged anymore. He said that maybe it wasn't all that different, and that's when he started telling me about his friend from the Great War and that whole business."

Jonathan paused while the waitress refilled his coffee first, and then Joseph's.

"Anyway," Jonathan continued, "it sounds like you had a few gals over in England before you were shot down. So like Pop said, things got all screwy with the war and everything. But the war's over now, and things will probably get back to normal with men and women and all that. So maybe if you and Abby have a good talk when you see her, you should at least take her out for coffee or a movie. Otherwise you might be like Pop's friend, looking back a couple years later and saying that you wish you had given her another chance."

"Ma?"

Irene Coleman looked up from the stove, where she had just checked on a potful of boiling potatoes for tonight's supper. The kitchen clock now showed a time of 4:45. Outside the late December day had already given way to darkness, helped along by the thick layer of soot in the air, courtesy of the area's many steel mills.

"Yes?" Irene asked Charlene, who had just been dropped off at home ten minutes earlier by Jack Leonard. Jack had taken Charlene to see a matinee at the Liberty Theater in the city's East Liberty section.

"Are you busy?"

Irene was about to reply with a detached "I'm making dinner" but the look on her daughter's face instantly told her that Charlene wanted to talk.

"I can talk" was instead Irene's response.

Only Ruthie was home, and she was upstairs in her room. Gerald would be home around five o'clock today, with the boys soon to follow. Tonight all three of the boys were going to the U.S.O. Canteen with Jack Leonard and Marty Walker…a sort of low-key, harmless bachelor's party for Jonathan. Where her sons were right at this moment, though, was something Irene didn't know; the feeling was an unsettling one…but one she knew she would have to get used to.

"What movie did you go see?" Irene asked Charlene as she put the cover back onto the pot. She started towards the kitchen table but then halted midstride. She took a couple of steps over to one of the kitchen drawers, opened it, and extracted a pack of Old Golds before resuming her original path.

"Funny you should ask that," Charlene replied as mother and daughter both sat down at the kitchen table. Irene offered Charlene a cigarette after taking one herself. One large wooden kitchen match was sufficient to light each of their cigarettes.

"We went to see *Fallen Angel* over at the Liberty Theater," Charlene continued. "Did you ever hear of it?"

Irene shook her head. She and Gerald didn't go to the movies much, and other than the movies her daughter appeared in, Irene wasn't very up to date with the popular films of the day...or for that matter, the popular actors and actresses beyond a couple dozen or so names such as Clark Gable, Jimmy Stewart, Gary Cooper, Bob Hope and Bing Crosby, Betty Grable...

As it happened, Irene's indifference towards the world of movies and plays had been one of the major points of controversy back in late 1942 when Charlene first was bitten by the show business bug. An offer to accompany Dorothy Lamour on a War Bond Tour? The name had meant nothing to Irene Coleman, nor did the opportunity itself.

"Alice Faye starred in it with Dana Andrews," Charlene continued, pausing to see if either name was recognized by her mother.

"I've heard of Dana Andrews," Irene nodded, "but not Alice...what was her name?"

"Alice Faye," Charlene repeated. "That's actually who I want to talk to you about."

Irene Coleman cocked her head, extremely puzzled where this conversation with her daughter was headed.

"I've met her – Alice – a few times," Charlene proceeded. "She is with Twentieth Century Fox but lots of actors and actresses from different studios know each other. Especially during the war with U.S.O. Tours and War Bond Tours."

"Uh-huh," Irene nodded, still somewhat perplexed, as she took a puff from her Old Gold.

"Please don't tell anybody what I'm going to tell you..."

"Who should I tell?" Irene interrupted. "Beatrice Leonard? Sally Donner? Your Aunt Lois? The movie magazines?"

Charlene chuckled.

"I'm not a gossip," Irene gently chided her daughter. "Especially about all of this show business."

"I know," Charlene replied, feeling a little chagrined at even raising that point with her mother.

"Anyway," she continued, "Alice was upset that the studio cut a lot of her scenes from this movie we just saw, and she just walked away after it was done. You know, quit show business altogether. I ran into her about a month ago and asked her if she was going to come back to the studio and she said no, that she was really enjoying just being a housewife and mother. Maybe she would do some radio later on, but she really didn't miss the movies at all."

Charlene paused as her mother started to get an inkling where her daughter was headed with this conversation.

"I'm a lot younger than her," Charlene added. "I think she's thirty."

Irene nodded as she decided that tiptoeing around the heart of the matter was not the best strategy for this late

December afternoon. Gerald and the boys would all be home soon and for the first time in years, Charlene was actually opening up to her mother about something important to her.

"And you're thinking the same thing about yourself? About you and Jack Leonard?" Irene came straight to the point.

"I don't know," Charlene sighed as she looked away from her mother. She crushed out the dwindling remains of her Old Gold and stared morosely at the ashtray for a few seconds, before looking back at Irene.

"I've only known Jack for a little more than a week," Charlene continued. "But when we're together all I can think about is being with him. And when we're not together, all I can think about is when I'll see him next. It's as if going to Hollywood and making movies and going on those U.S.O. and War Bond Tours was all just a dream."

Charlene took a deep breath.

"And what's worse is when I think about the movies and Hollywood, suddenly it's not that important to me anymore. It's almost as if I did it for the war effort and I went on tours to entertain all those G.I.'s, but now that the war is over something is…I don't even know how to say it, but it's as if everything is all of a sudden different now. Like the war is over and I was serving just like Jonathan and Joey did, but now it's time to get back to regular life."

Charlene's face had almost a pleading look as she gazed at her mother.

"Does that even make any sense?"

"It does," Irene nodded as she snuffed out her own cigarette. She reached for another one and offered the pack to Charlene, who declined this time around.

"Are you thinking now about quitting the movies?" Irene asked pointedly.

Charlene took almost five full seconds to answer her mother's question.

"I don't think so," she shrugged. "I don't know. I mean, ever since last weekend, and especially since Christmas, I keep asking myself 'What if I didn't have to go back to California?' Or 'What if Jack could come with me to Los Angeles?'"

After a few seconds of silence, Irene asked the one-word question: "Well?"

"I don't know, Ma," Charlene shook her head. "That's what I'm trying to tell you. Besides, it's not just Jack, either."

Charlene proceeded to finally confess to her mother what her nagging concerns now were with regards to her movie career via an abbreviated version of the tale; how perhaps her day in the sun as the "sweetly seductive girl next door for the servicemen to come home to" may be in the past now with the war's victorious conclusion.

"Maybe meeting Jack is…I don't know, some sort of a sign to me that I really am finished in the movies," Charlene pondered. "You know, something like one door opens while another one closes."

"Maybe," Irene shrugged. "I'm not sure, though."

"What would you do, Ma?" Charlene blurted out what was the most unthinkable question from about the time she had entered Schenley High School. For years now, her very soul was comprised at least in part by her stubborn refusal to seek out any such advice from her mother.

"You're asking me if I think you should quit show business and get married to Jack Leonard?" Irene stared hard at her daughter.

In response to that brutally blunt declaration, Charlene looked away once again.

"When you put it like that…" Charlene's voice trailed off.

During the next five seconds a thousand thought streams, a thousand more conjured still images, and dozens of short "Newsreel in the Mind" clips flew through Irene Coleman's mind as fast as lightning.

"No," Irene suddenly said, gazing intently at Charlene. "I don't think you should quit the movies."

Charlene, absolutely certain her mother would have seized the opportunity to make exactly the opposite declaration, was stunned into silence.

"Even though I don't necessarily understand the appeal of show business and life in Hollywood and all of that business, you've worked very hard. I will admit back when you first brought up that idea of going on the War Bond Tour with Dorothy Lamour I thought it was a silly idea, because I was worried about you traveling to New York and Washington and Philadelphia when you were just a high school girl. I was worried that Mister Gene Kelly had filled your mind with nonsense and fantasy dreams. And then when you left for Hollywood I thought there was no way anything but heartbreak would come your way."

Irene paused to take a final puff from the remains of her Old Gold before crushing it into the ashtray in the center of the kitchen table.

"But when you told us about your U.S.O. Tours way out there in the Pacific, and how Jack was in the hospital wounded on…which one of those islands?"

Knowing which one of Jack Leonard's battle wounds her mother was referring to, she responded with:

"Saipan."

"Saipan," Irene nodded. "When he was in the hospital at Saipan while you were there with Mister Bob Hope at the same time…well, I think all this Hollywood business is more than just making movies, or at least it has been. All during the war we would hear about all of the entertainers who went all over the world to perform for all of those poor boys who were doing the fighting. Back before you left, who was that actress; you know, Clark Gable's wife…"

"Carol Lombard," Charlene quickly answered.

"Uh-huh," Irene nodded again. "She was killed in that plane crash on a U.S.O. Tour, right?"

"War Bond rally," Charlene corrected her mother. "But I know what you mean; it was still for the war."

"And then Mister Glenn Miller's plane crashed," Irene continued. "And Mister Bob Hope must have entertained a million men himself. Because you were so insistent on going to Hollywood and joining the movies, you helped the war effort like your brothers did. Well, maybe not exactly the same, but you didn't stay home."

Irene couldn't quite get out what it was that she wanted to say, but she persevered.

"I think it's wonderful that you met a nice boy like Jack Leonard back here. I don't know if he is the right boy for you; maybe he is, or maybe some other nice boy right here in Pittsburgh will be. Or maybe you will meet someone nice out there in California and fall in love with him."

At the sound of the front door opening, Irene made her final declaration.

"The one thing I do know now, though maybe I didn't know it before, is that you shouldn't just quit the movie business all of a sudden right now just because you met Jack Leonard and you've been going to the movies and having coffee with him, and you enjoy his company. I don't know what will happen with the two of you after you go back to California, but you *should* go back."

At the sound of Gerald Coleman's "Irene?" coming from just inside the front door, Irene called out in reply "I'm in the kitchen with Charlene."

She lowered her voice to conversation-level tones once again as she finished that final declaration to Charlene.

"The choice is yours," Irene said as she stiffly rose from her kitchen chair, "but you asked me what I think you should do, and I've told you."

❄ ❄ ❄

"I'm not real good at making toasts…"

"Well you better get good before Saturday," Marty Walker interrupted his cousin Joseph Coleman. "The best man has to make a toast at the wedding reception, right?"

"Yeah," Joseph diverted his attention to his cousin, then back to the entire group of five – including himself.

"Anyway," Joseph continued, still raising his glass of Duquesne, "I want to make a toast to Jonathan and Francine, and their life together."

"Great toast," Tommy Coleman muttered, sarcastically but also good-naturedly.

"You weren't kidding," Marty Walker chimed in. "Hopefully you get a lot better before Saturday."

"Shut up and drink," Joseph said with mock anger to both his younger brother and his cousin. All five – Jack Leonard filled out the quintet – took healthy swigs from their respective glasses of Duquesne.

Over the past week, many of Jonathan's high school friends suggested a full-fledged bachelor party was called for in the face of their buddy's impending nuptials. Jonathan graciously yet firmly declined all such suggestions. Instead, the proxy for a bachelor party would be this much more subdued gathering at the U.S.O. Canteen next door to Pittsburgh's Penn Station. The end of the war meant that the future of the Canteen was in doubt, though for the foreseeable future with so many returning servicemen – and so many more to follow – the Canteen would likely remain open well into 1946, if not longer.

The gathering of the three Coleman brothers, their cousin Marty, and Jack Leonard began at seven o'clock. Word spread to Harry Spitz, Reuben Goldfarb, Stan Greenfield, Walter Dennison, Chuck Manelli, and many Schenley High buddies and football teammates that they were welcome to join the festivities any time after eight o'clock. Even Old Man Weisberg's sons who used to lug boxes alongside Jonathan before the war were informed.

But no wild party; no girls jumping out of a cake; no trips to less-than-reputable establishments on the outskirts of Pittsburgh; nothing of the kind would be in the mix for tonight.

Until then, this core group of five – the same group of five that had gathered under different circumstances on Christmas Eve afternoon out in Fox Chapel – would have a quiet, reflective celebration together. Marty had driven his father's Buick in from Fox Chapel, while Jack Leonard had swung by the Coleman house to pick up the three brothers for the short drive to the Canteen.

"So what's the story with this girl Abby?" Jack Leonard asked Joseph. "Is that the same one you met before you left for pilot training?"

"During Thanksgiving furlough back in '42," Joseph corrected Jack's inaccurate timeline. "But yeah, that's the one. Why? did Charlene say something?"

"Sort of," Jack shook his head. "When I got to your house to pick up you guys, she told me that you heard from Francine she ain't engaged anymore."

"That's pretty much the story," Joseph shrugged. "I guess at the wedding we'll see if we talk, or somethin' like that."

Joseph took a swig from his Duquesne as he added:

"I'm not gonna give it much more thought till then."

The conversation gravitated towards tomorrow's wedding rehearsal, scheduled for Saint Michael's at one o'clock in the afternoon.

"You really think I should go?" Jack asked Jonathan in response to Tommy asking Jack if he was going to be there.

"I'm not in the wedding or anything like you guys are," Jack added.

"You don't have to come, but you're invited," Jonathan assured his friend. "You know, because of you and Charlene. You can sit and watch us if you want."

"Well sure," Jack nodded. "As long as I'm not intruding or anything."

"Nah," Jonathan shook his head. He almost added "You're almost like family now, anyway" because during the past week it certainly seemed that way, given how much time Jack and Charlene had spent together...including with each other's family. But given the somber circumstances of Charlene's impending return to the Land of the Silver Screen, such a sentiment could only result in sorrowful feelings, no matter how well-intended. So Jonathan choked off that part of his reply.

"Here's to long-awaited new beginnings," Tommy raised his glass and suddenly offered his own toast. The U.S.O. Canteen technically was required to adhere to Pennsylvania's drinking age laws, but given how many servicemen were under the age of twenty-one, the local authorities typically turned a blind eye to anyone in uniform being served a beer or two. And tonight all five members of this party were wearing their respective service uniforms, even though three of them – Marty, Jack, and Thomas – were now more accurately classified as veterans rather than servicemen. And come Monday, both Jonathan and Joseph would join the other three as former servicemen following their discharges from the USAAF.

"Long-awaited is right," Marty chimed in. "Now that you're almost to the altar I guess I can say it, but four years ago if anyone had told me that you and Francine would be getting married right after Christmas of 1945, I woulda bet anything they woulda been wrong."

A sharp look from Jonathan immediately sent Marty into damage control mode.

"I mean with you being gone for the war for so many years," he quickly added, realizing that his original statement had caused one and all to think of Jonathan's original offer of marriage to Francine that had been aborted by the Donnie Yablonski incident.

Jonathan realized that his cousin hadn't meant anything malicious in his statement.

"Same goes for all of us gathered here," Jonathan seconded. "Honestly, right after Pearl Harbor and then for the next couple of months with the way the war was going, I'm not sure I would have bet anything that four years later we all would have made it back here okay. Same with all of the other guys who are gonna show up later."

Jonathan looked over at Joseph.

"Joey, you remember when you and I stopped by Schenley when we were on that Thanksgiving furlough? How lots of guys were there?"

"Uh-huh," Joseph nodded.

Jonathan looked over at Jack.

"You were already over on Guadalcanal by then."

Jack felt an involuntary shudder run through him as a flood of unpleasant memories hit him at once. He didn't respond as Jonathan looked back towards Joseph.

"You remember how none of us would say anything like 'See you after the war' or 'Let's get together after we all get back home'? Like we didn't want to jinx it?"

Jonathan paused for a brief moment before continuing.

"I remember Tommy Bonnaverte was there that day..." he added gloomily as his voice trailed off.

"I don't know if this is appropriate for a bachelor's party," Joseph chimed in, "but I guess technically this isn't a bachelor's party so maybe it's okay."

Joseph paused but since he hadn't explicitly stated what he was referring to, no one reacted; so he continued.

"I think we should drink a toast to everyone we know from Schenley who didn't make it back from the war."

Jonathan nodded.

"Yeah; not just mentioning their names," Jonathan agreed, "but also a little bit about what we remember about them. As the years pass we'll probably start to forget about them, so this can be our tribute."

Just then Harry Spitz wandered up to the group, wearing the uniform of an Army Air Forces major; the same as Jonathan. But as with Jack and Marty and Tommy, Harry's uniform was in spite of him already having been discharged.

"Am I too early?" Harry asked.

Jonathan shook his head.

"Nah; in fact, just in time. We just decided we were going to toast all of the guys who didn't make it back, and talk about them a little bit."

"Maybe we should wait for some of the other guys to get here for that," Harry suggested.

"Yeah, maybe," Jonathan nodded. "Yeah; that's a good idea. This way we can all pay tribute to them, or whatever you call it."

For the next half-hour, as one by one others arrived and then joined the group, the conversation meandered among wartime experiences; what everyone had been doing since they had been home, however long that had been; how many Carla Colburn pictures each had seen; and a myriad of other topics. By a quarter after eight, the group had grown to nearly twenty uniformed servicemen and veterans. Joseph looked over at his brother, who nodded in return.

"Hey guys?" Jonathan said, but he had to repeat himself several times to get everybody's attention. Finally, the group had quieted enough for Jonathan to address all of them.

"First of all, I want to thank every single one of you for being here. I know you all wanted a girl in a cake or something like that" – laughs went up from everyone gathered – "but honestly, this is the perfect place for us to get together."

"Some of you picked up on this," Jonathan continued, "but we're going to make toasts and say a little bit about our friends who didn't come back from the war. You know, to remember them. I know this isn't the typical bachelor party but honestly, with all of us gathered here I think we should do this so it would be like Damian and Sebastian, and Bonnaverte, and Paul Rzepecki, and Kozlowski, and all those other guys were also here with us tonight. You guys okay with that?"

A wave of nodding heads and murmured "uh-huhs" signaled unanimous agreement with the idea.

"Let's start with Paul Rzepecki since he was the first...well you know, at Pearl Harbor," Jonathan stammered.

The toasting and remembrances of lost friends, though bearing great merit and unanimously agreed to, would not be easy.

9 – Friday, December 28, 1945

"I, Jonathan, take you, Francine, for my lawful wife, to have and to hold…"

The words were merely practice ones. They carried no force of mortal law nor God's law. Yet listening to their son put voice to those words caused instant waves of bittersweet memories to wash over both Irene and Gerald Coleman.

Irene saw a much younger version of herself bringing her baby home from Magee Hospital, already determined that his name would be Jonathan after the Biblical friend of King David.

Gerald watched two-year old Jonathan rush to the front door to greet his new baby brother Joseph; his legs churning so fast that he tripped and fell face-first, resulting in his first split lip.

Fourth-grade Jonathan already standing out as one of the best baseball players of his age among the boys in Polish Hill, and then two years later showing even greater prowess at football.

High school Jonathan excelling in varsity baseball and football while carrying grades of almost all A's in every subject, each year.

Jonathan and Francine dressed for the Schenley High senior dance, the way they looked at each other already indicating the first hints of love.

Eighteen-year old Jonathan forcing himself awake in the darkness almost every morning – yet not complaining – as he trudged off to work at *Weisberg's* to help the

Coleman family make ends meet as the Depression years stubbornly clung to life.

Gerald watched his wife's tearful goodbyes to Jonathan and Joseph as they boarded the train at Penn Station that would begin their journey to Air Corps training all the way out in Arizona, and he could actually feel himself choke back his own tears on that long-ago morning as he struggled to give his sons a stoic, manly sendoff.

Irene Coleman watched dozens of V-Mail letters written by Jonathan dance before her eyes; each one of them signifying that at least as of the date Jonathan had written the letter he had still been alive and well.

Tomorrow, in front of the gathered celebrants in this very same place, both Gerald and Irene would be cognizant of their respective designated roles in the wedding ceremony. There would certainly be occasion for additional reflection then. Today, though, watching one attempt after another to put the finishing touches on the wedding ceremony, was for both of Jonathan's parents the time to lose themselves in years of memories.

10 – Saturday, December 29, 1945

This time, the spoken words did carry the force of both man's law and God's law.

"I, Jonathan, take you, Francine, for my lawful wife; to have and to hold, from this day forward; for better, for worse; for richer, for poorer; in sickness and in health; until death do us part."

Father Nolan nodded slightly and shifted his gaze from Jonathan to Francine.

"I, Francine, take you, Jonathan, for my lawful husband; to have and to hold, from this day forward; for better, for worse; for richer, for poorer; in sickness and in health; until death do us part."

Father Nolan nodded again as he addressed Jonathan and Francine together.

"You have declared your consent before the Church. May the Lord in his goodness strengthen your consent and fill you both with his blessings. What God has joined, men must not divide."

Another chorus of "Amen" went up from those seated in Saint Michael's this Saturday morning.

The priest then turned to untie the delicate ribbons binding the two rings that were lying on the ceremonial pillow that Francine's five-year old cousin Alexander, the ring bearer, had carried. As Father Nolan accomplished his handiwork, Joseph stole another glance into the fourth row where Abby Sobol was sitting. Unlike the past three times he had gazed at her, this time Abby did not make eye contact in return. She wasn't ignoring Joseph; she obviously was intent on watching the priest retrieve the two rings that within the next couple of minutes would wind up on Francine's and Jonathan's fingers.

So far this morning, Joseph and Abby had not said anything to each other. Joseph had been busy before the ceremony with the final preparations for the wedding Mass, while Abby had eased her way into Saint Michael's – alone – about fifteen minutes before the Mass began. She had caught the streetcar from her parents' home in East Liberty to a connecting one that stopped half a block down the street from Saint Michael's. During her entire twenty-minute journey Abby couldn't help but think what a beautiful winter day God had provided for her friend's wedding. The sun was shining and the thermometer had hovered right around forty degrees all throughout the night. If it weren't for the grayish-brown slushy mess that had pervasively covered Pittsburgh's streets for the past four weeks, one might even mistake today for one in early spring rather than one of the few remaining dying winter days remaining in this momentous year of 1945 that most everyone would remember for the rest of their lives.

Abby first saw Joseph when he accompanied Jonathan, both brothers marching with military precision from the side door to join Father Nolan at the altar. As Joseph executed a smart "left face" to face the congregation, his eyes locked with hers for a split second before he looked away.

Twice more – once during the processional, and once during the Mass – Joseph's eyes had sought out Abby. The first time she was already staring at him, but the second time she had been looking at Francine and something told her to look over at Joseph. Sure enough, he was looking at her and this time they held the shared glance for a good two seconds before each looked away.

Meanwhile, Charlene and Jack Leonard were doing much the same, though without the uneasiness of years apart that hallmarked Charlene's brother and Abby Sobol. Charlene was well aware that many people beyond just Jack Leonard were staring at her – actually, staring at the famous Carla Colburn. Like the other bridesmaids, Charlene wore a bluish gray floor-length dress that eased its way in a "V" pattern down from her shoulders (but still a safe distance above her bust line). Charlene was not only widely known by one and all as a movie starlet; she was also easily the most attractive of all the women on the altar this Saturday morning. For these reasons, almost as many eyes were on her as were on Francine.

Ruthie, standing next to Charlene, did her best to ignore the many people gaping at the starlet throughout the ceremony...even though Ruthie's close proximity to her sister made her feel as if all of those stares were actually directed at herself. She did her best to concentrate on the wedding ceremony itself as it progressed.

"May the Lord bless these rings which you give to each other as the sign of your love and fidelity," Father Nolan intoned, interrupting Joseph's and Charlene's thoughts and forcing their attention – and vision – back to the ceremony taking place only a few steps away from where they stood.

"Amen," came the reply.

"Lord, bless these rings which we bless in your name. Grant that those who wear them may always have a deep faith in each other..."

Father Nolan continued his blessing of the wedding rings as Joseph again glanced at Abby – he couldn't help himself! – but this time she was already staring at him when his eyes settled on her. The priest's just-spoken words – "may always have a deep faith in each other" – seemed to mock this shared glance. Joseph immediately told himself that he was being entirely unfair. Abby had not been governed by any such covenants following their whirlwind romance of only a few days. The logical side of Joseph's mind insisted that especially in light of such a short time the two of them had shared, the girl had had every right in the world to begin a romance with someone else while Joseph was across the ocean.

"Lord, bless and consecrate Jonathan and Francine in their love for each other. May these rings be a symbol of true faith in each other…"

Knowing that within seconds Jonathan and Francine would exchange rings, Joseph again forced his attention back to the ceremony.

Following one more "amen" Father Nolan handed Francine's wedding ring to Jonathan, who quickly placed it onto his bride's finger as he promised:

"Francine, take this ring as a sign of my love and fidelity. In the name of the Father, and of the Son, and of the Holy Ghost."

Francine watched the ring slide onto her finger but then she looked up at Jonathan and smiled as her eyes began to glisten, just as they had yesterday during the rehearsal. She ordered herself not to cry, but the glistening gave way to a few streaming tears of joy – again, just as a day earlier – as she reached for Jonathan's ring. She was able to choke out her own promise:

"Jonathan, take this ring as a sign of my love and fidelity. In the name of the Father, and of the Son, and of the Holy Ghost."

She finished sliding Jonathan's ring onto his finger, locking eyes with him the entire time…though her vision was slightly clouded by her tears.

Both Jonathan and Francine fervently wished for the ceremony to end right then and there (as did most everyone else gathered at Saint Michael's, except perhaps for the zealously religious congregants), but the full wedding Mass still had a ways to run. Jonathan and Francine frequently smiled at each other as Father Nolan proceeded with the General Intercessions, the Liturgy of the Eucharist, the Memorial Acclamation, and more for another half-hour. Finally arriving at the Nuptial Blessing, the priest began:

"Let us pray to the Lord for this bride and groom, who come to the altar as they begin their married life…"

The entire time, Joseph and Abby exchanged glances at least a dozen more times. This last time, just before the Nuptial Blessing began, she finally accompanied her look with a smile that caught Joseph off-guard. Joseph returned a tight, almost unnoticeable smile and then willed himself to stop looking at Abby until the ceremony had concluded. He instead glanced over at his brother Thomas, who happened to catch this latest visual tête-à-tête between Joseph and Abby. Thomas caught his brother's eye and smirked knowingly.

❊ ❊ ❊

For a few seconds, Joseph seriously thought about stepping out of the receiving line and quickly scurrying…well, anywhere away from where he wouldn't have to come face to face with Abby Sobol. She was next

302

in line to greet Francine's parents at the beginning of the receiving line, which meant that within the next minute she would make her way to Joseph. For a split second Joseph had a flash of anger that he had allowed himself to be talked into joining the receiving line in the basement reception area at Saint Michael's. He had heard that for the best man, such a duty was not required. Father Nolan had been the one, following yesterday's rehearsal, who all but ordered Joseph to stand next to his brother in the line. Joseph was certain that the priest saw some sort of symmetry in the brothers, each wearing their Army Air Forces uniforms, standing together. Joseph had just shrugged and agreed to the idea rather than get into some sort of ruckus with Father Nolan.

Now, though, he cursed himself for not insisting that he be excused from this duty. Here she was…almost here…

"Oh, Francine!" Abby cooed when she reached the bride and embraced Francine. "It was all so wonderful! I'm so happy for you!"

Francine held Abby's embrace for a few seconds, and since her head was on the side of the receiving line where Jonathan next stood followed by Joseph, both brothers could see Francine's lips slightly move as she obviously whispered something into Abby's ear that neither one of them could hear. A second later the girls released each other and Abby moved on to Jonathan.

"You look so wonderful in your uniform!" she gushed as Jonathan leaned forward to embrace her.

"Thanks," was Jonathan's one-word reply.

"It was all so wonderful! I'm so happy for you!" Abby repeated exactly what she had said to Francine.

Jonathan was about to offer a reprise of his one-word "Thanks" response but he caught himself and instead said:

"It's almost hard to believe, isn't it? Doesn't it seem like a lifetime ago that we all went to see *Thunder Birds* down at the Senator?"

Jonathan looked over at Joseph as he spoke. He obviously was doing his best to ease the inevitable awkwardness that was about to take place when the wedding ceremony glances between Joseph and Abby gave way to actually speaking to each other.

And now, the moment was here.

"Hello, Joseph," Abby smiled as she took a few steps to face this man of her past.

"Hi Abby," was Joseph's tight reply. He could feel his heart pounding as if it were about to explode through his chest.

They stood there in awkward silence for a good ten seconds.

"I'll see you at the reception?" Abby finally said, the smile coming back to her face.

"Uh-huh," Joseph nodded as Abby moved on to greet Lorraine Walker, who was next in the receiving line.

"That's it?" Jonathan muttered in the lowest tones he could manage; hopefully so Joseph could hear him but Abby couldn't.

Joseph stole a quick glance over at Abby and then looked back at Jonathan.

"I'm not sure what to say to her," he replied in an equally subdued voice.

❄ ❄ ❄

"Everyone was staring at you," Jack Leonard said to Charlene as they took their seats for the reception luncheon. Many of the merchants in Polish Hill had given Jack Donner special considerations for his daughter's wedding to the Air Corps major who was one of their own. As a result the menu for the mid-afternoon meal was more scrumptious than the railroad worker might otherwise have been able to afford.

"*You* were staring at me, you mean," Charlene teased Jack Leonard in response. "Every time I looked at you during the entire ceremony, you were looking right back at me."

Jack chuckled.

"Yeah, but not just me. Everyone wanted to get a good look at Carla Colburn the Bridesmaid."

"I guess," Charlene replied, her voice carrying a touch of discomfort.

Charlene changed the subject.

"I can't wait to dance with you," she offered. After the luncheon one of the neighborhood bands would set up and play for a couple of hours. Polkas would of course be the highlight – this was Polish Hill – but Jonathan and Francine had ensured that the band would play some of the current popular songs, and other songs from during the war years, as well.

"Then everyone will be staring at me," Jack said good-naturedly.

"Well, they should," Charlene said in all sincerity. She took in the image of Jack Leonard as if she were seeing him for the first time today. His Marine Corps dress uniform; his staff sergeant's stripes; his rows of battle ribbons, including his Purple Heart...her heart fluttered as she stared at him with fresh eyes.

With Joseph approaching the head table, Charlene lowered her voice.

"What about Joey and Abby?"

Jack quickly eyed Joseph and then his eyes sought out Abby Sobol, who was seated four tables away at a table that was populated by several of Francine's aunts and uncles and a few of her cousins similar in age to Francine...and Abby.

"I dunno," Jack murmured back. "Not sure what to think. She seems like she wants to talk with him but Joey..."

He broke off his response as Joseph came within earshot.

"Have you talked to Abby yet?" Charlene asked her brother, fully knowing the answer.

Joseph shot her a sharp look.

"Just in the receiving line," he answered tersely.

"Uh-huh," Charlene responded, innuendo hanging heavily in the air.

"What's that supposed to mean?" Joseph asked.

"Nothing," Charlene answered.

Joseph was about to challenge his sister's noncommittal response when he realized that the rest of the head table had already taken their seats. He walked over to the remaining empty chair on the other side of

Jonathan from where Francine sat, and quickly eased himself into his chair.

Father Nolan rose to offer the blessing over the meal, after which platters of food began appearing from the Saint Michael's kitchen that adjoined the large basement gathering hall. The bounty commenced and by the time the next hour had passed, nearly everyone present felt his or her clothes were suddenly a size or two smaller.

As the hour wound down, Joseph's nervousness appeared once again. This time it had nothing to do with Abby Sobol. His toast to the bride and groom was looming. He thought he had a good handle on what he was going to say, but as the moment ticked nearer and nearer Joseph felt his mind become emptier and emptier.

A few minutes later Joseph felt a nudge from his brother and knew the time was at hand. He stood and clinked his water glass with his knife until the murmuring throughout the hall died down enough for Joseph to be heard over the few who stubbornly persisted in their conversations.

"This moment is a long time in coming," Joseph began. "Back at Schenley High School my brother and Francine began dating at the beginning of their senior year, and before long they were going steady. Everyone looked at Jonathan and Francine as the perfect couple: the football and baseball star and one of the most beautiful and popular girls in school."

Joseph had chosen his words carefully. Even as he proceeded with his opening thoughts, part of his mind was doing its best to make sure he didn't continue on and inadvertently say something he really shouldn't...specifically, the schism of almost a year between Jonathan and Francine.

"We all know what happened in late 1941 when the war came. Almost every one of us here had our lives disrupted, and many of us in this very room were called into the armed services to fight in the war. Jonathan and I joined the Army Air Forces – as you can tell from our uniforms, even if you don't know us" – Joseph's words brought a light chuckle from a few of the celebrants – "and we both went out to Arizona to officer's school and pilot training."

He paused for a second before continuing.

"During the war Jonathan and Francine wrote to each other almost every day for three years. Someday their children will find those letters and see that their father kept telling their mother almost every single day how much he missed her, and that their mother wrote the same thing to their father."

Joseph paused again for a couple of seconds.

"Finally, Jonathan came home from the war and couldn't wait a second longer than he had to before he and Francine got married. That's why we're all here today: to celebrate the triumph of love over time and distance and hardship."

Joseph then raised his glass of *nalewka* and was quickly joined by everyone else present except – per custom – the bride and groom themselves.

"Here is to the health and long life of the newly married Mister and Mrs. Jonathan Coleman," Joseph said. "Na *zdrowia!*"

"Na *zdrowia!*" came the enthusiastic response from one and all.

❄ ❄ ❄

The voice came from behind him.

"You've been avoiding me," Abby Sobol said.

Joseph felt his heart begin to pound once again as he slowly turned around.

"No I'm not," he answered defensively. The band was almost finished setting up, and dancing would soon begin. "I had to do all of this best man stuff..."

"Okay," Abby interrupted, her voice clearly conveying her disbelief in Joseph's tepid, defensive rebuttal. "But you're done now; can't we talk?"

Joseph let out a deep sigh.

"I'm not sure what there is to talk about," he finally said.

Abby gave him a mournful smile.

"Then how about just letting me apologize to you," she offered.

"You don't have to apologize," Joseph quickly answered.

"I do," Abby sadly nodded. "Not for starting to date Jeffrey, but for not having the courage to tell you about it."

Joseph thought to himself: Jeffrey, huh? So that's the guy's name.

"Tommy told me that you were going to but when he heard about it he told Francine to talk you out of writing me," Joseph retorted. "So you don't have to apologize," he repeated.

"I should have told you anyway despite what Francine said," Abby countered. This was the first Abby had heard that Joseph's brother had played a role in those events, but by this point Tommy Coleman's involvement was irrelevant.

Joseph let out another deep sigh.

"Look, Abby. The whole time I was in the Luftstalag I kept thinking about you, and honestly if I had heard about you and…Jeffrey, I might not have…I don't know, endured things as well. So just forget about it; I'm fine and you don't owe me an apology, okay?"

Abby seemed to struggle with what she wanted to say next.

"When I heard you were shot down, before anyone knew you were a prisoner of war, I cried myself to sleep every night. I was convinced that God was punishing me for jilting you for Jeffrey…"

"You didn't jilt me," Joseph interrupted. "We had a couple of days together back during that Thanksgiving, and then I went away. I know we wrote each other a lot and you talked about waiting for me, but I really didn't expect you to…"

"Really?" this time Abby's eyes flashed angrily. "So you think I was just saying that in my letters because it was what I thought you wanted to hear, but I really didn't mean it?"

"Abby, that's not what I said," Joseph answered.

"That's *exactly* what you said," Abby rebutted.

"Okay, that's not what I *meant*," was Joseph's own rebuttal.

Just then, Harry Spitz wandered over to where Joseph and Abby stood. The close presence of another person – any other person – was enough to tamp down Abby Sobol's anger. She smiled sweetly at Joseph as she said "I'm going to find Francine," and began to walk away from Joseph.

Abby was almost out of earshot – almost – when Joseph blurted out:

"I'll talk to you later, okay?"

No response.

❄ ❄ ❄

"I understand you had a lot to do with this wedding actually happening," Stan Walker said to Jack Donner. The two workmen who labored on behalf of different railroads were each nursing a tumbler of *krupnik*, the honey-spiced vodka popular at heavily Polish celebrations such as this one.

The two men knew each other well enough from when the Walkers had lived in Polish Hill, and Stan's employment with the Pennsylvania Railroad and Jack Donner's with the Pennsylvania & Lake Erie line had formed a bit of a bond between them.

"You mean talking to Francine about Jonathan going to college and all that?" was Jack Donner's response.

"Uh-huh," Stan replied as he took a healthy drink of his *krupnik*. "I know that was a problem for both of them, and I felt a little like I was to blame for telling Jonathan I thought he should use that government money to go to college."

"Nah," Jack Donner replied, taking his own healthy swig as he did. "I told Francine the same thing, that it was the best for both of them if that's what he did."

Francine's father looked around to make sure that his daughter wasn't within earshot.

"Francine likes to have things her way," he said, "and she got it in her mind that Jonathan was going to buy her a house right away. I told her…well, I guess pretty much the same thing you told Jonathan, I guess. And probably Gerald as well."

Jack Donner paused to swallow the rest of his drink.

"Look at us," he said to Stan Walker. "You and me. You got that nice house out in Fox Chapel now, I hear, and I want that for my little girl. I don't want Jonathan to have to work for such little money like you and I did all our lives. Don't take no offense to this, but without going to college, unless Jonathan got lucky playing the stock market like you did, him and Francine would…well, things would always be tough for them, you know?"

"No offense at all," Stan nodded as he swallowed the rest of his own drink. "I don't want to sound like I'm some know-it-all or nothing, but I swear I can almost see the future for all of these guys who came back from the war. I was telling Jonathan that just like my own boy, and his brothers, and all these other boys, the ones who go use that government money now to get their diplomas are the ones who will buy the nice houses and have the easier jobs in four or five years."

Stan looked over at Jack Donner.

"I'm glad you see it that way, and convinced Francine to go through with the wedding," he said.

"I just want the best for my little girl," Jack Donner said, his voice beginning to choke up.

❄ ❄ ❄

The band played for almost forty-five minutes – polkas mostly – before they took a short break. Captain Joseph Coleman seemed immune from the steadily increasing gaiety of the occasion. Outwardly he frequently smiled and shared short bits of conversation with many of those gathered here. But inside, Joseph felt little else other than overpoweringly melancholy in the aftermath of his dissatisfying conversation with Abby. As far as he was concerned, this day – actually, this gathering – couldn't end soon enough.

Several times he looked around in hopes that Abby had departed, but each time he eventually caught a glimpse of her talking to someone, or dancing to one of the polkas. She never looked in Joseph's direction...at least while he was looking in hers.

Oh well, Joseph thought to himself. He had no expectations whatsoever from Abby's presence at his brother's wedding. Until two days earlier, he had presumed that she was well on the way to her own wedding with "4-F Jeffrey." Then, even after learning from Jonathan via Francine that Abby's engagement was no longer, it wasn't until Jonathan brought up the idea that a second chance might be in order that Joseph even gave that idea any credence.

But now, things were back to exactly where they had been two days earlier. Abby Sobol was a distant memory from the past that had been blown far away by the blustery December Pittsburgh wind.

Then why did Joseph feel so down at the moment?

"Can I talk to you before I leave?" Again, the voice came from behind Joseph.

He slowly turned around to face Abby.

"You know, you shouldn't come up from behind on any guy who had been in the war," he said only half-jokingly. "We're all on a hair-trigger and you never know what might happen."

"So are you going to attack me now for sneaking up on you?" Abby said in the same half-joking tones Joseph had just used.

"Not for sneaking up on me," Joseph blurted out, instantly regretting his words.

Abby fought back a sharp retort. She wanted to say her piece, and then be at peace.

"Do you know why I broke off my engagement?"

Joseph shook his head.

Before continuing, Abby looked over at an empty nearby table.

"Can we sit down for just a minute?"

Joseph shrugged.

"Sure, I guess."

After taking a couple of seats – leaving one buffering chair between them – Abby continued.

"Jeffrey and I went downtown for V-J Day," she began her tale. "It was the biggest celebration I've ever seen."

Abby looked at Joseph.

"Were you back in the States by then?"

He shook his head.

"I was still over in Europe. We had been liberated from that last prison camp but the war was still going in the Pacific, and they were thinking about taking a lot of us pilots and sending us over there. So they didn't start shipping any of the P.O.W.'s back to the States until after V-J Day, unless a guy was really in bad shape or something and wouldn't be able to fly."

"Well anyway," Abby continued, "we were downtown and everybody was carrying on like…well, you know. I said something like how wonderful it was that everybody would be coming home and wouldn't have to fight anymore and face getting killed all the time."

She paused for a couple of seconds before continuing.

"Jeffrey had been classified 4-F because of some kind of bone deformity or something. You couldn't tell anything to look at him, but apparently when he took his draft physical they found whatever it was, and gave him 4-F."

Abby paused again, as if what she had to say was particularly painful.

"He had been drinking quite a bit, and when I said that about everyone coming home he said to me – and I'll never forget what he said – 'I can't tell you how glad I am that I was 4-F. I really don't have anything wrong with me but because the Army gave me 4-F, I was here and that's how I got to meet you."

Abby shook her head, as if desperately wanting to shake away unpleasant thoughts.

"I guess he wasn't really being a jerk about it; you know, what he said. But the more I thought about it, especially the way he said 'I really don't have anything wrong with me', the more I started to not really like him all that much anymore."

She sighed and looked away from Joseph when she continued.

"I started thinking a lot about you, and how you had been shot down and for a while everybody thought you might be dead. And then finding out that you were in a Nazi prison camp. I kept thinking about what you had gone through, and I also kept thinking about what Jeffrey had said."

Abby paused for another couple of seconds, then looked directly at Joseph.

"And the more I thought about you and him, I realized that I couldn't marry him."

Abby dropped her head slightly then looked back at Joseph.

"That's why I wanted to apologize to you; for thinking that…I don't know, that I wanted to date him and then to marry him, rather than waiting for you like I said I would. I just figured that you would come back from the war and maybe you would bring back a wife from England or France and I would feel so stupid to have been waiting for you. So when Jeffrey asked me to go to the movies that first time, even though I felt like I was cheating on you, I said yes. And things just…well, they progressed from there."

"If it wasn't for the war," Joseph muttered.

"What?" Abby had only heard the word "war" because Joseph's voice had been so muted.

"I said that if it wasn't for the war," he repeated. "You know, if I didn't have to go back to Thunderbird Field right after we met, then maybe...well, you know."

"Do you remember," Abby seemed to be peering directly into Joseph's very soul, "that first afternoon we met? At Jack Canter's?"

Joseph snorted.

"Jonathan and I were just there two days ago; right after Francine told him about you not being engaged any more, and being back in town; and also coming to the wedding."

"You went there?"

"Well, it was Jonathan's idea. We walked there and we were talking about...something else, and I wasn't paying attention until we just about walked in the door."

"I see," Abby nodded. "Well, do you remember that when I met you that was also when Jonathan and Francine saw each other for the first time in something like nine months? And that was after all that..."

Abby looked around to see if anyone was within earshot. Still, bringing up Francine's indiscretion with Donnie Yablonski on her friend's wedding day, at her friend's wedding reception, seemed blasphemous so she didn't finish the sentence. Still, Abby was certain that Joseph knew what she would have said.

"I talked to Francine after we all left and before we went out to the movies," she continued. "She instantly wanted to get back together with Jonathan, but I asked her how she expected him to want to do that after what she had done. You know what she said to me?"

Joseph shook his head.

"She said that despite everything that had happened, she was absolutely certain there was still this little piece of what they had that was still alive. And if she didn't give up, she was sure that he would realize that too. And no matter what she had done, or anything that he had done, they would end up together."

Joseph's eyes sought out Jonathan and Francine on the dance floor. The band had started playing again, but this set had shifted from polkas to popular big band music. They were halfway through *Till the End of Time* – the popular Perry Como song – and Jonathan and Francine were now dancing together, smiling lovingly at each other as if they were the only two people in the world despite a dozen other couples on the dance floor and so many other people in the hall.

"I guess she was right," Joseph said.

"Do you really think so?" Abby asked.

Joseph looked back from the newly married couple to this girl from his past.

"Sure," he nodded. "Look at them. Jonathan didn't see her at all for more than three years, and he's only been back since last week, but it's like the two of them actually spent every second together the whole time."

Abby nodded as well.

"I think that also," she said. "And you know what else I think?"

"Huh?"

"I think the same thing applies to more people than just your brother and Francine."

Joseph looked at Abby with sad eyes that started to slightly glisten.

"I don't know," he muttered, knowing exactly what Abby was getting at.

The band finished their rendition of *Till the End of Time* and after a few seconds began their next song. After only a single note Joseph knew exactly what they had just begun to play.

"Will you dance with me?" Abby Sobol asked Captain Joseph Coleman as *It's Been a Long, Long Time* began to play, her eyes now glistening just as Joseph's were.

❄ ❄ ❄

Gerald Coleman strolled – actually, he staggered, considering how much *krupnik* and *nalewka* he had consumed today – over to where Irene had just finished talking with Sally Donner half a minute earlier. The two mothers would never become bosom buddies; of that Irene Coleman was absolutely certain. But now that the wedding ceremony was over, and this day of marriage celebration was nearing its end, an alliance of sorts had formed between the two women with regards to Jonathan and Francine. They each would keep an eye out for the couple's well-being, and without stating as much, they would share information as necessary to keep the youngsters on track.

Irene took one look at her husband and shook her head. Not in disgust; after all, it was his eldest son's wedding day and if Gerald Coleman wanted to drink in one afternoon what he would normally consume throughout an entire month as part of the celebration, that was his right. He would pay for his celebratory imbibing later tonight perhaps, and certainly tomorrow.

Gerald said nothing as he stopped next to where his wife stood. He turned to gaze out on the dance floor that still was populated by a dozen and a half couples. Over in one corner, three couples were not only dancing close by one another but they also seemed to have a barrier of sorts around them, since no other couples were in the immediate vicinity of them.

Gerald and Irene Coleman stood in the basement hall of Saint Michael's and watched Jonathan and Francine; Joseph and that girl Abby Sobol; and Charlene and Jack Leonard all dancing to the nostalgia-tinged sounds of *Thanks for the Memory*.

Epilogue

The Pittsburgh Press – Monday, December 16, 1946
Middle of Page 1

Pittsburgh's Carla Colburn, UCLA Football Star Tie the Knot

Pittsburgh's own Carla Colburn married UCLA football star Jack Leonard last Saturday at Saint Michael's in Polish Hill. Miss Colburn – whose real name is Charlene Coleman – graduated from Schenley High School in 1943 before gaining fame in Hollywood during the final years of the war.

Her new husband, a veteran of the Marine Corps who rose to the rank of Staff Sergeant, earned the Bronze Star and three Purple Hearts while fighting on Guadalcanal, Tarawa, Saipan, and Tinian. He originally matriculated at the University of Pittsburgh after returning from the war, but won a scholarship to UCLA this past spring in time to join the Bruins for the 1946 season. Like many other returning war veterans who have since gone to college on the G.I. Bill, Mister Leonard is older than most of his teammates but still went on to become one of the stars of this season's undefeated and untied Bruins team that will face Illinois in the Rose Bowl on New Year's Day.

Mister Leonard was a varsity football star at Schenley High School where he was a teammate of his wife's brother before enlisting in the Marine Corps shortly after Pearl Harbor. Despite being a college freshman – normally ineligible for varsity college football – Mister Leonard earned a spot on the UCLA roster as a wingback due to a special exception for returning war veterans with more than two years of service and who are over the age of twenty.

Mister and Mrs. Leonard selected this past Saturday in between the bride's filming schedule and in time for Mister Leonard to return to Los Angeles in time for the Rose Bowl.

Mister Leonard's best man was his younger brother Mort Leonard, recently returned himself to Pittsburgh from the occupation forces in Japan. Carla Colburn's cousin, Lorraine Walker of Fox Chapel, served as her maid of honor. The actress' bridesmaids included her younger sister Ruth Coleman, the groom's two sisters Lenora Wijoski and Stella Majorskech, and also the bride's sisters-in-law Francine Coleman and Abigail (Abby) Coleman.

On the groom's side, in addition to his brother were the bride's three brothers: Major Jonathan Coleman and Captain Joseph Coleman, who both served as pilots in the Army Air Forces during the war; and Private Thomas Coleman, who served in the Marines near the end of the war. All three brothers are currently studying at the University of Pittsburgh. Completing the groom's side were his two older brothers, Arthur and Walter Leonard.

The bride's parents are Mister and Mrs. Gerald Coleman of Polish Hill, and the groom's parents are Mister and Mrs. Antoni Leonard, also of Polish Hill.

A reception was held following the ceremony at Webster Hall, where Pittsburgh's Gene Kelly joined in the festivities and toasted the newly wed couple after the best man's toast.

After the Rose Bowl, the couple will honeymoon in Key West, Florida before the new Mrs. Leonard begins to film her next picture.

A final note from the author about real-life personalities in this tale

Several real-life Hollywood personalities are referenced in **The First Christmas After the War** in fictional settings, interacting with our story's characters.

As in **Thanksgiving, 1942,** Gene Kelly – one of the most famous entertainment personalities ever to come out of Pittsburgh – is mentioned as the catalyst for Charlene Coleman becoming Hollywood actress Carla Colburn. Mister Kelly's role in the story is of course fictional.

Actor Wayne Morris was, as portrayed in this tale, a World War II naval aviator and ace who shot down seven enemy planes. His challenges in securing movie roles in the immediate aftermath of the war, as referenced in the story, are taken from online sources. His referenced conversation with the fictional Carla Colburn is likewise fictional.

Actress Alice Faye did, as portrayed in this tale, abruptly walk away from her film career following 1945's *Fallen Angel,* and was reported as not missing Hollywood very much in favor of a "normal" life with her family. (She did return to the screen nearly two decades later in 1962's *State Fair* and appeared in films several more times over the years.) As with Wayne Morris and Gene Kelly, the story's reference to her interaction with the fictional Carla Colburn is of course fictional.

Beyond Hollywood and the world of entertainment, and as in the first two novels in this series, several of my great-uncles have unnamed cameos as former co-workers of Jonathan Coleman. The *Dedication* of **Thanksgiving, 1942** noted that by time that book was published, all of my great-uncles had passed away.

In a final literary tribute to my great-uncles, the photograph on the cover of this book was taken shortly before a family wedding in late 1945. That real-life wedding is the foundation for Jonathan's and Francine's wedding in this novel. My great-uncles Joseph Weisberg (Army uniform, left); Larry Weisberg (Navy uniform); Bernie Gomberg (Marine Corps uniform); and Nathan Weisberg (Army uniform, right) all served in the military during the Second World War. This novel is dedicated to each of them, along with approximately sixteen million other Americans, who made so many sacrifices – for some, the ultimate sacrifice – on behalf of others in their generation and for generations to come.

The First Christmas of the War – the sudden attack on Pearl Harbor brings about a troubling Christmas like none other for the Coleman family...

Thanksgiving, 1942 – Jonathan and Joseph Coleman return home for a brief, bittersweet family holiday before heading off to war...

The First Christmas After the War – World War II is over, and new journeys begin for the members of the Coleman family...

The saga of our Coleman family is far from over...

Stay tuned as the family's saga continues into the 1950s with the next book in the series! If you would like to be notified when the next title is available and also stay up to date with other titles from author Alan Simon, contact us at info@alansimonbooks.com to be added to our mailing list. You can also visit our website at www.alansimonbooks.com to learn more about our books.

Also by Alan Simon

A USA TODAY Bestseller

July 1-3, 1863: The famed Battle of Gettysburg turns the tide of the Civil War, but not before approximately 50,000 soldiers from both sides become casualties during those three terrible days of carnage.

June 29-July 4, 1913: To commemorate the 50th anniversary of The Battle of Gettysburg, more than 50,000 Civil War Veterans ranging in age from 61 to more than 100 years old converge on the scene of that titanic battle half a century earlier in an occasion of healing that was known as the *Great Reunion*.

Abraham Lincoln had incorrectly surmised in his famed Gettysburg Address that "the world will little note nor long remember what we say here" four months after the battle itself, but those very words could well be said about the Great Reunion that occurred half a century later. At the time the 1913 gathering was a well-known, momentous commemoration with 50,000 spectators joining the 50,000 veterans, but the grandest of all gatherings of Civil War veterans has been all but forgotten in the 100 years since that occasion.

Until now.

GETTYSBURG, 1913: THE COMPLETE NOVEL OF THE GREAT REUNION

(originally published as a three-part serialized novel; this complete edition, now a USA TODAY bestseller, contains all three parts)

Travel back in time to meet and spend the months leading up to the Great Reunion with the following unforgettable characters in this meticulously researched tale:

Doctor Samuel Chambers, a young unmarried Philadelphia physician thrust into great responsibility as Pennsylvania's chief planner of medical and aid facilities for more than 50,000 Civil War veterans, averaging 70 years of age...all of whom will be spending the duration of The Great Reunion encamped in outdoor tents under temperatures expected to approach or even exceed 100 degrees.

Louisa May Sterling, a Gettysburg nurse and the young widow of a West Point-educated Army officer whose untimely death from typhoid left her alone with only her son Randall for companionship...but for whom The Great Reunion opens up an unexpected second chance at happiness when she meets Samuel Chambers.

Angus Findlay, now just past his 85th birthday but during the Battle of Gettysburg a dashing cavalry officer serving with the Army of Northern Virginia directly under the legendary J.E.B. Stuart...and who became a leading figure in Virginia politics during Reconstruction.

Chester Morrison, a classic Gilded Age Titan of Industry (and recent widower) from Philadelphia who decades earlier had been a green private facing battle for the first time at Gettysburg.

Edgar and Johnny Sullivan, brothers from Illinois who had been members of the Union Cavalry Division that arrived at Gettysburg the day before the battle began.

Years later, the Sullivans became allies of the Earp brothers in Tombstone and were first-hand witnesses to the evolution of Arizona from Old West to the early 20th century.

Devin McAteer, who was at Vicksburg with Ulysses Grant's Army of the Tennessee rather than Gettysburg during those first days of July, 1863 and who stayed in the Union Army for another decade during Reconstruction. Devin reluctantly attends The Great Reunion because of the personal plea of his aging cousin Seamus despite feeling out of place because he hadn't fought at Gettysburg.

Philip Roberdeau from New Orleans, a former Confederate officer who had resigned from West Point shortly before graduation because of the start of the Civil War and who had previously attended the much smaller 25th reunion of The Battle of Gettysburg back in 1888.

Ned Tomlinson, a Confederate veteran from Norfolk, Virginia who lost his left leg during the ill-fated assault known ever since as Pickett's Charge before being taken prisoner by the Yankees.

John K. Tener, the real-life Governor of Pennsylvania - born in County Tyrone, Ireland, only weeks after the Battle of Gettysburg - who was a former Major League baseball player and under whose leadership The Great Reunion was planned and held.

Made in United States
North Haven, CT
01 February 2022

15421815R00198